AN INVITING KISS

Cymberly lifted her head slightly, deliberately inviting Geoffrey to seek her lips.

"My sweet," he murmured.

Her hands crept up to pull his head closer.

He pulled back to gaze at her. Embarrassed by the intensity of her own response, Cymberly had never imagined being overwhelmed by sheer need for another person. Or that satisfaction of such need might make one feel safe, complete—whole.

"I-I-we should not have done that," she said.

His smile was tender, his words soft. "It felt supremely right to me. I want you, Cymberly, as I have never wanted anyone before. I cannot believe you are indifferent to me."

"But it is not right," she said, evading his implied question. She turned her back to him, but she did not move away. . . .

Books by Wilma Counts

WILLED TO WED

MY LADY GOVERNESS

THE WILLFUL MISS WINTHROP

Published by Zebra Books

THE
WILLFUL
MISS WINTHROP

Wilma Counts

ZEBRA BOOKS
Kensington Publishing Corp.
http://www.zebrabooks.com

ZEBRA BOOKS are published by

Kensington Publishing Corp.
850 Third Avenue
New York, NY 10022

First Printing: October, 2000
10 9 8 7 6 5 4 3 2 1

Printed in the United States of America

This one is for
Audrey, Brenda, Helen, Judy,
Mary, Mona, Nancy, Ramona, and Rowene

I have always been incredibly lucky in my friends.
These ladies are among the best!

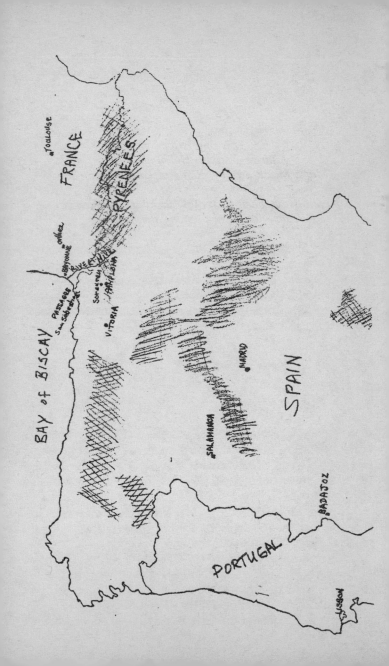

One

"You did *what?*" The Viscountess Renfrow fairly sputtered at the young woman seated across from her in the elegant drawing room of the Renfrow townhouse.

"I refused Lord Taraton's offer." Miss Cymberly Winthrop looked her godmother in the eye, noting the other lady's posture, rigid with frustrated anger and genuine alarm. "We would not suit, you know."

"It matters not whether you would suit. The damage has been done. Your reputation will be in shreds. 'Twas commendable of Taraton to do the right thing by you, considering your lack of dowry and that you are not precisely in the first bloom of youth. Renfrow did not even have to pressure him."

After a year in the other woman's household, Cymberly scarcely noticed her godmother's bluntness. "Lord Taraton and I were stranded at a country inn for a few hours while his curricle was being repaired. I do not see that as a basis for marriage."

"During which time the two of you were sequestered in a private parlor. You had no suitable chaperon, not even a maid. It simply will not do, my dear."

"The entire event was an unfortunate accident! The rest of our party had gone ahead. It took much longer to repair the wheel than anyone might have anticipated."

"And you were alone together all that time."

"The innkeeper and his wife could not spare a maid for

us. Heavens! They barely managed a simple meal. We were lucky they had a private parlor. The taproom was overflowing with farmers and tradesmen."

"That is neither here nor there," Lady Renfrow said dismissively. "You have been compromised. You must marry him. You will send round a note telling him you have reconsidered. He is a gentleman. He understands that girls often say no when they mean yes."

Cymberly sighed. She sat with her hands clasped in her lap, trying to think how she might make her godmother understand. Then she raised her clear-eyed gaze to Lady Renfrow's and spoke firmly, but softly.

"No, madam, I will not send round such a note. At three and twenty, I am hardly a green girl who knows little of her own wishes. Lord Taraton is an amiable man, but I will not condemn us both to a life of misery by accepting his suit because of an accident."

"A life of misery? How *can* you speak so? Taraton is one of the richest young men of the *ton*. He is a very good catch. You should deem yourself lucky."

"Did I love him, I should certainly feel lucky. But I do not, nor is he especially enamored of me. He partnered me for a few dances. We enjoyed a few outings in the park and the picnic. But I repeat, madam, that is no basis for marriage."

Cymberly did not add that David Taraton had sought her company for the picnic precisely because—as he told her in his joking but honest manner—he knew she, at least, was not seeking to ensnare him in matrimony. He was a friend. Period. Now society would spoil their friendship by springing the very trap the viscount sought to avoid. Cymberly Winthrop was not going to allow it. Her hazel eyes snapped with determination.

Her godmother considered her silently for a moment, then tried a different tack. "Have you any idea how your selfishness will affect the rest of this household once the scandal really breaks? So far there are only whispers."

"Selfishness? I cannot consider it selfish to refuse the suit of one who would never have offered under ordinary circumstances."

"I was not thinking of you or Lord Taraton. I was thinking of Amabel. Her father and I have gone to a great deal of trouble to ensure her come-out is a success. Now your behavior will spoil her chances at a suitable match."

"Oh, I do hope not."

Lady Renfrow went right on as though Cymberly had not spoken. "Is this how you are to repay our hospitality? With your grandmother off digging into old Egyptian graves, it was my duty to take you in when your mama died—a duty I was glad to perform. When your time of mourning was over, I was happy to bring you out along with Amabel. Indeed, I was convinced—and rightly so!—that your dark good looks and outgoing personality would be the perfect complement to my fair Amabel. But now . . ." She finally wound down.

"I am not unmindful of all you and Lord Renfrow have done for me, and I am deeply grateful. Mama would have been also."

"Well then . . ."

"But I cannot do as you wish."

"Surely you can. Think of the scandal. And Amabel."

"Amabel is a lovely, conformable girl. She is very sweet, not to mention that she will have a generous dowry. I cannot doubt she will survive any talk about her parents' houseguest, especially if that houseguest is no longer in England."

"No longer in—why, whatever can you mean by that?"

"I plan to join my father in the Peninsula."

"You would follow the drum? Oh, my heavens!" Lady Renfrow drew back in shock and put her hand to her ample breast. "It was bad enough when your mother took her baby and went off to India with Captain Winthrop, but at least she was married. Trailing behind the army is no place for an unmarried young woman—not a respectable one."

Cymberly laughed. "My dear godmama, have you not just suggested that my refusing to marry Lord Taraton will make me less than respectable in London society? And," she added in a very firm tone, "I do assure you I shall not change my mind on that question."

"Ohhh." Unaccustomed to having her wishes ignored, Lady Renfrow wailed her frustration. "Where on earth did I ever get the idea you were a biddable young woman?"

Although it was clearly a rhetorical question, Cymberly responded. "I truly regret that I cannot please you, ma'am. Nor would I willingly hurt Amabel. The gossip will prove a nine days' wonder once I have gone."

"That is probably correct," Lady Renfrow admitted grudgingly. "Well, if you absolutely refuse to marry Taraton, I wash my hands of the situation. I cannot say I will be happy to see you go, but . . ."

For the next few days Cymberly avoided social outings, in part to spare her godmother's having to deflect gossip, but also because she was caught up in arranging the details of her removal to Portugal. Viscount Renfrow offered to check on ships challenging the French blockade of British sea traffic. He would try to determine which ships—and which captains—would stand the greater chance of success. As it happened, Mrs. Horton, a bosom friend of Lady Renfrow, was traveling to Portugal to meet her colonel husband.

Mrs. Horton was reluctant to allow her own consequence to lend an air of respectability to a young woman who was currently the talk of the town. However, Lady Renfrow, with little regard for subtlety, reminded her old friend of a nearly forgotten social debt, and Mrs. Horton was persuaded to accept Miss Winthrop as a cabin mate.

Cymberly made one important morning call on Lady Suzanne Allenby, the Earl of Kirkwood's countess. Within weeks of confinement with her first child, Lady Kirkwood received very few visitors, but she welcomed Cymberly with an eager hug.

Greetings over, Cymberly asked, "How are you feeling?"

"Fat and clumsy." The normally lithe and slender blond woman lowered herself awkwardly into a chair and waved her visitor to a seat. "Three more weeks, the doctor says."

"I am truly sorry I will not be here to welcome the Kirkwood heir properly."

"I heard. Oh, Cymberly, I shall miss you so." There was genuine distress in Suzanne's tone, and tears filled her eyes.

"And I you." Cymberly smiled sadly and then said more lightly, "Amazing, is it not, that we became such close friends?"

"Amazing," Suzanne agreed. "You seemed so standoffish—so superior—when we met in the common room of Miss Sutherby's Select School for Girls."

"I know. I was miserable. I desperately missed my parents. I had quite made up my mind to hate the school and the teachers and the other girls. I was especially determined to hate you."

"Me?"

"You. You may recall you were late returning to school that year."

Suzanne nodded. "Because of my sister's wedding."

"Prior to your arrival I heard 'Lady Suzanne this' and 'Lady Suzanne that' until I was heartily sick of the name. In my infinite wisdom, I knew full well no real person could live up to such a picture of perfection."

"Oh, dear. You must have thought me insufferable."

"I did, at first. You seemed entirely preoccupied with your own circle of friends, none of whom had time for a provincial like me."

"Girls of twelve and thirteen years can be so cruel," Suzanne said regretfully. "Actually, we envied your having lived an exotic life in India. *We* were the provincials. You intimidated us because you *knew* so much."

" 'The Bluestocking.' Barbara Frankton used to whisper it so I would hear. Reading and learning had always been such a joy to me. They still are, actually."

"I know. And I am glad we did not kill that in you."

Cymberly laughed. "There was little danger of that. I took refuge in my books and envied the popular Lady Suzanne."

"Thank goodness for the insight of Miss Kilby."

"Or for her sensitivity—which is probably the same thing. Her pairing us for extra study was quite simply the best thing that happened to me at school."

"I learned to conjugate French verbs," Suzanne said, "and that you were more lonely than snobbish."

"I learned to read music properly, and that you were not only as shy and vulnerable as I, but you really did live up to that picture of perfection!"

Suzanne looked embarrassed. "You hear that, young sir?" She patted her protruding stomach. "Your mama is the picture of perfection."

"She is clairvoyant, too, I surmise." Cymberly's voice held a gurgle of laughter.

"How so?"

"You seem certain this child is a 'young sir'!"

"Kirkwood hopes so."

"And you do, too," Cymberly teased. "Honestly, Suzanne, you seem more besotted with him than ever."

"I know. I am. Unfashionable of me, is it not?"

"I think it is charming."

"Oh, Cymberly, I do hope you find someone as wonderful as my Richard."

Cymberly sighed. "Most unlikely."

Then they talked of other things, promised to write faithfully, and bade each other a tearful farewell.

A few days later, Cymberly boarded a ship, one of a convoy bound for the Iberian Peninsula on a journey that could take as long as six weeks, depending on weather and the captain's skill in evading the blockade.

She stood at the rail of the ship as it sailed out of Plymouth harbor and loneliness crept over her. She had experienced the same isolation when her parents sent her from India to school in England. Expecting to be reunited with her parents when she finished school, she'd received only half a loaf. Papa was posted to the Peninsula, while Mama, already suffering the wasting sickness, returned to England to share a cottage with her daughter. Mother and daughter had lived quite simply, with only Mr. and Mrs. Bartlett as live-in servants. Her mother lamented the fact that her health would not allow her to provide her daughter a proper come-out.

"There will be time enough for that when you are feeling better, Mama," Cymberly invariably replied. Both mother and daughter knew this to be a polite fiction.

When her mother died, Cymberly longed to share her grief with her father, but such was not to be. Weeks later the two of them visited Mama's grave and shed resigned tears, but it was not the same as having his sturdy shoulder to lean on at the time.

She loved her father too much to blame him for her loneliness. Instead, she directed her resentment at that great anomalous entity that kept him from his family—the army. As a soldier, his first duty had ever been to king and country. She understood this, as had her mother. But understanding did little to lessen the feeling of being utterly alone again.

Well, she reassured herself, it would not be for long. She would be joining her father soon, army or no.

She nurtured this thought throughout the voyage, which turned out to be miserable. Summer squalls on the Atlantic and dodging Napoleon's warships, combined with the judgmental coolness of her cabin mate, intensified the discomfort of the trip.

Cymberly tried to befriend the woman she had known fleetingly in London society, but Mrs. Horton obviously found her position distasteful. She made it clear she resented Lady Renfrow's bullying her into chaperoning a young woman society had rejected.

Finally, Cymberly gave up, retreated into formal civility, and spent as much time on deck in the fresh air as weather permitted. However, inclement weather often confined passengers to their quarters. Mrs. Horton, prone to seasickness, seemed to resent Cymberly's robust good health and only reluctantly submitted to the younger woman's ministering aid.

There were fewer than thirty women on board this ship, which carried nearly four hundred soldiers to augment Wellington's forces. Two of the other females were wives of army officers and billeted on the same deck, sharing the captain's table with Cymberly, Mrs. Horton, the ship's officers, and higher ranking army personnel. Young, newly married Juliana Williams was traveling with her equally young lieutenant husband. Mrs. Gordon-Smythe, whose colonel husband outranked Mrs. Horton's spouse by a few months, much to the latter's annoyance, traveled in relative style with two of her servants. She shared Mrs. Horton's superior demeanor, and the two of them often had their heads together, probably comparing negative opinions of the inferior beings around them, Cymberly thought.

The other women were wives of lower ranks. They, and in some instances their children, shared cramped communal quarters on the lower decks. Feeling isolated by the Williams' preoccupation with each other and the distinct coolness of her other companions, Cymberly was drawn to these women when she encountered them on deck. She sympathized with their plight, particularly with that of Mrs. Peters, who tried to keep her two-year-old son under control as she suffered with the early stages of another pregnancy. The woman's husband, always busily engaged in man-talk, never seemed to be available to help. Cymberly occasionally took the little boy, Tommy, from his grateful mother to give the poor woman some respite.

Friendly, talkative Mrs. Peters revealed more of herself than a discreet tongue might willingly have disclosed. Thus, Cymberly learned Mrs. Peters was the daughter of a wealthy cit. Her father had forbidden the marriage, but Mary Beth and her dear Johnny had run off to Gretna Green to be married anyway. They just knew Papa could not withhold his approval once the deed was done. But he had.

" 'You made that bed. Now you must lie in it.' That's what he told us," Mary Beth said sadly. "Oh, my. Johnny was that unhappy about it. He had thought to quit the army, don't you know? But we have managed, mostly because my mama sneaks us funds now and then from her pin money."

The basic elements of Mary Beth's story—young lovers marrying in spite of a disapproving father—paralleled Cymberly's mother's story. Though, of course, Papa was the child of the cit and Papa had adequate, if not ample, funds of his own to care for his wife and daughter. The Winthrops had never again seen the Earl of Chadwyck, Mrs. Winthrop's father. Cymberly remembered once journeying with her mother to the earl's country seat. She must have been about six years old. The butler had been surprised but pleased to see them at the door. A few minutes later he had returned, looking sad and embarrassed.

"I am sorry, Lady Elise. He will not see you."

Mama gripped Cymberly's hand tightly and turned back to their hired carriage. Cymberly twisted around to look again at the imposing house and saw a drapery pulled back on the ground floor. It was quickly dropped, but not before the child glimpsed a shock of white hair. Mama wept silently all the way back to the inn where Papa waited. He had refused to approach the old earl himself and had not encouraged his wife's doing so, though he could not bring himself to deny her wish to go on her own. Her disappointment saddened him, but in Papa's arms, Mama soon recovered her good spirits.

Cymberly gave herself a mental shake. *Pay attention to business, my girl,* she admonished herself. She was observing the frenzied activity of unloading boats ferried to the dock from the ship now anchored in Lisbon's bay. There had been seven ships in their convoy and Cymberly noted other ships in the harbor as well. The captain of "her" ship had been incensed at the presence of three of them.

"Damned Americans," he muttered. Then he saw the ladies standing at the rail and apologized for his language.

"I did not know we traded with them now that we are at war with the former colonies," Cymberly said.

"We don't," the captain replied firmly. "But the Portuguese traders do. *They* sell the goods to us. The Americans know very well where all those goods are going, but where there is a profit . . ."

Later, Cymberly found standing on the firm foundation of the dock after weeks of the motion-filled deck of a ship disconcerting. Mrs. Horton spied her husband immediately and hastily moved off with him, not even bothering to introduce the man to her traveling companion. Aware of the cut, Cymberly felt a twinge of pain, but she refused to let a mean-spirited woman dampen her reunion with her father.

Along with the white garb and red sashes of Portuguese dock workers, the busy wharf sported various military uniforms. The blue uniforms of the British navy were overwhelmed by the red tunics of the British army. There was a sprinkling of green among them, which Cymberly recognized as the color of rifle regiments. Other uniforms, she surmised, belonged to the Portuguese and Spanish armies.

Her father's familiar figure did not appear. She experienced a moment of panic, alone in a whirling sea of humanity. No. He *would* be here.

As the chaos on the dock thinned, some semblance of order began to appear. A tall man in a rifleman's uniform seemed to have firm control of his area, issuing crisp orders in what Cymberly took to be Portuguese. It certainly was neither Spanish nor French. His uniform suggested officer status, as did his ordering others about. However, she saw him share one hapless soldier's burden and leap to the rescue of another who nearly dropped a load.

The Peters family stood on the other side of the dock, near this officer and his crew. As usual, Corporal Peters was laughing and horsing around with other newly arrived soldiers while his wife oversaw their belongings and their son. Mary Beth sat her son on a leather bag and Cymberly saw rather than heard her telling him to "stay put." The harried mother turned her attention to getting the rest of her family's belongings together.

Of course the child immediately scrambled down from his perch and toddled on his chubby little legs toward the edge of the dock. Just as Cymberly started toward the Peters group, knowing her voice would not be heard over the din, she saw Tommy reach for the tail of a scruffy stray dog. He tumbled off the dock into the brackish water below.

The sequence of events that followed seemed to move at a maddeningly slow pace. Mary Beth screamed. Her husband looked around in annoyance. Cymberly tried to rush across the dock, but it had suddenly gained the dimensions of a large field filled with people conspiring to impede her movement. The tall officer whisked off his hat and dived in after the child.

As Cymberly reached the edge of the dock, the man's head popped up from the scummy water. He took a deep breath and his head disappeared. Was he never coming up again?

Finally, the head appeared—no, *two* heads—and the man began to swim somewhat awkwardly toward a rowboat propelled by another quick-thinking bystander.

The audience on the dock watched as the rescuer worked with the inert child. Finally, the little body twitched. They could not hear his cough, but they did, indeed, hear his howl of protest. They let out a unified sigh of relief.

Cymberly, standing next to Mrs. Peters, put her arms around the crying mother.

"He is all right. He is safe," Cymberly murmured soothingly.

"Why were you not watching him properly? That's what I want ta know," Corporal Peters demanded of his wife.

"I—I was," Mary Beth sobbed. "I was looking after your gear, is all. I only glanced away for a moment."

"Woman's s'posed to look after her young'un," Peters grumbled as the dripping officer approached with the little boy in his arms.

"Your property, madam?" He had a deep voice laced with just a hint of laughter. "He is very wet, but otherwise seems to be in fine shape."

"Oh, thank you. Thank you. Thank you." Mary Beth reached for her son.

"Mama, I falled," Tommy said with a note of surprise.

"Yes, darling, you did. But the nice man rescued you." She hugged him fiercely to her.

"Mebbe now you'll take better care of 'im," her husband said curtly. He turned to his son's rescuer, held out his hand, and said in a deferential tone, "I thank you, sir. Sorry about your getting wet like that. My woman will see to your clothes, sir. She shoulda been watchin' the boy."

The tall officer stared at Corporal Peters for a moment before taking the offered hand.

"Never mind my clothing. My batman will handle it. Your wife seemed to have her hands full. She could have used some help." His voice was soft, but the reprimand was clear, and Johnny Peters colored up slightly.

Mary Beth still hugged her child. "I cannot thank you enough, sir," she said. "I'd 'a' died if I lost Tommy. You are a real hero, Captain—uh, Major?"

The man smiled, obviously embarrassed, but it was a genuine smile, showing a flash of strong, white teeth. "Major. With the Portuguese Army today."

"But you are clearly English," Cymberly blurted without thinking.

He turned a pair of mesmerizing slate gray eyes on her and Cymberly felt a strange stillness within her. For a split second—or was it an eternity?—nothing else existed but this man and his presence.

"Yes, ma'am, I am. With General Beresford's Portuguese force." He pulled his gaze away from hers and addressed the group around him. "If you all will excuse me . . ."

He was interrupted by a voice clearly used to a parade ground—one Cymberly knew well.

"Cymberly! Cymberly, my girl."

"Papa!" She threw herself into the arms of the beloved stocky figure and hugged him warmly. "I was sure you had forgotten me."

"Never." He kissed her cheek and clasped her tightly, repeating her name. Finally, he drew back. "Let me look at you. Ah, yes. Still one of the two most beautiful ladies of my acquaintance, your mama having been the other one."

The familiar line had thrilled a little girl, and now brought back warm memories, but Cymberly blushed all the same.

"Oh, Papa. The most extraordinary thing just occurred." She related Tommy's fall and rescue. But when she looked around for the officer who had retrieved the child, he was nowhere to be found.

Two

Geoffrey Alan Hayden Ryder, British rifleman and major attached to General Beresford's Portuguese forces, rescuer of little Tommy Peters, sat staring at his glass of watered-down wine. Major Ryder never drank heavily when he could be called to action at any time.

Hours later, and still the image of that woman on the dock floated through his mind.

The sun had picked out reddish highlights in her dark brown hair. Her hazel eyes, intelligent and observant, had shone with warmth and compassion for the little boy and his mother. Would she be equally expressive in showing passion for a man? He surmised that her traveling costume was in the latest London fashion. That marked her as Quality, yet she had befriended an ordinary soldier's wife.

General Winthrop's appearance answered the immediate question of who she was. Old "Cuss 'em and Cuff 'em Charlie" had a daughter! Geoffrey had known General, then Colonel, Winthrop when they both served with Wellington, then Wellesley, in India, though a lowly lieutenant did not fraternize much with field-grade officers. Ryder knew the sobriquet was a term of grudging admiration rather than disparagement from men who had learned that rigid discipline and training saved many a soldier's life.

Would the daughter be as tough as her father? She would have to be to survive for long in the Peninsula. Good God!

Who in his right mind would bring a woman into this particular substitute for hell, especially one of those pampered darlings of the *ton* such as Winthrop's "Cymberly" appeared to be?

Ryder mentally shrugged his shoulders. It was none of his concern. Finishing the wine, he sought the comfort of a cot in the less-than-elegant facilities he shared with three other officers. He fell asleep promptly. Experienced soldiers learned to sleep when they could. Sunlight-filled brown hair, sparkling hazel eyes, and lips that promised to be infinitely sweet swirled through his dreams. He woke in the middle of the night thinking it had been too damned long since he had a woman. That must be the reason this one continued to invade his thoughts.

Cymberly knew her father had mixed feelings about her being in Portugal. He was pleased to see her, but he would have worried less if she were still in England.

"You will find my quarters not nearly so luxurious as what you are used to, my dear," he apologized as they rode in the open carriage through the streets of Lisbon, lined with buildings of whitewashed stucco and red tile roofs.

"They will be fine, Papa." She patted his hand. "Amitabha is still your batman, is he not?"

"Yes, indeed. I do believe that man would follow me to the gates of hell!"

"He has always been grateful that you rescued him from those selfsame gates years ago."

"He will be glad to see you again."

"Amitabha," she said fondly. "He used to push me for hours in that swing you fashioned for me in Malabar."

"I have also hired a maid for you. Maggie Osborne. Her husband was killed a few months ago. So far she cannot bring herself to accept any of the offers of marriage she has received."

"Thank you for thinking of that necessity for me."

"Be sure to take her with you whenever you go out. The locals are *very* conservative in dos and don'ts for unmarried females. Wellington likes us to accommodate their views insofar as possible."

"Very well. You have only Amitabha and Maggie?"

"And Senhora Domingo, the cook. She came with the house when I rented it."

"That was lucky."

"Very. She is an artist in the kitchen. A gardener and another maid come in during the day, but they live out. When my regiment moves north, I shall take Amitabha with me, of course, but I will leave the others with you, and perhaps hire another man to help look after my females."

"Wha-a-at? I shall not stay in Lisbon if you are not there." There was a trace of panic in her voice.

"Of course you will. You cannot follow a fighting army around—not a girl like you."

"I most certainly can. And I will."

"Cymberly, no." He said it as though he were admonishing his little girl about touching a hot fire. "I would you had stayed in London, but since you are here, you must remain in Lisbon."

"No, Papa. I will stay with you." She knew she sounded just as she had as a young girl when stubbornly asserting herself. "Others manage. So shall I."

"My dear, you have no idea what you would be in for. The hardships."

"I shall learn. And I shall cope with whatever comes my way." She lifted her chin obstinately.

"We shall speak of this again," he said, as they arrived at their destination.

With four or five bedchambers, a large drawing room, dining room, kitchen, a small library, and servants' quarters, the rented house was quite elegant. There was even a stable that would accommodate as many as six horses. The rooms had high ceilings and thick outer walls to keep the building cool in summer. The furniture was dark heavy wood that contrasted with tiled floors and whitewashed walls. Cymberly found it altogether charming.

The three live-in servants stood in the foyer to greet her. Cymberly put her palms together and held her hands in front of her in the traditional Indian fashion as she bowed to her old friend, a tall, thin Hindu man of indeterminate years.

"Namaste, Amitabha. How wonderful to see you again."

"Namaste, Missy Sahib. Welcome." He grinned widely, showing strong white teeth against dark skin. His eyes, so brown they were nearly black, were warm and friendly.

Her father introduced her to the two women and they exchanged greetings. Middle-aged Senhora Domingo had black hair streaked with gray. Maggie was an energetic woman of perhaps thirty; she had light brown hair and deep blue eyes.

Two days later, Cymberly found herself at a lavish party hosted by General Lord Boynton and his wife. The Boyntons had rented a villa on the outskirts of the city with a large drawing room and lovely formal gardens. Lady Boynton had achieved a "crush" that would have cast a greenish tinge of envy on the cheek of any London hostess.

Cymberly entered on the arm of her father and—no, it was not her imagination—there was a long, pregnant pause in conversations as all eyes focused on her momentarily. Then proper manners triumphed and conversational murmurs resumed. The gossip mill was grinding away even in distant Portugal. Mrs. Horton and Mrs. Gordon-Smythe had been busy.

Cymberly had no fear she would sit out any dances. After all, she noted ruefully, there were about ten smart military tunics for every ball gown in the room. In a splendid creation of antique white silk, she knew herself to be in especially good looks this evening. She wanted to make a good impression for her father's sake. So much the better if doing so helped restore her self-esteem, which had taken a bruising from that business in London.

The Boyntons' drawing room had been denuded of most furniture and the carpets taken up. Several musicians played in a far corner. After greeting their hosts, Cymberly and her father stood momentarily on the sidelines. Then Juliana Williams approached on the arm of her lieutenant husband.

"Miss Winthrop, how nice to see you again." Howard Williams bowed over her hand as his wife murmured her greeting. Cymberly knew very well their goal was not merely renewing their transitory acquaintance with her. As one of Wellington's aides, General Charles Winthrop was in a position to put in a good word for ambitious young officers. Nevertheless, she was grateful to them for breaking the ice. Greeting them warmly, she made them known to her father.

Soon a few other young officers, some accompanied by ladies, joined them. Her father excused himself as Cymberly chatted amiably and flirted mildly, just as she might have done in a London ballroom. Then a newcomer, a very smartly turned out lieutenant, approached them.

"I say, Williams. You *must* introduce me to these new paragons of female beauty." Carefully arranged blond hair and confident sky-blue eyes marked one of the best-looking men Cymberly had ever beheld.

"Go away, Fleming. You ain't needed here," one of the other young men joked.

Lieutenant Williams had little choice. "My dear, and Miss Winthrop, may I present Lieutenant Reginald Fleming of the Twenty-First Foot? My wife, Mrs. Williams, and Miss Cymberly Winthrop."

"I do hope you ladies each have at least one dance left that I may claim. Be a shame if you were relegated to dancing only with these clodhoppers." He laughed and gestured toward his fellow officers.

"Fleming . . ."

"I say . . ."

The injured gentlemen growled at him.

"Just because your Pa's a general doesn't give you first rights to all the pretty girls," one of them said, but there was no animosity in the protest.

"No. My charming, handsome self assures me that privilege," he said smugly. "Come, Miss Winthrop, say you will allow me to be your shining knight, here to rescue you from such as these."

"Perhaps later, sir." Cymberly laughed at his brazenness. "I have the set after supper open. Do you think all that charm will keep until then?"

"I will store it up just for you, dear lady."

At this point, the first dance was announced and General Winthrop claimed his daughter.

"Sorry, gentlemen. A father takes certain priorities, you know," he said. As they waited for the set to form, he asked her softly, "Is everything all right?"

"There is some slight restraint. I cannot think the dowagers like me overmuch, but the others seem amiable enough."

Cymberly had told her father the complete story of her London disgrace. He had been lovingly indignant on her behalf, sorry about her fall, but he supported her decision to refuse Taraton's offer.

"Your Lord Taraton sounds a decent lad," he had said, "but I would not have you marry where your heart is not engaged. Nor would your mama have wished such."

"Thank you, Papa. I do hope one day to have what you and Mama had in your marriage." They had hugged each other tightly and Cymberly knew both of them had in mind a vision of the dear lady who also would have approved her decision.

Now her father smiled down at her on the dance floor. "I see you met Lieutenant Fleming."

"Yes. He is an amusing fellow, is he not?"

"Makes a big hit with the ladies, young and old alike," he agreed. "Very charming."

Cymberly laughed. "That is what *he* said."

"Did he now? Sounds like him."

"Captain Wilson said Lieutenant Fleming's father is a general."

"He is. Good man. Serving in North America now. We could use him here. The son has yet to prove himself."

"Now, Papa," she chided. "This is a party. Stop soldiering for a little while."

"Yes, miss," he said with mock submissiveness. "For what it is worth, young Fleming is an excellent dancer."

As the set swung into action, it occurred to Cymberly that her father was quite adept in a ballroom himself.

She went into supper with Captain Wilson, who reminded her slightly of David Taraton. Friendly and easy to talk with, Wilson answered her questions and shared information with her as though she were a thinking human being, not merely a decorative sounding board for male witticisms.

Cymberly and Wilson shared a table with two other couples. A nearby table accommodated five or six single gentlemen who seemed to be enjoying the wine more than the food. At another table within the same circle, General Winthrop sat with other high-ranking men and their ladies.

During a lull in conversation, one of the young men at the next table asked, "Where is Ryder tonight?"

At the name "Ryder," Cymberly caught her father's eye. He mouthed the word "later" to her.

"Doubtless still out playing soldier with the locals." This voice was Lieutenant Fleming's.

"He has been in town these last several days," someone else said. "Told me he would be here a fortnight."

"Well then, he probably just does not want to be with *real* soldiers. Not after that fiasco at Salamanca," Fleming said.

"Reggie!" The pretended shock came from one of Fleming's companions, Ensign Warren, who seemed to hang on Fleming's every word. "You are surely not suggesting that our Portuguese brothers in arms are not 'real' soldiers!"

A calmer voice cut in with, "General Beresford has his work cut out for him, forming a national army in this country. The Royals took a good many of the most able people with them when they fled to Brazil."

"He ain't likely to succeed if Ryder is typical of the help he is getting," Warren's scornful voice came again.

The voice of reason responded, "Wellington personally assigned Ryder to Beresford. Old Nosey must have some regard for the major's ability."

Fleming snorted derisively. "More likely ridding his own ranks of a coward."

"I am not sure we heard the whole of that incident at Salamanca," the reasonable one said.

Another voice deliberately changed the subject.

"Say, George, I hear you happened upon a find in terms of horseflesh."

"I surely did. A real goer. Half Arab."

At Cymberly's table Juliana Williams remarked, "They do not hold this Major Ryder in very high esteem, do they?"

Captain Wilson cleared his throat. "As Beauchamp said, they do not know the full story. Best give a man benefit of doubt."

"Something must have happened on that battlefield," said Mrs. Johnstone, wife of the third man at the table. "Ryder was sent over to the Portuguese almost immediately."

"Now, my dear," her husband admonished. " 'Tis possible that was just coincidence."

The conversation turned to local sights that the newcomers might find interesting. But Cymberly could not get the name Ryder out of her mind.

In the end, Lieutenant Fleming claimed Miss Winthrop for two dances despite the protests of his fellow officers. Cymberly was immensely attracted to this handsomest of men. Flattered by his obvious efforts to charm her, she did not hesitate to accept his invitation to go driving the next day.

In the carriage as she and her father returned to their quarters, she said, "Ryder was Mama's family name. Is there a connection, Papa?"

"A very remote one. When Ryder was in India, he and your mother met once at a social function. Seems the second or third earl, about eight generations back, married twice. Your mother was descended from the first wife and Geoffrey Ryder belongs in the lineage from the second wife."

"Oh, well . . ." she said dismissively.

"The Chadwyck earls never had much luck producing heirs. Lots of girls. Not many sons. The present earl—your grandfather—lost his only son when you were about four. Seems to me Major Ryder's brother is the heir."

"Seems to me," she said, echoing his tone, "the major must have inherited negative traits from the Chadwyck line. Those men tonight did not think very highly of him."

"I am not personally well acquainted with Ryder. Knew him only briefly in India. He was mostly assigned to work with locals there, too. He acquitted himself well, though."

"Do you know what happened at Salamanca last year? Someone said he behaved in a cowardly manner."

"I would not credit gossip overmuch," her father said evasively, and Cymberly knew he would say no more on the matter.

But she had already reached her own conclusions. On the one hand, she found it disconcerting—not to say embarrassing—to have any connection, however remote, with a man other soldiers considered a coward. On the other hand, what she had heard merely confirmed her preconceived impression of anyone named Ryder. She despised the family who had contrived to make her mother's life miserable.

She hoped never to meet the man.

Three

In some respects, transfer to Portugal wrought few changes in Cymberly's life. The weather was warmer and more dependable, allowing use of an open carriage in making morning calls. She reluctantly made such calls, though often as not they occurred in midafternoon, after the siesta hours.

"Trust us true sons and daughters of 'the sceptred isle,' " she mused, "to turn a foreign location into a grand imitation of home."

Making social calls, even in England, was not a task Cymberly had ever welcomed. She enjoyed good conversation springing from the discussion of books or world events, but deep discussions of which braid looked best on which ball gown bored her to the point of distraction.

Now it was even worse, for she was likely to find her reception somewhat chilly, especially if she called alone. Her father was rarely free to escort her, but Lieutenant Fleming eagerly performed the service. Cymberly delighted in his company and was drawn to him that much more for his willingness to befriend her despite whispers of scandal.

A good conversationalist, he entertained even as he conveyed vital information about her new life. She learned the English community in Lisbon was rather a tight-knit group, larger than usual because much of the army had wintered in this location. Troops would be moving out soon now that supplies brought by the convoy were being readied for transfer to the north and east.

"What will the wives do when the army marches?" Cymberly introduced this topic as she and Fleming rode in an open vehicle to attend an afternoon tea. She knew that in India, soldiers' women were likely to stay in the compounds when their men went out on military sorties.

"Some will stay here," Fleming said. "A few will return to England—Lady Boynton, for instance, has been here only for the winter lull. She prefers winter weather in Lisbon to that in Northhamptonshire."

"And the others?"

"Those who stay will carry on pretty much as they do now. You know, making calls, afternoon teas, that sort of thing. There will still be a good number of troops to handle supplies as they come in, so there will even be a ball now and then." He grinned at her.

"And those who choose neither to stay in Lisbon nor return to England?"

He shrugged. "They will follow the army as they always do. Whenever a military contingent goes out, the baggage train is filled with women and children. As long as they do not hamper the march, they are tolerated. Welcomed, actually. The women cook, do laundry, and mend. And they have other uses," he added mischievously.

"Lieutenant Fleming!" A twitch in her lips negated the mild reprimand. She steered his attention back to the topic by asking, "What of the officers' wives? I cannot imagine Mrs. Gordon-Smythe performing such mundane tasks as cooking and laundry."

"Lord, no. She will travel with a full staff of servants, to be sure. Some have four or five, but most make do with one or two."

"Why do they not simply wait here for the men to return?" Cymberly had been unable to discuss the details of this issue with her father, who still insisted his daughter stay in Lisbon.

"Because," Fleming answered, "their men may not return."

"Oh."

The concern in her voice caused him to look at her. "No. That is not what I meant. I simply meant the troops may not return to Lisbon. They may sail from some other port." He turned his attention back to the horses.

"Oh." She silently cursed her ignorance of the geography of the Iberian Peninsula. "I understand. I also understand a woman's desire to stay close to her man."

"Would you be staying close to your man in such a case?" he teased.

"Of course." Her firm tone held no trace of teasing.

He looked at her, startled. "I say, Cymberly—Miss Winthrop. You are not of a mind to follow the army? Surely your father would not approve."

"He does not approve—yet."

He started to reply, but suddenly his attention was diverted by a cluster of men on the side of the street. They were traveling through a rather run-down section of the city, safe enough in these daylight hours, but dangerous after dark.

"Did you see that?" His voice was excited and disapproving.

"See what?" She looked and saw a group of Portuguese peasants standing off to one side.

"That fellow who took off down the alley."

She had a fleeting impression of a big man, taller than the other peasants, but with hair equally as dark.

"What about him?"

"It was Ryder," Fleming said excitedly. "Now what would *he* be doing with fellows like these? And dressed like them, too! Up to something havey-cavey, I'd wager."

She looked again, but the man was gone.

"If only my father could see his pet boy now!" Bitterness and triumph sounded in his voice. "Salamanca. And now this."

"Your father?"

"My father thinks Ryder is *the* perfect soldier. Used to hold him up as a pattern card for me to follow. Father's favorite. Lost some of his shine now, though."

"I do not quite understand."

"First, he sneaks off in the midst of a major battle and now he is consorting with what are probably criminal elements. 'Wrecking Ryder' appears to be wrecking himself."

"Could it not be an innocent meeting?"

He snorted. "In this neighborhood? I think not."

They left the unsavory area and emerged onto a street of black and gray cobblestones laid out in intricate patterns— like a Roman mosaic, Cymberly thought. Soon they arrived at their destination, the home of a major who served with her father.

Cymberly knew some of the women she met socially did not approve of her. They tolerated her out of deference to her father's rank and his close friendship with Wellington. Her social acceptance correlated directly with her hostesses' concern for their husbands' military careers.

She also knew Lieutenant Reginald Fleming's interest in her helped smooth the feathers of some of the old hens before they had even been ruffled. Fleming was as popular with all the ladies as her father had said. He flirted outrageously with every female he encountered. He even had Mrs. Horton giggling over the hearts she was supposedly breaking among his fellow officers.

He seemed to enjoy a high degree of popularity with men, too. At a social function, if he were not entertaining and flattering the ladies, he would be the center of a group of men, telling a joke or story. From the tone of the laughter, Cymberly surmised that these were often ribald tales. She knew Fleming had a following among certain younger men. His daredevil willingness to bet on anything from sporting events to which of two raindrops would course down a pane of glass first insured his dominating this group. Chief among his male admirers was Ensign Warren, who ostentatiously aped Fleming's dress and mannerisms and echoed Fleming's views.

Fleming injected life into every gathering he attended, Cymberly observed. The company seemed to heave a collective sigh on his arrival to indicate that *now* the fun could begin. When this handsome, merry fellow singled her out for attention, she was flattered. Nor did his pursuit of her go unnoticed. There were subtle indications that others had begun to think of them as an "item." She did not discourage him, for she quite simply and quite thoroughly enjoyed his company.

Her father, too, noticed the growing friendship.

"Young Fleming seems rather marked in his attentions," General Winthrop commented one morning at breakfast. "Should I be demanding to know the nature of his intentions toward my daughter?"

"No, Papa." Cymberly smiled her acknowledgment of his teasing tone. "Not yet, at least. Heavens! We have known each other only a matter of days."

"Sometimes it takes much less than that, my dear. Maybe only an instant."

Now why did the image of a tall man with slate-gray eyes and wearing a sopping wet uniform pop into her mind? "Was it like that for you?" she asked to divert his interest from the subject of Fleming. She knew full well it was, for the story of her parents' meeting and courtship had fascinated their little girl.

" 'Twas, indeed. I knew the moment I saw your mama at a country assembly she was the only girl for me."

"Did she know, too?"

"I think so. Told me she did. Of course, I had no idea she was an earl's daughter. But it was already too late for that to matter."

"That hateful old man," Cymberly said fiercely.

Her father nodded. "A disagreeable fellow, but once I had a daughter of my own, I understood his attitude better."

"I cannot imagine your being so cruel. I do not care that he is my grandfather. He treated Mama abominably."

"That he did. And she never quite got over it," he said sadly. Then he brightened. "You need not fear such rejection from me. If I dislike your choice, I will simply call out the army and chase the bounder off! So choose where you will, daughter of mine."

She chuckled. "I shall not be making such a choice any time soon, I assure you."

"By the by, speaking of Chadwyck, I just learned that Major Ryder—we spoke of him after the Boynton ball, you recall?—Ryder is now Chadwyck's heir."

"Indeed?"

"Seems he has been for some time. His brother died over a year ago when his horse refused a fence."

"Oh, my."

"Old Chadwyck is apparently in quite a dither because our major refuses to do his bidding."

"Do his bidding?"

"Give up his commission and come home to play his proper role as heir."

"Why would the major not do so?"

"I have no idea. Sense of obligation? Duty?" He shrugged. "Well, I must be off, my dear."

He rose, gave her a quick kiss on her forehead, and left her musing. She dismissed the news about the Chadwyck earldom. It had nothing to do with her. But how *did* she feel about Fleming?

That evening the Winthrops were to attend what was said to be *the* social event of the season. Napoleon's invading French troops had, six years ago, forced the Portuguese royal family to flee to Brazil. In their stead, the Council of Regency, the acting government, sponsored a grand ball to celebrate the expulsion of French forces from Portugal and to honor officers of the British army and of the Portuguese army, reorganized under Britain's General Beresford. Also present would be officers of the KGL—the British King's German Legion—and those of the Spanish army who fought with the allies against the forces of Spain's puppet King Joseph, brother of Napoleon Bonaparte.

Cymberly dressed carefully in her favorite ball gown, an apricot silk trimmed with cream-colored lace. With it she wore a gold topaz pendant and matching earrings, her father's wedding gift to her mother. He smiled approvingly as she pulled on the long gloves and wrapped herself in a finely woven woolen shawl the color of the lace on her gown.

The festivities started with a reception line consisting of the highest ranking government officials and generals commanding the honorees. Cymberly was overwhelmed by the array of colorful uniforms, sashes, and gold braid.

"I will never be able to keep them all in order," she said softly as she and her father left the receiving line. "I had expected Lord Wellington to be at this grand affair. I look forward to meeting him."

"He is readying the army to move against French forces in northern Spain. His headquarters is over a hundred miles from here now. He has been known to attend a ball until the wee hours and report for duty the next morning none the worse for wear, but that would be a long ride even for him."

"Such a pity our army boasts so few superior horsemen." Cymberly's voice was laced with irony.

Her father gave a bark of laughter. "Ah, my dear, there Wellington would agree with you wholeheartedly."

Circling the edge of the ballroom, they approached a cluster of officers and ladies. Most of the men were in her father's regiment.

"Ah, General Winthrop. Just the man to answer our question," said a short, rotund man with a shining face.

"Reese. Good evening, ladies, gentlemen. Have all of you met my daughter Cymberly?"

There were some murmurs of assent, but a tall man standing to the side turned slowly and said in a deep voice, "No, I have not."

Colonel Reese laughed. "Geoffrey, dear boy, where *have* you been? Unlike you to allow others to get a march on you. Miss Winthrop, allow me to present Major Geoffrey Ryder."

Extending her hand, Cymberly looked up and caught her breath. The man from the dock! He took her gloved hand in his own and bowed over it. Cymberly felt something she thought must be akin to a lightning bolt course through her. Then those wonderful eyes were smiling directly into hers.

"Miss Winthrop," he murmured.

"You—you—are Ryder?" she stammered rudely, disengaging her hand from his.

"Yes, for over thirty years." His voice held a hint of laughter. "You were expecting someone else of that name?"

"No. I . . . that is . . . no, sir." The cool Miss Winthrop was flustered. "I had not thought to meet you at all." This sounded harsher than she intended, so she quickly added, "I remember you from the dock."

"I have the advantage of you, Miss Winthrop. I knew who you were when your father greeted you that day. General." He acknowledged her father's presence.

"Now, General," Colonel Reese said before the conversation could take another turn, "we were just discussing Wellington and supplies."

"That so?"

"Chester here says we cannot leave for another week."

"Can't," Chester asserted. "Need more donkeys and more carts. Wagons ain't practical for the mountains."

"Chester has the right of it," Winthrop said. "We need more donkeys and more carts, but we should have them in two or three days. We leave as soon as we have them."

"Three days!" Cymberly blurted.

"We will discuss it later," her father said.

Three days, she thought. *Three days.* Her mind was in turmoil. Surprised and hurt, she wondered if her father still meant to leave her behind.

Also, she had not realized how much the man on the dock had preoccupied her mind. Now to meet him and to learn he was a Ryder came as a shock. Distracted though she was, she made appropriate small talk, politely agreeing to dance later with Major Ryder. Soon Lieutenant Fleming claimed her for the opening set.

Well, now he had actually met her, Geoffrey Ryder told himself. Perhaps if he came to know her, she would stop haunting his dreams. One thing was certain, his other remedy had not worked. Another woman had not made this one less of a presence in his musings.

He watched her walk away with Fleming and he wondered how much substance there was to the rumors in that quarter. Surprised by a twinge of jealousy, he gave himself a mental shake and turned his attention to an ongoing discussion of military tactics.

When it came time to claim his dance with Miss Winthrop, it was very late in the evening. He had watched her stand up twice with Fleming and take supper with him. Never much of a ladies' man, Geoffrey had danced only with Mrs. Reese and the wife of a Portuguese officer with whom he worked.

He positioned himself to be near her father as she was returned to his side. "I believe the next dance is mine."

"So it is," she agreed, looking at her card.

They waited for the music in awkward silence. At the first bars, she started and consulted her card again.

"Oh! It is a waltz," she squeaked.

"Yes. Are you uncomfortable with a waltz?"

"No. Oh, no. It is just a surprise. I have not seen it here

before and I thought perhaps it had not yet arrived in Portugal."

"The Germans introduced us to it, though I must admit Portugal's dowagers do not approve."

"I should think not. Shocking display." She imitated a tone of staid disapproval.

He smiled and opened his arms. And there she was—in his arms, her head just beneath his chin, and it felt so right to have her there. The scent from her hair reminded him of India. What was it? Ah, sandalwood and something else. Something flowery and spicy, but very light. He knew instantly that, as a means of getting her out of his system, this had been a mistake. A big but very wonderful mistake.

Neither said anything as they danced for several moments, each seemingly absorbed in the music. Then she looked up at him.

"It is customary, Major Ryder, to make small talk as one dances."

"Hmm." He pretended to think about this. "Yes. I suppose you are right. Unfortunately, I am not proficient in that particular art."

"Oh? And in just what arts are you proficient, sir?"

I kill other men very proficiently, he thought. *And I am accredited a capable spy.* But one did not discuss such dubious skills in a ballroom. "I ride and fence and shoot. Those are gentlemanly skills, are they not?"

"Very much so," she said with a great show of false enthusiasm. "Are you an accomplished orator, too? I am told true gentlemen make great speeches in the House of Lords."

"I *knew* there was something I was missing!" He looked down into her laughing eyes and then his gaze went to her lips. He nearly missed a step. He drew her ever so slightly closer and thought she leaned in to him. He swept her in a great circle of the dance. "Your turn," he said.

"My turn for what?"

"You must tell me of the arts at your command."

"I am not sure there are any."

"Come now, Miss Winthrop. I thought all ladies could draw, paint, embroider, play the pianoforte, and flirt outrageously with the flutter of a fan."

She laughed. "Such important skills you impute to ladies! Alas. I fear I am a miserable failure, for I do none of those things well."

"But you do do them."

"I sketch—not well—and play the pianoforte, but only for my own amusement."

"Not such a very miserable failure, then. A lady fit for any London drawing room."

"Please tell me you are not one of those gentlemen who feel women have nothing to contribute outside a drawing room."

"That is not what I said." He could think of another room he would dearly love to have this one in. *Down, boy,* he admonished himself. Aloud, he added, "I must admit women are delightful creatures, but in war they are likely to be more hindrance than help."

She stiffened. "Pray, do explain."

He began to feel he had opened a container best left sealed, but he plunged on. "During a campaign they sometimes get in the way of a marching column. A man worried about a woman's welfare cannot devote himself properly to his job of soldiering."

"So the army truly has no use for all those women who seem called upon to follow it around?"

"Very little, I would say."

"I am told they cook, mend, and do laundry on the trail— are those not useful functions?"

"Of course. But they are mere conveniences."

"Much better to leave the woman home to wait for her soldier." Her tone was derisive.

"I think so, yes," he said stubbornly.

"Are we not fortunate, then," she said, the sweetness of

her tone belied by her snapping eyes, "that yours is not the prevailing view?"

Suddenly, the dance was over. As he returned her to her father, he groped for a more amenable note on which to end the conversation, but found none. Against his better judgment, he wanted—even now—to ask permission to call on her, but he was leaving before daylight to meet with partisans in the north.

He thanked her for the dance and silently regretted what might have been. He was amazed at the intensity of his thwarted desire. Lord! When was the last time he had entertained the notion of paying court to a woman like this? Years. Not since Georgina . . .

Cymberly and her father were both quiet as they rode home, each seemingly occupied with troubling thoughts. She was astonished at her reaction to Major Ryder. She had not wanted to dance with him. He was a Ryder. One of *those* Ryders. Chadwyck's heir.

And he was an insufferably arrogant know-all! His attitude toward women was nothing short of insulting. Moreover, the man lacked basic social skills. Why, he had deigned to dance only three times and had taken supper at a table with other men only. He had mostly stood around talking to fellow officers the entire evening. What did *he* know of women?

But, Lord, he was attractive. No getting around that. Why else would she have been aware of where and with whom he was all evening? He was not handsome like Reginald Fleming. No, Fleming, blond, blue-eyed, with perfect features, was just short of beautiful, as a Greek statue is beautiful.

Ryder, with his high cheekbones and straight black brows, looked more rugged. He had a wide mouth and a hint of a dimple on the left side when he smiled. His nose was not precisely straight, having probably been broken at some time.

The only real blemish on his face was a scar that angled from just above the inner corner of his left eye through the edge of his eyebrow and into his hairline. She thought he must have come very close to losing his eye. More than his looks, a sense of solid strength and controlled power commanded one's attention. She recalled a faint spicy scent, probably his shaving soap, and the rough texture of his smooth-fitting uniform tunic.

She tried to remember what had been said of him at the Boynton affair earlier. Something about an act of cowardice at Salamanca, was it not? She could not reconcile this idea with the image of a man diving into the scummy water of a bay to rescue a little boy, but it might fit a man who thought women so useless. She deliberately steered her mind to other matters.

"Papa?"

"Hmm?"

"What was that business about leaving in three days?"

He sighed. "I was going to tell you when the time came."

"You mean just as you were going out the door?"

"Not exactly."

"I am going with you."

"Cymberly, be reasonable. You know it is impossible."

"No, Papa. I do *not* know that. I have discussed this with others and I see no reason I cannot accompany you. Maggie has agreed to go with me. She has had experience and can help me. So will Amitabha when you have no need of him."

"It is not that I dislike the idea of having you with me," he said patiently. "I am trying to spare you the hardships. You should stay here where you can enjoy life."

Enjoy life? Good heavens. Did her own father share Ryder's view of women?

"I understand your concerns, Papa. But how could I possibly enjoy being a useless fribble here in Lisbon when I might be of some service to you and others? Besides," she said, playing her trump card, "without you to smooth the way for me here, my social consequence is likely to diminish appreciably. Especially as Lieutenant Fleming will be going, too."

"What makes you think you have so little consequence on your own?"

"Papa, those tabbies remember that I was compromised in London."

"I thought they had gone beyond that. Lord knows you are invited out often enough."

"No, Papa. *You* are invited and you are welcome to bring your daughter along. It is not the same thing. I am received civilly when I call, but unless I am with you or Lieutenant Fleming, the reception is decidedly cool."

"I was not aware," he said softly as the carriage arrived at their quarters.

"I know. I did not want you to worry about me. But can you not see how difficult it would be for me here without you? I would prefer the hardships of the campaign to the icy atmosphere in, say, Mrs. Horton's drawing room."

General Winthrop jumped from the stopped carriage to hand her down. "Well," he conceded, "we had best see about getting you a sturdy horse and some more pack mules for our gear."

"Thank you, Papa." She gave him a quick, tight hug.

"I hope you will still feel like thanking me when this is over."

Four

A week later Cymberly thought of the Lisbon interlude as a pleasant sojourn and life in London as a dream of the distant past. Her present was a blend of dust, sweltering heat, and bone-deep weariness. She had confidently thought of herself as a capable rider, but being on a horse all day, day after day, was quite different from leisurely outings in Hyde Park.

General Winthrop had procured a sturdy little Spanish mare for her. His own two horses and five mules, one of which pulled a small cart, completed their traveling stable. Besides baggage for four people, the animals carried a two-day supply of food for themselves and their human companions. The general allowed himself only one luxury—a set of books.

Cymberly was amazed at the size of the army and its vast "tail" as it finally came together two days from Lisbon—and they had yet to connect with the main elements of Wellington's forces, which were already deep into Spain. Infantry and riflemen marched in front, with officers and cavalry riding on either side. Close behind came the artillery and ammunition wagons, bandsmen, and the commissariat with its dozens of carts and pack animals. The commissariat carried foodstuffs and soldiers' baggage and drove a herd of cattle to provide the daily rations of meat. There were also the entrepreneurial sutlers who would, for a price, provide any number of extras the soldiers and their families might require.

In the rear of this vast tail were additional baggage wagons, pack animals, a few men, and dozens of women and children. Some rode on or drove the wagons, but most marched alongside. These were servants, camp followers, and wives and children "following the drum" of Wellington's army.

Cymberly, along with Amitabha and Maggie, traveled with this group. Maggie drove the Winthrops' cart; Amitabha, on one of the mules, controlled the other animals. Cymberly usually traveled off to the side to escape some of the dust. Occasionally, she rode with Fleming or with her father, though both men were usually occupied with their respective regiments.

In the evenings, Lieutenant Fleming often made an appearance at the Winthrop tent, but in the first days, Cymberly was simply too exhausted to entertain him properly.

Overnights were made in towns and villages when possible. The quartermaster officers would ride ahead and determine which buildings would provide suitable lodging. As the army arrived each evening, the quartermasters greeted the marchers at the outskirts to give directions. The best houses were reserved for officers and their families.

In strict obedience of Wellington's orders, the British army, unlike their French adversaries, paid for what they took in the way of food for themselves and their animals. Often, the village would be too small for all the army, so many would be set up in tents on the outskirts. If no village or town were available, everyone established camp out in the open.

While the general saw to the needs of his regiment or met with staff officers, Amitabha and Maggie erected small tents—one for Maggie and Cymberly, one for the colonel and his batman. Cymberly would begin preparations for their dinner, which Maggie completed. Frequently another officer joined them, sharing some treat such as fresh vegetables or fruit.

As the army crawled its way north and east at a rate of twelve or fifteen miles a day, the terrain became more harsh. They were not into the mountains yet by any means, but the hills they encountered slowed progress considerably. Often the route was narrow, with a steep embankment on one side and a precipitous drop on the other.

Cymberly was thankful for her surefooted little mare, but frequently she and other riders were forced to dismount and lead their animals.

Major Ryder reappeared when Cymberly and her father had been on the road about a week. At the time, she was riding beside Reginald Fleming, enjoying one of his amusing tales. Reggie's stories always centered on himself, but, as he had a remarkable ability to laugh at everything, including himself, he never appeared conceited. Cymberly threw back her head and laughed gaily and then there *he* was, right in front of her on a sleek-looking gray stallion.

"Miss Winthrop." Ryder touched his hat in salute. "I had not expected to see you in the wake of our forces."

"Hello," she replied. A flash of white teeth against sun-bronzed skin and searching eyes the color of a summer storm cloud caused her to take in her breath sharply and lower her gaze. She had not realized how much this man had dominated her thoughts since that encounter on the dance floor. "No, I suppose you did not expect me to be here. But then your own appearance is something of a surprise, sir."

Fleming crowded his horse closer to theirs. "Ah, Major Ryder. Come to join the army, have you?" Cymberly thought only the most discerning listener would detect the slight edge to Fleming's voice. A barely perceptible change in Ryder's expression indicated he had not missed it.

Ryder gave the other man a mechanical smile and said, "For a while. If I might have a word with you and," he raised his voice slightly, "Ensign Warren and Captain Wilson . . .

you will excuse us, Miss Winthrop?" He gave the men a nod that amounted to an order.

"Yes, sir, Major." Fleming's tone stopped a syllable short of being insubordinate.

"Of course," Cymberly murmured, but she was incensed at this peremptory dismissal. Of all the arrogant, rude . . .

She retreated back along the line until she joined Juliana Williams, who was riding beside a cart driven by Molly Mac-Iver, wife of a rifleman sergeant. Mrs. MacIver, sturdy, middle-aged, and possessing a no-nonsense optimism, was a fountain of information for the young women new to this way of life. They rode along in the comfort of developing friendships until the way narrowed and steepened. Juliana and Cymberly dropped behind and separated.

An hour later, the road—little more than a wide path now—had become rougher and the drop below frighteningly deep and steep. Cymberly tried not to look down. Even dependable Dolly was having difficulty keeping her footing. Cymberly decided she should dismount and lead the mare, if only she could find a place to do so, what with the rigors of the road itself added to all the traffic sharing it. With this in mind, Cymberly freed her right knee from the tree of her sidesaddle in anticipation of dismounting.

Suddenly the mare stumbled, dislodging her rider. Cymberly screamed as she kicked herself free of the saddle and fell head over heels down the steep incline.

Out of breath, she came to a stop next to the roots of a small tree about fifty feet down from the trail. She lay there stunned for a moment, then lifted her head.

"Don't move!" a male voice shouted.

She twisted her head enough to see faces peering at her over the edge of the trail. A length of rope snaked down the bank and a man in a rifleman's tunic was rappelling himself down to her. As he did so, she averted her face to avoid the sand and pebbles he dislodged in his descent. Reaching her side, he placed his feet carefully and turned toward her. Major Ryder!

"Don't move," he said again. "That shrub might not withstand much jarring."

He had tied the rope about his own waist, leaving a great length dangling loose. He knelt gingerly beside her and slid an arm beneath her shoulders to clasp her to him. "Put your arm around my neck, if you can," he said. "There. We know that arm is intact. What about the other one and your legs? Is anything broken?"

She moved her other arm and her legs delicately. "I . . . I think not," she said.

"Can you stand?" He helped her to an almost upright position, still kneeling but managing to keep a grip on her.

"Yes."

"Good. Brace yourself against my shoulder." As she did so, he tied the extra length of rope about her waist.

His cheek brushed hers and she felt the stubble of his beard and his warm breath. A sensation that had nothing to do with the accident swept through her.

"There." He tugged the rope to be sure it was secure. "Now—" he smiled at her ruefully, then turned his back to her and spoke over his shoulder. "This may be a bit uncomfortable, but I want you to put your arms around my neck and brace your knees against either side of my waist. My horse and the men above will help draw the two of us up."

"I . . . I . . ." She could not control the fear in her voice.

He turned enough so that his eyes held hers in a speaking gaze. "I'll not lose you, little one," he said softly.

Reassured, she silently wrapped her arms around his neck and pressed her body to his as he had instructed. A few inches at a time, they made their way up the hillside.

Geoffrey was amazed at her calm understanding of the situation. Where were the hysterics one might expect of a pampered miss of the *ton*? Even as he concentrated on getting them up the steep, gravelly incline, he was aware of the soft contours of her body pressed to his and a faint whiff of the scent he remembered from the dance.

Finally, they were on the solid bed of the trail. As the onlookers murmured approval, he untied the rope from their waists. Then the shock of what had happened seemed to hit her and she swayed toward him with a sob.

He put his arms around her and whispered, "Now, now. You are all right. You are safe, my brave girl." Still she trembled and sobbed into his chest. He held her more tightly and stroked her back. "There, little one. It is over." Gradually, he felt her regain control of herself.

She stepped back and looked up at him shyly. He felt a brief sense of loss as she left the circle of his arms.

"Thank you. I know that is inadequate, but I do thank you most sincerely."

"You will be all right now?" he asked as others began to crowd around them.

"Dolly?" she cried. "My horse?"

"She be over there," a young boy said, pointing.

"Oh." It was a sigh of relief.

Geoffrey knew she was still in shock and he wanted to enfold her in his arms again, to protect her from all dangers, but by then her father, having heard of the accident, had ridden back down the line with Fleming close behind him. Geoffrey turned away as Cymberly sought the comfort of her father's embrace.

Cymberly felt a pain in her side where she had landed hard against the small tree. She knew her body would discover many another ache before long. Her gloves were shredded, as were her stockings. She had scrapes on her legs and hands, and there were two ugly rips in her riding habit. Her hat had been utterly lost. But she was alive! And she had Geoffrey Ryder to thank for that small detail.

The next day, despite disturbing dreams that mingled the terror of her fall with very mixed feelings about her rescuer, she was herself again. Life quickly resumed what passed for normalcy on the campaign trail. Cymberly saw little of Major Ryder.

Two evenings later, General Winthrop, enjoying a pipe after dinner, leaned back in his camp chair and looked down the long line of tents. "I must say, these tents were a good idea."

"I'm not so sure," Colonel Reese objected. He and his wife had joined the Winthrops for dinner. "Takes an unconscionable amount of time to raise them and take them down. Not to mention the extra pack mules needed to carry them."

"But, Reese, consider," Winthrop said. "We have lost far fewer men to fever since we got them." Her father ritualistically tapped the burned tobacco from his pipe, and refilled it as he continued. "Tents are definitely an improvement." He lit a twig in the campfire and relighted his pipe.

Reese grunted. "And they cost a great deal more—for tents *and* the mules, not to mention extra feed for extra mules, but you do have a point." He rose. "Come, my dear. You are tired and I still have a report to write." Offering his quiet wife a hand in rising from her chair, he added, "You heard the news, General? The advance patrol spotted French today. Maybe a regiment. Not a whole battalion."

"Yes. Cymberly, you stay close to the baggage train tomorrow. A skirmish is very likely."

"Yes, Papa."

The next day tension swept through the entire cavalcade at the expectation of a skirmish with the enemy. In early afternoon, the fighting began. Cymberly heard the bursts of gunfire and boom of artillery.

Those not engaged in the fighting immediately set about the task of establishing a campsite. The two doctors and their assistants—musicians who doubled as medical personnel during battle—set up a large hospital tent.

Cymberly felt at sixes and sevens, wanting desperately to

do something. She trudged over to the hospital tent and presented herself to Dr. Cameron.

"This is no place for a refined lady," the doctor said curtly. Cameron, a man of her father's generation, had sandy hair streaked with gray, piercing blue eyes, and, normally, an amiable, smiling disposition.

"I want to help."

"As soon as the wounded start coming in here—any minute now—we will have precious little time for females who faint at the sight of blood."

"I assure you, sir, I am not the type to faint at every little fit and start." Cymberly was not all sure she would *not* faint at the sight of a seriously wounded man, but she wanted to be of service, to contribute something to this great concern that was the war against the French.

"Very well. Suit yourself. I have no time to argue with you. Just try not to get in our way." The doctor continued to supervise setting up two makeshift operating tables and some cots in the rear of the tent.

Immediately, Cymberly removed her bonnet, donned an apron, and set about directing placement of the cots. Within minutes, the bandsmen began ferrying wounded from the battlefield. The first seriously wounded man Cymberly had ever seen was a frightfully young infantry private who had taken a musket ball in his stomach.

The young man, bleeding profusely, lay on a stretcher, the fingers of both hands laced over his midsection. The doctor lifted the boy's hands to glance at the wound. Blood pumped out over the patient's side. The doctor quickly placed a pad over the gaping, pumping hole.

"Here, hold this," he said to Cymberly.

"I'll do it, sir," one of the bandsmen said with an apologetic look at Cymberly.

"Miss Winthrop wants to help. She can do it. They need you out there."

"Yes, sir."

Cymberly knelt beside the wounded boy. He replaced his hands over his stomach, but, with his strength weakening, he could not exert enough pressure to slow the flow of blood. Cymberly placed her hands over his.

"Press down firmly," the doctor told her.

Rivulets of sweat and tears streaked through dust and grime on the young man's ashen face. His mouth was rimmed with black gunpowder from loading and reloading his weapon.

"Please, miss," he croaked. "Water. A drink, please."

"Bring me some water, please," she said to one of the two bandsmen bringing in another man on a stretcher.

She was handed a canteen which she held to the boy's lips with one hand, keeping the other in place on his midriff. Unable to hold his head up, too, she allowed a dribble of water to pass over his lips.

The bandsman reached for his canteen and looked at the wounded boy "That one's a goner," he said, his voice matter-of-fact, but soft. Cymberly found the comment all the more horrifying for its mildness.

"Mama. Mama. Don't let me die, Mama." The boy stared at Cymberly, his eyes beseeching, but unfocused. "Please, Mama."

"Doctor!" Cymberly called as Cameron hurried by. "Can we do nothing for him?"

Dr. Cameron paused and shook his head sadly. "You are doing as much as we can—letting him go gently."

She smoothed the boy's brow and swallowed a sob.

"Mama!"

"Ssh. It's all right, darling." She stroked his head and cheek. Finally, he gave a great shuddering sigh and was still.

Cymberly sat unable to move. The only other death she had witnessed had been her mother's. But that had been different. Her mother had been felled by some inexorable supernatural force. This boy barely out of childhood had been cut down by his fellow man before he had a chance to taste life fully.

"Ma'am?" One of the stretcher-bearers paused and touched her shoulder. "Ma'am? He's dead." The speaker pulled a blanket over the dead boy's face.

Cymberly rose as in a trance. Looking at the blood on her hands, she shuddered in horror. She hastened toward the entrance and heard someone say, "I knew she'd never last."

Outside she bent over, her hands on her knees, and took several deep breaths.

"Here you go, dearie." Molly MacIver handed her a canteen. "Take a drink—'tis only water." Cymberly took a long swallow and thought of the last drink the boy had had. "Hold out your hands," Molly said. She poured more water over Cymberly's hands, washing away the blood. "There. Mayhap you should go and lie down."

"No. I am all right. I mean to help." Cymberly squared her shoulders, took another deep breath, and reentered the hospital tent. "I am sorry, Dr. Cameron. That will not happen again. What may I do now?"

The doctor looked at her keenly and she thought she saw a spark of approval in his gaze. He finished tying off the last stitch of a long laceration in another young soldier's arm. "You can bandage this young fellow's arm and fashion a sling for him. That man," he pointed at a nearby cot, "needs his head cleaned and bandaged. He needs no stitches, but watch him, for he took quite a blow to the head."

It was after dark before the last of the wounded had been cared for. Cymberly had helped set a broken leg and had watched unflinchingly as the doctor gently patted one man's innards back into his slit belly and stitched it closed. She had bandaged the stump of an amputated arm.

She stepped outside the hospital tent and paused to arch her back, cramped from bending over wounded in cots. Hawkins, the second doctor, handed her a cup of tea. He was younger than Cameron by at least a decade, but both men had been recruited to the medical services by James McGrigor, whom Wellington had personally chosen to take charge of those services for his Peninsula army.

"Here you go, miss," Hawkins said.

"Thank you." She looked around, surprised that the rest of the world went about its business routinely as the human beings in the tent behind her faced that greatest of all crises, death.

"You've been a great help to us today, Miss Winthrop— you and Mrs. MacIver. The men always respond to a woman's touch."

"I was glad to do what little I could." She gestured toward the tent. "Those poor men. And so many of them."

"We lost only six of them here. That's good. Maybe ten or twelve out on the field. Most of these," he nodded in the direction of the wounded, "will survive. That's good, too. But then, this was just a minor skirmish. A real battle is something else altogether."

Five

The seriously wounded, accompanied by a small number of troops, were sent behind the lines to a hospital, from which the permanently disabled would be sent back to England.

"Are so few troops considered adequate protection?" Cymberly had just bade "her" patients good-bye.

"They're not really for protection." Molly sounded surprised at the question. "More to see to their comfort and feeding, don't you know? Neither we nor the French would think of bothering wounded."

"Really?"

"Yes. Why, when they're not actually shooting at each other, British and French soldiers are quite friendly."

"I would not have thought it."

"MacIver has a marvelous story of a French sentry who was persuaded to buy cognac for his English counterparts on the other side of a bridge." Molly laughed. "Another time they were happily digging side by side in the same potato patch. Equally hungry, don't you know?"

"Do their officers not object?"

Molly shrugged. "Some do. Some don't. The Peer issued an order, but it is not enforced very effectively."

"Mortal enemies one moment, errant schoolboys the next—is that it?" Cymberly asked.

"You might say so," Molly agreed.

The next day the replacement battalions from Portugal and

their welcome supplies joined the rest of the army. Wellington's forces now swelled to immense numbers and moved like a lumbering beast under the hot summer sun of northern Spain. Vitoria was on the emotional horizon, though it was still three days march to have it in full view.

Rumors flew like birds scattered by gunshot: The French were in full retreat; they were barricaded behind the town walls. They outnumbered Britain and her allies by ten to one; for once Wellington had the edge in numbers. There was a great concentration of wealth in Vitoria; the town offered little in the way of treasure.

As usual, some rumors were true, some patently false. Sorting it all out was impossible.

That evening, Lieutenant Fleming appeared at the Winthrop camp to invite Cymberly to join him in a stroll along a nearby stream. With her father's nod of approval, she took the lieutenant's arm and they set off.

It was a lovely evening. The merciless sun had beat down on the slow-moving army all day. Dust had billowed and hovered in the windless, cloudless atmosphere. But now the rising moon and a soft breeze contrived to bring ease to weary travelers.

"This is so pleasant," Cymberly said. "It is hard to believe we are part of an army engaged in actual warfare."

"Yes." With his opposite hand, Fleming caressed her hand on his arm. "But for the stark terrain, we might be strolling in an English garden."

Soon they had wandered away from the noise of the camp and the light of the dozens of campfires. They could hear the sounds of insects, an occasional bird call, and a more disturbing sound.

"What was that?" she asked.

"An owl."

"No. Something else. A howl."

"Oh, that. Just a wolf."

"A wolf? Are you sure it is safe to be out here?"

"There are sentries posted. Besides"—he moved his arm to encompass her shoulder and pull her closer—"I should never allow any harm to come to you."

His voice was a soft murmur at her temple. Slightly uncomfortable, Cymberly tried to withdraw, but he held her tightly. She did not struggle. After all, she welcomed his embrace, did she not? Handsome, charming Reggie. She looked up at him.

"Ah, Cymberly." He turned her toward him and pressed his lips to hers. Startled at first by his intensity, she stood very still, then consciously returned the kiss, but immediately pulled back when she felt the wetness of his tongue explore the seam of her closed lips.

"No," she said, shoving her hands against his chest.

"Don't be a tease, my dear." He wrapped both arms around her, effectively trapping her. "You surely knew I wanted to kiss you. And I think you wanted it, too."

"Well, yes," she admitted, never one to deny an obvious truth.

He put his mouth to hers again, caressing and pulling softly at her lower lip. "Please, my darling," he whispered.

Again she returned the pressure of his lips. Something in her wanted to respond as he wished her to, but something stronger kept her from doing so. She turned her head away.

"No. Please. I'm sorry."

He sighed and loosened his hold on her. "It's all right, my dear. I am a patient man. Shall we go back?"

They returned to find Major Ryder sitting with the general in earnest conversation. A nearly full bottle of brandy and two empty glasses sat on a small folding table along with a map. Both men rose as Cymberly and Fleming approached. She dropped her hand from the lieutenant's arm and hoped her blush did not show in the uncertain light from the dying campfire and the lantern.

"Miss Winthrop. Fleming." Ryder nodded to them. Was his voice a shade warmer at uttering her name? He turned to General Winthrop, held out his hand, and said, "I must go. Thank you, sir."

The general took Ryder's hand in both of his. "You take care, my friend. This could be dangerous."

An unusual degree of concern in her father's voice caused a tremor of alarm in Cymberly. She looked at Major Ryder, but he was smiling calmly.

"It's *all* dangerous, sir. But my 'friends' are clever."

"All the same . . ." Winthrop admonished.

"We are careful, General. I shall see you again in two, perhaps three days." Nodding his farewell to Cymberly and Fleming, Ryder left.

Later, Cymberly lay on her cot, listening to Maggie's soft snores, and mulled over her reaction to Reggie's kiss—or, rather, her lack of reaction. She felt warmed by the fact that he cared for her, but his kiss was curiously unmoving—like kissing a brother or an uncle, though no relative would have offered quite *such* a kiss. Reginald Fleming was a most attractive man. She should be thrilled by his very touch.

Unbidden, another image entered from the backstage of her mind. She recalled the feel of Ryder's arms as he comforted her after her fall—the spicy smell of soap mixed with sweat and how that fleeting, not-quite-rough stubble of beard had felt against her cheek. Seeing him had brought it all back.

Do stop! she silently scolded herself. She was being silly. She had merely been frightened and upset at an accident. Why, the man had scarcely noticed her tonight.

She pounded her pillow into a more comfortable shape and finally slept.

Major Ryder returned to his own campsite in a decidedly negative frame of mind. He had recognized the surge of jealously he felt on seeing Miss Winthrop and Fleming emerge from the shadows. He told himself it was none of his business and threw aside his tent flap with more force than he intended.

"Go and tell MacIver we are leaving," he instructed his batman. He gathered up his own gear and made his way to the MacIver tent.

"Ready?" he asked the burly sergeant.

"Yes, sir."

Molly emerged to hand MacIver a haversack, which he slung over his shoulder. She smoothed the lapel of his jacket and said, "Be careful."

The sergeant picked up his rifle and said, "I will." He gave her a quick, husbandly kiss good-bye.

Geoffrey felt a twinge of envy at the casual adoration these two had for each other. Good God! He was in a mood, wasn't he? He turned away to give the couple a modicum of privacy.

There was a burst of laughter from a group at a neighboring campfire. He recognized Fleming sitting very close to a pretty Spanish girl named Florencia. Geoffrey could not hear what was being said, but he saw the girl toss her long black hair and look suggestively at Fleming. Fleming then pulled her head toward him and kissed her. She and the others laughed heartily as they passed a wineskin around. Fleming whispered something to the girl, which brought forth a flirtatious giggle.

"I know you'd rather walk," Geoffrey said to MacIver, "but we'll have to ride this time."

"I expect my backside will complain, but so be it."

Locating their animals, saddling, and bridling them took but a few minutes. As they swung onto their mounts and headed away from the camp, Geoffrey saw Fleming disappear into some bushes with the Spanish girl.

"That bastard," Geoffrey muttered, thinking of the way Cymberly Winthrop had looked at the other man. *And what has it to do with you?* he asked himself. He shrugged and deliberately focused his mind on the mission ahead.

* * *

The routine was the same even for the leviathan the army had now become. The camp began to stir at first light. Some stopped to heat water for tea. Most started packing up immediately. An hour later, they would again be on the trail. There was a general sense of urgency now. Everyone knew a major battle was in the offing; they just had no idea exactly when.

Her father having warned her to stay close to the train despite the dust, Cymberly rode beside a supply wagon that carried a few women and children. Others walked along the side. Among the walkers was Mrs. Peters, carrying her son astraddle one hip. Tommy was fussy, pushing at his mother to let him down.

"Trouble, Mrs. Peters?" Cymberly asked.

"Oh, miss. Hello." Mrs. Peters' head was partially obscured by her son. She shifted the child higher on her hip. "Tommy won't ride on the wagon. He wants to walk, but I can't allow that—we'd fall behind." She looked up with a sigh of frustration.

Cymberly gave a sharp gasp of surprise. "My heavens! What happened? Your eye, your cheek, what happened?"

Mary Beth Peters put a hand to her face gingerly and colored under the bruises there. "I . . . I, uh, fell. Tripped over a tent rope. Stupid, eh?"

"Painful, I should say," Cymberly said.

"Down," Tommy demanded and pushed at his mother again.

"This child has a mind of his own," Mary Beth said.

"Here. Let me take him for a while." Cymberly reined in her horse and extended an arm. "Would you like to ride the horsey?" she asked Tommy.

"Horsey!" he said, trustingly reaching toward Cymberly. His mother handed him over and he was seated somewhat awkwardly astride the animal in front of Cymberly.

"Thank you." Mrs. Peters gratefully handed over her burden.

Tommy chattered gaily as they rode at the side, out of the worst of the dust. Cymberly understood about every fifth word, but pointed out things to amuse the boy as they rode. She kept her arm tight around his little body and wondered how she could possibly feel greater warmth and protectiveness about a child if she herself were its mother.

The midmorning rest stop allowed soldiers and followers alike to sit for a few minutes. They broke their fasts at last with bread and cold meat or cheese. The beverage of choice—or necessity—for most was water. Warm water from a canteen grown hot in the sun, but welcomed for being wet. Cymberly turned her sleepy passenger over to his mother.

The next day proceeded much as the days before it had. During the midmorning break, two riders approached far to the left of the column. As they came closer, they emerged from the background as Major Ryder and Sergeant MacIver. The sudden flip of her heart caught her by surprise.

"Miss Winthrop." Ryder touched his hat at they came within speaking distance.

"Sir." She inclined her head, glad to be able to hide whatever emotion might show in her eyes.

"General Winthrop is ahead, I assume," the major said in a manner that was almost abrupt.

"Yes. He is with the Ninety-Sixth, I believe." She tried to keep her tone neutral, flat.

"And the Peer?"

"Lord Wellington is some distance ahead—on the right, I think." Cymberly waved the direction.

"Thank you, Miss Winthrop. Mac, see if you can find Winthrop and give him our report. I'll find the Peer and tell him."

"Yes, sir." MacIver touched his hat in a gesture intended, apparently, as a salute.

Major Ryder rode beside her in silence after MacIver left. Cymberly wondered why he did not immediately make his way to the front to find Lord Wellington. She glanced at him several times. He was, of course, wearing the usual green jacket of a rifleman, now covered in dust.

"And how do you like life on the trail now, Miss Winthrop?" He might have been in a London drawing room asking about the weather.

"How do I like it? I would not say I *liked* it at all. I hate the fighting and what it does to people." She brushed the long sleeve of her dress, sending up puffs of dust. The oppressive heat had caused her to give up her heavy riding habit in favor of a full-skirted dress. "And I truly detest the dust."

He chuckled sympathetically. "Fighting is what an army is all about, Miss Winthrop, and dust is a great hazard—and annoyance—of war, I'm afraid."

Cymberly smiled. "You know, I don't believe you are."

"You don't believe . . . ?"

"You are afraid."

He was suddenly serious. "Only a fool would be unafraid in war. Fear is always there—a beast seeking to attack. But one manages to overcome it from time to time."

"Like when one is rescuing damsels in distress?" She laughed softly and looked at him only to find him considering her very seriously. His gaze was warm and somewhat questioning.

"Sometimes the sheer urgency of the moment pushes fear out of the picture entirely," he said.

"I see." She did not see at all, but she was still grateful for whatever had motivated him that day.

"I must make my report," he said, abruptly changing the tone of the conversation. "Perhaps I shall see you later?"

"I hope so."

Now, why in the world had she said that? She could have given him a cool, "Perhaps."

Wellington rode off with Ryder and three other high-ranking officers to hear Geoffrey's report. Major Ryder and Sergeant MacIver had sneaked into the walled city of Vitoria to reconnoiter the enemy's probable defenses.

"My lord, we seem to be seriously outnumbered." General Travers voiced the concern of all.

"We are," Wellington conceded. "However, our troops are better trained than French soldiers. Furthermore, ours are by and large veterans. The French regiments that we face are mostly inexperienced conscripts. Napoleon has most of the veterans with him in the east. And," he added sardonically, "I trust their Spanish troops are no better trained or more courageous than the ones with us. Our Portuguese troops have come along quite nicely, however. Gentlemen, I doubt not we shall prevail this day."

Geoffrey spent the rest of the day relaying Wellington's new orders. Camp would be made in a large valley through which a small stream flowed. The sun was lowering toward the horizon as Geoffrey made his way back along the line looking for his batman.

Suddenly Cymberly Winthrop appeared before him. Had he really been thinking of her most of the day? Her greeting was polite. He wanted to believe it held special warmth just for him, but he could not be sure.

"Come," he said impulsively. "Let me show you something quite amazing."

"What?" There was curious skepticism, but no suspicion, in her tone.

"It is a surprise. But we must ride to the top of that hill." He gestured toward one of the higher points.

"All right. Lead on, oh, mysterious knight."

He smiled, surmising her teasing tone was meant to offset her nervousness at going off alone with him. He turned his horse in the direction he had indicated and she followed at an easy gait.

By the time they reached the top of the hill, the sun was a huge red disk sitting on the edge of the visible world. Geoffrey dismounted and reached to help Cymberly down. He resisted an urge to enfold her in his arms and felt a slight emptiness as she stepped away.

Below them in the dimming light, the army resembled a mass of moving ants, the disorder making little sense to observers. There was also a small Spanish village whose church spire towered over the convent attached to it and the humble dwellings that surrounded it.

"Turn this way." Geoffrey touched her shoulder to turn her from the sight below. It was darker in the direction they now faced, though trees and vegetation were clear in the unreal, just-before-dark light that brings objects out in such sharp relief.

"It will be a lovely evening," Cymberly said. Was she just making conversation to cover uneasiness? But surely she had nothing to be nervous about.

He glanced over his shoulder, then said, "All right. You may turn around and look."

There below, where disorder had reigned, three distinct and very orderly bivouac areas had arisen next to the quaint and ancient village. In a matter of minutes, tents had been erected in precise rows with wide boulevards. Cooking fires twinkled brightly.

She gasped. "It is simply amazing. One moment there is chaos and the next . . ."

"You have a whole city at your feet." He finished her statement, pleased at her reaction. He stepped closer to her and put his arm around her shoulder to direct her gaze as he pointed out certain features. He showed her where the animals were located, the sutlers' wagons, the headquarters tent—and, off in the far distance, the locations of some of the enemy and their gun emplacements.

" 'Tis incredible, is it not?" She turned toward him, wonder in her eyes and voice.

"What?" He could not take his eyes from hers.

"This. This transformation shows people capable of such

creative powers to build, yet this is done for the express purpose of destroying other beings like ourselves."

"I suppose it would be irrelevant to draw your attention to the fact that *we* did not start it?" There was a note of laughter in his voice, though he understood fully her point of view. It was, after all, an echo of his own thinking.

"Yes. It would be irrelevant," she said softly. She seemed as incapable of looking away as he was.

Slowly, silently, he pulled her closer and touched his mouth to hers. He kissed her tenderly, tentatively, but then her arms were around his neck. She murmured a small moan of surrender and leaned in to him. He intensified the kiss, surprised and pleased at the vehemence of her response. She hesitated momentarily when he stroked her lips with his tongue, but then, amazingly, she welcomed his exploration of her mouth.

He knew instantly the moment she came to her senses. He drew back and she pushed against him, trembling. He loosened his hold on her, but did not let her go. They both spoke at once.

"How could I . . ." The reproof seemed directed at herself.

"Cymberly—Miss Winthrop—I apologize. I should not have . . ."

"Don't." She pressed her fingers to his lips. "Neither of us should have." She laughed, though it was a far from care-free sound. "Under the circumstances, perhaps it should be 'Cymberly.' "

"And 'Geoffrey,' " he said quietly.

"And Geoffrey," she repeated and disengaged herself from his embrace. "We must get back."

He cupped his hands to give her a lift into the saddle and mounted his own horse. Both were quiet on the ride back to camp, but her silence seemed more thoughtful than accusatory or regretful.

They turned the horses over to the troops responsible for

their care and Geoffrey helped her locate her father's camp. Fleming was there.

"There you are," the general said.

"Where were you?" Fleming demanded and flashed a venomous glance at Geoffrey. The general seemed surprised at the lieutenant's tone.

"We started to worry, Miss," Maggie said.

"I am sorry. I never meant to worry you, Papa. Or you, Maggie."

Geoffrey noted with some satisfaction that her apology did not include Fleming. "It was my fault. I dragged her away to see the view."

"No harm done. I am sure she was safe with you," the general said.

If you only knew, Geoffrey thought. Even in the uncertain light, the color seemed heightened in her cheeks, but her voice was cool.

"Thank you, Major Ryder. It was a spectacular sight. And I thank you for your concern, Lieutenant."

With that she retreated to her tent.

Six

Cymberly was furious.

She was angry with herself for her wanton behavior with Major Ryder. Good heavens! She might as well have worn a banner announcing her eagerness for his touch, his kiss. And he with such close ties to Chadwyck. What was she thinking? Obviously, she was *not* thinking! Why? Why would she respond to Geoffrey Ryder with such abandon and be unable to allow herself a warm response to the more attractive Reggie Fleming? It simply did not make sense.

She was also angry with Reggie. He had no right to demand she account for her behavior. A kiss or two did not carry such obligation. *It would in London if it became common knowledge,* she reminded herself. *Look what happened with Lord Taraton.*

She washed her face and hands, recombed her hair, and brushed the worst of the trail dust from her clothing. During dinner, both she and her father were too pensive to care much about the meagerness of their meal.

"Is something wrong, Papa?" she finally asked. "You seem on another continent."

"What? Oh. Perhaps I was, at that. I was thinking of a camp and a battle in India."

"A successful campaign?"

"In the end. But hard won. This engagement tomorrow

will not be easy. I hate having the men go into battle on empty bellies."

"Is it truly that bad? I heard some of the women complaining, but I thought it was the usual grousing."

"We have pushed the men so hard that we have outrun the supplies we should have received." He ran his hand across his face. "But if reports are correct, we have prevented the French from getting the reinforcements they anticipated."

"It is difficult for women. Some lag behind."

"I know. We lost two, I think." His voice was bleak. "It will get worse as we cross the mountains. The French are on the run, but they will not—dare not—allow us over that border without doing all they can to stop us, or at least slow us down considerably."

"Will it be so very bad, then?"

"Yes, my dear, it will. Please, Cymberly, I ask you again, will you not take Maggie and go home to England? Once the supply caravan reaches us, they will return to port, taking wounded and prisoners with them to await the next convoy of supply ships. You would be safe if you went with them."

"I would be more miserable in England without you than I can imagine being here. Besides, I have only just rediscovered my father. But if it will ease your mind, I promise to *consider* going back to England."

He rose and cupped her chin in his hand. "Do it for me, daughter." He kissed her on the forehead. "Wellington has called a meeting. Sleep well, my dear."

He left and Cymberly sat for a few minutes, sipping weak tea as weariness dragged at her. Finally, she rose and prepared for bed.

The village was about a mile from the central bivouac area. A small settlement, it had grown up around its feature attraction, a convent that had been overrun and looted by French troops. It was now taken over by British medical personnel who appropriated the chapel, the courtyard, the cloisters, and the dining hall, cleared of its customary furniture.

"Still not enough room," Dr. Cameron worried. "We'll set up more tents outside the convent walls."

"So many?" Cymberly asked.

Against the appalling background music of cannon bursts and distant rifle fire, she had reported to the surgeon early in the morning.

"This will be a major encounter, my girl. This courtyard will be a sea of blood. Severed arms and legs will be tossed about as garbage. Many will die before we can even get to them. Pardon my bluntness, Miss Winthrop, but this will be no place for a gently bred young woman."

Cymberly drew in a breath and lifted her head. "Nevertheless, I must do what I can to help. I simply cannot stand by idly."

Cameron sighed. "So be it, then. Report to Captain MacDonald. He is McGrigor's man, and he will assign you a post."

She smiled. "Is the whole medical corps made up of Scotsmen, then?"

"Nay, Miss." Cameron's eyes twinkled as he exaggerated his brogue. " 'Tis only, ye ken, that we Scots have a dram maer compassion in our wee souls."

"And a dram maer deviltry, too, I ken." Her tone changed from teasing imitation of his to serious curiosity as she asked, "What happened to the nuns who were here?"

"Some are still here, trying to carry on as best they can. You know the French attacked them? Killed the abbess."

Cymberly found MacDonald directing the placement of beds in the chapel. He was a huge man of perhaps forty with graying hair and a plethora of freckles on his face and hands. He put his hands on his hips and surveyed her slight figure disinterestedly.

"You? *You* want to volunteer your services? Here? Have you any idea at all what such a madcap idea involves?"

"Yes, I do," she replied with more confidence than she felt in the face of his intimidating stance. "I have helped Dr. Cameron and Dr. Hawkins before."

"A skirmish. I heard about it. Well, ma'am, this is likely to be a good deal different."

"So I have been told."

He inclined his head in an as-you-wish gesture and said, "So be it. God knows any extra set of hands will be welcome." He gave her some terse instructions and left her on her own to direct the placement of beds, basins of water, and other necessary items.

Actually a church serving the village as well as the convent, the large gothic chapel had a soaring nave with aisles on either side of it. The altar held a huge, startlingly realistic wooden crucifix, the figure of Christ sporting blood-red wounds. In niches here and there were figures of saints and the holy family. Cymberly worked alone for a while. Then she became aware of another person in the nave. A nun. The woman knelt and crossed herself in front of the altar and then turned toward Cymberly.

"I . . . w-will . . . um . . . help?" she offered in the unsure manner of one who had learned her English only in a classroom and rarely practiced it.

Cymberly looked into the face of the most beautiful girl she had ever seen. Her hair was, of course, completely covered by her headdress, but raven black eyebrows arched fetchingly over dark brown eyes. A very soft olive complexion was highlighted by naturally pink cheeks and a perfect rosebud mouth. Her hands were small, well-shaped, and moved gracefully.

"Why, yes, if you like." Cymberly was embarrassed at being caught staring.

The girl pointed to herself. "I be—am—Sister Angelina. These," she gestured, beckoning to the shadows, "are Sister Alicia and Sister Elena."

"Welcome. I am Cymberly."

"Kimm-ber-lee," they said almost in unison, rolling the strange syllables over their tongues. The other two were of an age with Angelina—seventeen or eighteen, Cymberly guessed.

"Well," Cymberly muttered to herself, "this is going to be interesting."

"Troubles, Miss Winthrop?" Captain Wilson called from the doorway.

"Oh, just the man I need," Cymberly said. "You speak Spanish—mine is so poor. They want to help. This is Captain Wilson," she said to the three.

"El capitan . . . Wil-son," they said, inclining their heads prettily. Alicia and Elena blushed and giggled.

He swept the three a courtly bow and said in Spanish, "How may I be of serv—" He stopped mid-sentence, open-mouthed, clearly stunned as he finally really looked at Angelina.

"Madre de Dios!" he exclaimed.

Cymberly laughed. "I think not, Captain. But she might as well be, as far as you are concerned."

He quickly recovered himself and apologized to the three young nuns. He chatted with them several minutes, translating as necessary for Cymberly.

The three did, indeed, want to help. *Sí*, they understood this would be a hospital and might be quite horrible, but the brave soldiers were trying to free their homeland. They would help. This, too, would be serving God.

"It appears you have some helpers, Miss Winthrop. And I leave you to them. I came only because his lordship wanted a firsthand report on facilities here."

When he left—after another lingering look at Angelina—Cymberly and the three continued to communicate in pidgin English and equally pidgin Spanish. Their talk was facilitated by the universal language of hand signals and punctuated periodically by gunfire.

Cymberly learned that the French soldiers had not only

taken all the food supplies of the convent, but had stolen everything of value—a gold reliquary set with jewels, the silver chalice and plate from the altar, and even silver crosses on the walls of some cells. Two other young nuns had been raped before a French officer put a stop to that particular offense. The Mother Superior had hidden these three in the crypt beneath the altar.

They lamented the death of the abbess and told Cymberly that many of the sisters had returned to their families. Those who stayed lived off the generosity of the villagers, who had also been systematically robbed.

"Tanto dolor," they murmured. So much pain.

At this point, their socializing came to an end as the bandsmen took on their alternate roles as field medics. The wounded they could get to were brought in on hospital wagons. Other wounded had to be left in the field to crawl to safety where possible. Some would simply bleed out their lives into the Spanish soil where they lay.

Some would lie on the field for hours, desperately aching for a drink of water, their extreme thirst caused by the salt-peter of the gunpowder in the packets of shot and powder they opened with their teeth in the rapid reloading of muskets and rifles. If they were lucky, no chance shot or misfired cannon would set the dry grass afire around them. Infantrymen, Cymberly knew, feared two things above all others— cavalrymen with their flashing sabers and lying helplessly wounded in a burning field.

Angelina and Cymberly stayed in the chapel to work; the other two were sent to the cloisters. Other nuns joined the bandsmen in the dining room or worked in the kitchen helping to prepare meals. Molly MacIver and several other women and servants, followers of the drum, also helped.

The afternoon wore on and the wounded kept coming. They put two men to a bed and placed straw pallets at the bottoms of beds along the wall and anywhere else there was space to accommodate a broken, suffering body.

Some men cried out in pain. Some simply cried. Many, especially those nearer death, called for their sweethearts or mothers, reverting to a time and person who offered sanctuary from all life's dreadful hurts.

Cymberly bent over a sergeant who had just lost his left leg at the knee.

"Well," the man said philosophically, "looks like I'm to be a bootmaker like me pa, after all."

"Miss Winthrop!" a bandsman called at the door.

"Over here." She stood and waved the man over.

"Dr. Cameron said I should come get you right away."

"But he told me to stay here."

"All's I know is 'e told me to come get you."

"All right." Puzzled, she followed the courier, stopping first to tell Angelina she was going.

Cymberly had not been outside the chapel since the first patients had arrived. Emerging into the bright sunlight, she squinted her eyes. When they adjusted, she was stunned by the scene before her. The courtyard was filled with men lying on blankets. There did seem to be some order in where certain ones were placed, but the sheer numbers were overwhelming.

Dr. Cameron was right, she thought wonderingly. *There is blood everywhere.* It dripped from injuries and ran over and between the uneven cobblestones. There was, indeed, a pile of severed limbs tossed haphazardly near the operating tables set up under large tarpaulins. Her stomach lurched at the sight. She looked away and took a deep breath.

"Over there, Miss," her escort said, directing her along the wall to where Cameron was making quick decisions on where to send newly arrived wounded.

"Dr. Cameron?" she said.

He rose from a stooped position. She noted great splotches of fresh and dried blood on his apron. "Ah, Miss Winthrop." The worry in his eyes alarmed her. She held her breath.

"There's no way ever to say this gently," the doctor said. "Your father's been wounded."

"Wounded? My father? Where?" She looked around her.

Cameron put his arm firmly around her shoulder. "We put him in one of the empty cells off the cloister. He took a musket ball in the chest. It is quite serious, my dear." His voice was very gentle.

"Is he . . . dead?" Her lips trembled.

"No. He is still alive." The sadness had not left his eyes.

"Serious. You mean he will not survive, do you not?" she asked with that amazing insight that occasionally comes in the midst of great crisis. Tears stung her eyes.

"No, he will not. I am so sorry. He's a good man. The missile penetrated too many vital organs. Hawkins is with him."

"Take me to him, please." She made a concerted effort to still the tremor in her voice. "And send someone for Amitabha, please. He has been with Papa for many years."

He called a bandsman over and gave him instructions. Then, calling another to take her to the cloister, Cameron turned back to his task.

General Winthrop lay on his back, his eyes closed. Dr. Hawkins sat in a chair by his side. Cymberly gasped, then was pleased to see her father open his eyes. She knelt at the side of his bed and took his hand in hers. Already it felt cool and dry. Dr. Hawkins touched her shoulder and quietly left.

"Oh, Papa," she whispered. "This is so unfair. I only just got you back."

"I see they told you, love. I . . ." He took a ragged, painful breath. "I'm sorry we had . . . so little time together. . . . I loved you and your mama very much."

"I know, Papa. And we loved you. Don't talk now. Conserve your strength."

"Can't," he gasped. "There's no . . . time. Papers in Indian box . . . London solicitor . . . everything yours. Amitabha . . . knows."

She followed his gaze as he looked toward the opening door, and there was his Indian batman. Amitabha was out of breath. He must have run the whole way, Cymberly thought. Tears had turned his eyes to shiny bits of obsidian. He squatted on his heels in the manner common to Indian men and women alike, rocking back and forth and crooning softly.

The general smiled faintly and reached to touch the servant's hand. "Not . . . yet, Amitabha. Not quite . . . yet." He looked at Cymberly. "You must keep him . . . with you . . . always. He cannot . . . return . . . India."

"I understand," she said, stroking her father's hand. She could see him visibly fading and felt panic at her own loss. She choked it down.

"I wish you . . . return to England." He gulped in air. "But I . . . will not . . . impose my . . . will."

"Thank you, Papa, for trusting me so."

He looked again at Amitabha. "My . . . friend. Take care of . . . my little girl."

Amitabha nodded, his tears spilling over.

Her father turned his gaze to her again. "Forgive . . . Chadwyck. Ryder . . . good . . . man."

"Oh, Papa, I love you."

She felt him squeeze her hand in response and heard him take a deep gurgle of breath. Then he was eerily still. She and Amitabha looked at each other bleakly and let their tears flow.

The next day Cymberly watched with dry but red-rimmed eyes as her father was lowered into a grave in the churchyard, the only British soldier to be buried inside the cemetery walls and the only one accorded a coffin. Other casualties were buried in mass graves outside the walls with little ritual or respect. "Here, death is a far too common event to be treated with ceremony," one of the doctors had said. Cymberly was grateful to her father's cohorts, including his commander, who came to pay tribute to General Charles Winthrop.

The battle had eventually gone well for the allies, with the French, who actually had far greater numbers of men and arms on the field, fleeing in disarray.

"Everyone from drummer boys to generals was looking to his own safety," commented Colonel Reese at a gathering at General Winthrop's funeral.

"This battle surely spells the end of the French kingdom of Spain," another man said. "Parliament will have to take notice now."

"Wish Winthrop could have seen this day," another said.

"Well, yes and no," put in a third voice. "Charlie would have been as angry and dismayed as the Peer over the pillage and looting."

"Must say," the laconic Reese put in, "Lord Wellington had reason for his unusual display of temper. It was a grand triumph— and might have been grander had our boys pursued the frogs."

"Hundreds of abandoned wagons and carriages posed just too much temptation," General Lord Boynton said. "British men at arms have never been known to pass up a chance to plunder."

"Such plunder it was, too! The frogs and their Spanish puppets were stealing some of the country's greatest treasures."

"Now some British farmer will have it."

"More likely he'll sell it for drink."

"Right. It will take a week for their revelry to die down."

"Not if 'Nosey' starts hanging offenders tomorrow." The speaker referred, Cymberly knew, to just one of the nicknames the troops used for their commander.

"He will, too."

Cymberly moved on. She had received condolences from nearly everyone in the room. Lieutenant Fleming, having taken a proprietary stand next to her, reluctantly left when she asked him for a glass of lemonade.

Geoffrey approached and took her hand. "I am so sorry for your loss, Miss Winthrop. Your father was a fine man and a great commander."

"Thank you." She wanted to throw herself in Ryder's arms and sob out her loss against his shoulder as she had sobbed out her fear when she fell days earlier. Why did she not feel this way about Reggie? Ryder turned away—did he do so reluctantly?—and Fleming reappeared before she remembered her father's dying words about Major Ryder.

That afternoon she went back to the hospital.

"Good heavens, girl," Molly MacIver said. "You needn't be here now."

"Perhaps you are right, but I simply cannot bear to go through my father's things yet." She did not add that she could not bear any more well-wishers, especially those who asked not-so-subtle questions about her plans for the future and cast sly glances at Lieutenant Fleming. "I do need to be here," she said.

In the chapel, she was further saddened by the news that three of "her" patients had died. The obvious pleasure others showed at her presence cheered her, though. She was touched by their stumbling efforts to extend condolences to her. She was equally touched by Angelina's quiet, sweet acknowledgment of her loss and pleasure at her return.

"I pray for your papa," the nun said. "And for you."

"Thank you."

Back at her own tent that evening, she was visited by a delegation headed by Mrs. Gordon-Smythe and the Reeses. Mrs. Reese—she of so few words—spoke first.

"We have been wondering, my dear, what your plans are now."

"It should be clear you cannot stay on with the army now." Mrs. Gordon-Smythe's tone was haughty.

Cymberly was caught off guard. "I—I had not thought about my plans yet."

"Supply wagons arrived today. They will take wounded and prisoners to port at Passages. Can take you, too," Colonel Reese said. "Leave day after tomorrow."

"So soon? I shall have to think about it," Cymberly said.

"What could there possibly be to think about?" Mrs. Gordon-Smythe demanded. "You never should have been here in the first place, a single woman of your status. Now that your father is gone . . ."

"I appreciate your point of view, ma'am, but I cannot—I will not—make a decision today." Cymberly made little effort to hide her annoyance at the other woman.

"Ain't trying to get rid of you. Just thinking of your welfare, you know," Colonel Reese apologized.

"I know that, sir," she said more kindly. "And I shall let you know what I decide."

These visitors had barely left when Maggie announced, "Lieutenant Fleming would like a word with you, Miss."

"Tell him—no." She sighed. "Tell him I shall be right there."

Seven

"Good evening, Miss Winthrop." Fleming rose from the camp stool. She knew he avoided using her given name for the benefit of anyone who might be listening. He took her hand and continued, "I tried to see you this afternoon, but I was told you had gone back to that pest hole of a hospital."

"I am sorry to have missed you," she said politely.

"Yes. Well. You should not be there in any event."

Cymberly felt her hackles rise at this, but she was too tired, too distraught to put up a fight at the moment. She looked away and kept silent.

"Come, my dear. Walk with me a while. I would speak with you privately." He drew her hand into the crook of his elbow and steered her onto a path away from the camp. He sat her down on a stone near a small stream and knelt beside her, then cleared his throat.

"Cymberly . . . you must know how fond of you I am. Your father's death forces me to accept earlier a role I had hoped for later." He took her hands in both of his. "Will you marry me, my love?"

She sat stunned. Yes, she should have anticipated this, but it came as a surprise anyway.

"I am not unmindful of the honor you do me—"

"But you cannot refuse me," he interrupted, aghast. "You need a protector here."

"I have Amitabha and Maggie."

"Servants!" he said scornfully.

"Very good, very loyal people."

"But *not* a parent or a husband."

"Please, do not press me on this. I cannot think of marrying now. I have, after all, only just buried my father. A proper mourning . . ."

Again he interrupted. "Means nothing out here. Why, I know of one woman who buried three husbands in five months!" He rose and, pulling her to her feet, held her close. "Please, Cymberly. I want you—and you need my protection. Otherwise, you must return to England." He bent his head to kiss her.

She turned her face away and said, "That remains to be seen. In any event, I shall not think of marrying until I have accorded my father a suitable period of mourning."

"Have you no feeling for me at all?" His tone suggested this was a preposterous idea.

"That is *not* what I said. Of course I have some feeling for you. You are a most attractive man. You are amusing and you have been very kind to me. I value your friendship."

"Are you in love with someone else?"

"No." She refused to meet his gaze.

"I may continue to hope, then?"

"Reggie, please, do not insist on a response. I cannot make such a commitment now."

"Well, *I* can—and until I receive a flat no from you, I shall consider myself bound to you. I would, if you would allow me, take you back to England. Your father wished you to be there. I could sell my commission."

His comment about her father's wishes hit home. "No. I would never ask such a sacrifice of you. It would probably break your father's heart if you sold out."

"Not really," he said in a moment of candor. "My father does not think much of my soldiering."

Not knowing how to respond to this, Cymberly did not reply.

He sighed. "All right, my love, I shall not press you to marry immediately. I am, as I told you, a patient man."

"Thank you," she whispered.

With the palm of his hand, he raised her head and pressed his lips to hers. Conscious of his paying her singular honor in proposing to her, she returned his kiss, but again refused him the depth he silently sought. He sighed again, then returned her to her tent. He kissed her chastely on the cheek at the entrance to her tent. She blushed, hoping no one had seen him do so.

But someone had.

Geoffrey Ryder had stopped by her quarters to offer his condolences again, and he hoped to urge her to return to England. He knew it had been her father's wish. She would be safe in England and he intended to ask permission to call when he finally returned there himself.

This campaign would get harder as they went into the mountains. Many women simply disappeared. He knew of at least two who had drowned crossing streams. It was bad enough that men endured such hardships in answer to the demanding gods of war. It was untenable, unacceptable that any woman should, let alone a woman born to and schooled to a refined way of life—a woman like Cymberly Winthrop.

Perhaps if she were in England, he could perform his duties without having her image constantly in mind.

Then he spotted her with Fleming.

So *that* was the way the wind blew, was it? Not exactly the mourning daughter, was she? Not if she had been out in the bushes with Reginald Fleming! *Things are not always what they seem,* he told himself. Perhaps not, but this scene would be hard to misconstrue.

He returned to the tent he shared with Captain Wilson and dug around in his goods until he found the bottle of brandy he had long carried and never opened.

Here's to you, Ryder, ever the fool where women are concerned! he saluted himself silently and drank deeply.

"I say! I thought you were saving that for a special occasion," Wilson said as he arrived a short time later.

"Perhaps this *is* a special occasion. Join me."

"Victory in Vitoria? I suppose it is—and I will." Wilson poured himself a glass and looked at his friend speculatively. "Now why do I have the feeling this is not solely about our victory? Is it even a celebration?"

"Of course it is," Geoffrey lied, his voice full of false heartiness. He raised his glass. "To victory. And discovery."

"Discovery?"

"That's what I do—discover. I am quite good at it, you know."

"Yes, I do know. Just today I overheard Wellington say we owed this victory to information provided by your 'correspondents.' "

"And our partisan guerrillas. And a very efficient network of spies." Geoffrey's voice hardened. "Some pay a very high price to help us."

"Are they not helping themselves also?"

"Not always. Some act out of altruism, not selfishness."

"Serving a higher calling?"

"Something like that." Geoffrey refilled his glass.

"You are in a strange mood, my friend."

"You heard about the abbess?"

"The Mother Superior there?" Wilson gestured in the direction of the convent-turned-hospital. "Yes, I heard. Tortured. Terrible way to die. What could an old woman like that—isolated in a convent, yet—have to hide? She gave up all the convent's riches."

"She was one of ours."

"She was . . . what are you saying?"

"She was an important link in our network. She held out long enough to give us this victory, but we've problems ahead, believe me."

"My God. Those women—the nuns—they are not safe here, are they?"

"No. Hell. No woman is safe in this godforsaken war."

Later, Geoffrey congratulated himself on having turned Wilson's attention. Now if he could just turn his own. He remembered this sense of despair, of loss. But he had been in love with Georgina.

Good God! At eighteen, one could hardly have called that calf-moonling behavior love.

So why had it hurt so much when she transferred her interest to his own brother—his heir-to-a-title brother?

Fate had treated Georgina cruelly. She had been married so few years and managed to produce only two daughters, no heir to the title. She had scarcely shed her widow's weeds before settling for a viscount.

Any old title, eh, Georgie? he asked silently.

When he finally slept, it was not Georgina's silver-blond fragility that haunted his dreams, but a brown-haired, hazel-eyed sprite bravely facing her loss.

Arising early, he set off the next morning to meet with partisans in the mountains. With any luck, Cymberly Winthrop would be long gone when he rejoined the regiment. Once again Sergeant MacIver accompanied him.

After a restless night, Cymberly set about the task of sorting through her father's possessions. As was customary, his military equipment would be auctioned off in the afternoon. She needed to decide which of his personal effects to keep.

As she opened the trunk he had carried across India and into the Iberian Peninsula, she caught the blended scent of pipe tobacco and shaving soap she always associated with her papa. She held a piece of his clothing to her face and rocked back and forth in her grief.

"Oh, Papa, Papa. How I shall miss you."

In the bottom of the trunk that carried his precious books

was an inlaid wooden box containing his papers. On the top was a letter addressed to her. It was dated the day they left Lisbon.

My dearest daughter,

If you are reading this, one of my worst fears has come to pass—I have left you alone. I am profoundly sorry for the hardships and decisions I know you now face. At the same time, I have every confidence in your ability to handle them.

I should like to have seen you married, to hold my grandchild on my knee. Such is not to be. You are your mother's daughter—so many of your mannerisms are hers—and you have her courage and determination. You will be a wonderful wife and mother.

Choose wisely in selecting the father of my grandchildren. I will not be there to call out the army as I threatened. Even as a little girl, you know your own mind. I love that quality in you, but you must also learn to trust your heart. I did many years ago, and I never once regretted doing so.

Nor did she.

Your loving father

Also in the box were legal papers, including her father's will. She was surprised to learn she would inherit a substantial amount of money and a house in London. There were two other bequests, one to Amitabha and one to her grandmother.

The most significant find in the Indian box were the letters her parents had written each other. Apparently, each had saved every message ever received from the other. When his wife died, General Winthrop had put her collection with his own as a legacy of love for their daughter. Cymberly looked through them, reading bits here and there, but she could not bring herself to deal just yet with the emotional journey they represented. She put them away.

An hour later she finished sorting. She gave Amitabha her father's gold watch, then sent him off with the items to be auctioned. What was left was a pitiful showing for a man with such a distinguished army career.

Just after lunch, she was visited again by the Reeses.

"We have arranged for you to travel with Colonel and Mrs. Taylor and other wounded when the caravan leaves tomorrow, my dear," Mrs. Reese told her. "You may, of course, take your two servants."

"It is kind of you to have gone to such trouble . . ."

"No trouble. No trouble at all," Colonel Reese said expansively.

"But," Cymberly continued, "I am not going back to England just yet."

"But—but—you must. You simply must." Mrs. Reese clearly could not believe her ears.

"Your father wished you to go," the colonel said firmly.

"My father also said he would not impose his will on me. I choose not to go. There are other unattached females following this army."

Mrs. Reese harrumphed loudly. "Common trollops, you mean. You cannot mean to classify yourself as such."

"No, I do not. But I know I can be of use here."

"Won't look good in London for the Peer if he lets a single woman of your rank stay," Reese said.

"Well, that is a decision for Lord Wellington to make. I have made mine."

"We shall see." Colonel Reese took his wife's arm and they departed.

An hour later Cymberly was instructed to report to Lord Wellington. Flanked by four other officers, he was seated at a table in front of his tent. There was also a milling group of about fifty people, curiosity seekers who sensed something of interest about to happen. Besides the Reeses and Gordon-Smythes, she noticed Maggie, Amitabha, Molly,

Juliana and Howard Williams, Mary Beth Peters and her husband—and Reggie.

"Ah, Miss Winthrop," Lord Wellington greeted her, but he and the others remained seated.

"My lord." She dipped him a curtsy and stood proudly.

"What is this nonsense about your refusing to join the returning caravan?"

"It is not nonsense, my lord. It is the truth."

"Why?"

Expecting this question, she had prepared an answer in which she begged to stay and promised not to become a burden. She looked at the commander's impassive face and ignored her prepared argument.

"Why, Miss Winthrop?" his lordship repeated.

"Because Winthrops do not quit, sir. I started on this course of action and I should like to see it through."

"I see. Stubborn little thing, are you not?"

"I prefer to think of myself as persevering, my lord. Or even tenacious."

Lord Wellington's lips twitched.

James McGrigor, handpicked head of medical services for Wellington's army, sat at the commander's left. He cleared his throat and said, "If I may interject, sir?"

"By all means," the Peer responded.

"Doctors Cameron and Hawkins speak highly of Miss Winthrop's service to the wounded."

"Hear, hear," said someone in the audience.

Lord Wellington sat silent for a moment, withdrawn. Then he said, "I cannot allow a woman of your status to remain alone with the army. The War Office, the Horse Guards, the Prince himself would have a collective fit of apoplexy."

Cymberly felt her shoulders sag in defeat. She had not realized just how much she had counted on staying with the army. She should be eager to leave this monster that ever robbed her of her father and had now taken him permanently. But in some quixotic way, she took comfort from being among people who had known and respected him. Wellington was still speaking.

"I cannot allow you to stay—unless someone will accept responsibility for you."

Several voices spoke at once.

"I will."

"We will."

"Step forward," Wellington ordered.

Molly MacIver, Juliana and Howard Williams, Dr. Cameron, and Lieutenant Fleming all stepped forward.

Wellington seemed mildly surprised. "Eh? Fleming? What is your interest in this affair?"

"I hope to make Miss Winthrop my wife, my lord."

"Well, if she has accepted . . ."

"She has not, sir—yet."

"Miss Winthrop?"

Cymberly felt intense heat in her face—indeed, over much of her body. Drat Reggie Fleming anyway! She looked down at her hands, then up to meet Lord Wellington's eyes. "I cannot think of marrying now, my lord. I would not be so disrespectful to my father." That was certainly the truth. But was it the *whole* truth?

"Quite right," his lordship said.

Molly took a step closer to the table. "My lord, my husband and I should be glad to look after the lass."

"And you are?"

"Molly MacIver, my lord. My husband is Sergeant Mac-Iver, with the Ninety-Sixth."

"I know who MacIver is, madam," Wellington said. "All right, Miss Winthrop. I give you permission to remain under the joint care of the MacIvers and Dr. Cameron. Now be gone, all of you."

"Thank you, my lord." Cymberly curtsied and, turning away from Fleming's proffered arm, she hugged Molly. "And I thank you, Molly—and you, Dr. Cameron." She reached to take the doctor's hand.

"I hope, my dear, you will be thanking us when this is all over," Cameron said.

Cymberly felt a twinge of pain at this nearly perfect echo of her father's comment weeks earlier in Lisbon.

Eight

Several days elapsed before Wellington could marshal his forces to pursue the French. Many officers and their staffs had moved into the town of Vitoria. To celebrate his victory, the Peer hosted a grand dinner in an elegant palace that had suffered relatively little damage.

Cymberly had experienced a great deal of indecision about attending a social function so soon after her father's death. Persuaded by others that these were extraordinary times, she dressed in a hastily devised but nonetheless stylish black gown and went to the dinner, but she did not dance. Sitting in a secluded alcove, she overheard two generals in conversation with their host.

" 'Tis a shame we had to resort to hanging to restore order," General Travers said.

"It is, indeed," Wellington replied. "I cannot understand why such behavior as shown by our troops continues to surprise me, but it does. Talavera, Salamanca, now Vitoria. Each time they went berserk."

"We *should* expect it," General Baird said. "After all, they come to us as the very dregs of Britain's various folk."

"The king's shilling is not likely to entice gentlemen," Travers said scornfully, referring, Cymberly knew, to the paltry sum paid new recruits. "It brings us only country yokels and city scoundrels."

"However"—Wellington's tone was firm—"it is imperative that we control this pillage and mistreatment of local citizens. The French army alone outnumbers our forces very considerably. Our government does not allow conscription, so we are not likely to see an unlimited number of replacements. Quite simply, gentlemen, we cannot win without the support of local populations. This criminal behavior must stop—immediately."

"Yes, sir." Baird and Travers spoke in unison.

"Inform the provost officers they are to hang any man known to have raped local females and flog anyone appropriating food or property illegally."

"Will that not result in yet more desertions, my lord?" Baird asked.

"Possibly. And we have already lost far more to desertion than to enemy weapons. Send provosts out to round up deserters, too. Anyone who must be forcibly returned is to be flogged."

"But, my lord, that is not likely to encourage them to rejoin their regiments," Travers objected.

Wellington cast the man an impatient look. "I said flog those who must be *forced* to return. The others?" He shrugged. "Most of them will be back as soon as they sober up and realize how difficult life is in a place where the food, the way of life, the very language one must use is so unfamiliar to them."

"True enough, I suppose," Travers conceded, and the three moved off.

None of what they had said came as a surprise to Cymberly. She had been returning from the hospital with Captain Wilson the evening before when they had heard a scream from an alleyway.

"Stay here," Wilson told her and ran down the alley.

Knowing the street was not particularly safe and unwilling to have Captain Wilson face unknown danger alone, Cymberly followed him. After all, she carried a small but deadly pistol in her reticule.

Halfway down the alley, they found two British soldiers in the act of trying to strip the clothing from a young woman. Cymberly gasped in horrified shock. Had the assailants been less drunk, they might already have achieved their goal. Seeing a third man approaching, the girl's eyes widened even further and she screamed again.

"Tol' ya to keep 'er quiet," one of the miscreants said.

"Yipe! She bit me hand." The second assailant slapped the girl hard on the side of her head.

"Here! Stop!" Wilson punched one of the men who stumbled. The other loosened his hold on the girl and she lost her balance, sinking to her knees.

"Go 'n' find yer own piece. This'n's ours," said the one who had been bitten. Then his inebriated brain registered the authority of an officer. "Sorry, Cap'n. But we wasn't doin' anything wrong. She's the enemy."

Seeing that Wilson had the two attackers in hand, Cymberly knelt beside the whimpering girl. In the exchange of only a few words, she learned the girl was, indeed, French, abandoned by her soldier-lover in the French retreat.

"British soldiers do not wage war on women." Wilson's contempt was clear. "Now you two go on about your business—and that is *not* attacking innocent women."

The two hesitated, but seemed to consider both the captain's size and his rank. They staggered off muttering about meddlin' officers spoiling a feller's fun.

Helping the victim to her feet, Cymberly saw she was very young, perhaps only fifteen. "Good heavens," she gasped. "She is a mere child. And those men . . . they were . . ."

"Aye. They were. Now—what are we to do with her?" Wilson shook his head.

The girl had initially cringed away from him but now her expression became calculating as she boldly studied him. Cymberly watched, fascinated by the transformation.

"What is your name?" Cymberly asked her in French.

"Cosette," the girl replied, not taking her gaze from Benjamin Wilson's face. "I come from a small village near Lyon. You will help me to go home, *monsieur?*" She dipped her head flirtatiously and smiled only at him.

"Good grief," Wilson muttered. "I gather this one is no better than she should be."

"In answer to your earlier question," Cymberly said with an amused glace at Wilson, "I think the problem of what to do with her is not *ours,* but *yours."*

"Miss Winthrop! Never say you will desert me."

"No, of course not—though I daresay your damsel in distress would not be disappointed if I did. But come, let us take her with us. Molly will know what to do with her."

Molly did, indeed, know what to do with Cosette. She set the girl to work as a laundress. "But she won't be earning her keep that way long, I'm thinking," Molly said privately to Cymberly. "I give her a week and she'll have found an English protector to replace the Frenchman who deserted her."

It was not a week, but three days. It might have taken less time had Cosette not proved rather particular. Quickly determining that Wilson was out of her reach, she settled for a young sergeant.

Cosette had no sooner chosen the usually hapless Sergeant Miller when the handsome, amiable Lieutenant Fleming caught her eye. She made little secret of her new preference, but it seemed to Cymberly that the girl's lures met with indifference from Reggie. Fleming had even spoken of the situation to Cymberly, treating it as "a great joke on poor Miller."

"That girl is a bad bit of business, mark my words," Molly said. "There'll be trouble over her for sure."

Cymberly mumbled some sort of response to this. In truth, she was too preoccupied with her own concerns to care overmuch about Cosette, one of many French and Spanish women who had, in the aftermath of the battle of Vitoria, joined the ranks of British camp followers.

Cymberly continued to report to the hospital, and her friendship with Sister Angelina grew as the two young women worked together. Cymberly learned that Angelina, Alicia, and Elena had not yet taken final vows to devote their lives to the church. She also learned Angelina had little desire to do so.

"But why did you join a convent, then?" Cymberly asked.

"I had no choice. My father gave me over to the church when I embarrassed him."

"He abandoned you because you *embarrassed* him?"

Angelina shrugged. "He was very angry. I refused to marry his choice for me—one of his friends. But," she added defensively, "he was a very old man. He beat his other wives."

"Wives? How many did he have?"

"Three, I think. My maid told me about two mistresses also. He beat them, too."

"Your father knew this?"

"Oh, yes. I am sure he did."

"What about your mother? Could she say nothing on your behalf?"

"Spanish women have no authority in such matters. She told me it was my duty to marry as my father bade me."

"And you refused."

"I refused. And he sent me here. I think it was to allow me time to think over my misbehavior. But, truly, a convent is not so very bad—not when the alternative is sharing the bed of Don Jose."

"What will happen to you now? I am told the convent will be abandoned. The village cannot run it. I just supposed all of you would return to your homes."

"I cannot go home. I have no home. My father supported the French. The opposition forces killed him and my mother and took his property three years ago."

"I am so sorry." Cymberly put a comforting arm around the girl's shoulders.

Angelina smiled. "It is of no matter now. I accepted my circumstance long ago."

"Alicia and Elena?"

"They, too, have nowhere to go now. Perhaps we go to Madrid or another city to become maids in rich households." Angelina shrugged.

"Oh, no. You cannot." Cymberly knew this idea was wholly impractical. Not only were the cities in such turmoil as to make employment only a distant possibility, but three young women were unlikely ever to reach such a destination.

In the end, which came in a matter of days, the three young novitiates and four older nuns joined the "tail" of the British army. The soldiers were amazingly solicitous of their welfare, providing the nuns a tent, guarding their privacy, and giving them food. The women sought earnestly to return these kindnesses.

For Cymberly, the hardships of the trail took her mind off her own troubles. If she refused Reggie's proposal, what would her own future be? She supposed she might join her grandmother in London when that intrepid soul returned to England.

She could not rejoin the Renfrow household, had she even desired doing so. No. The scandal of a single woman following the army—not to mention working with wounded soldiers—would be far too much for Lady Renfrow's delicate sensibilities.

She decided not to decide, but to cross that bridge when necessity placed it squarely in her path.

Meanwhile there was a range of mountains to be traversed. The perils of the trail intensified. Now some of the routes they had taken prior to Vitoria seemed veritable boulevards. The trails became narrower and steeper, the vegetation sparser. There was little fuel for fires at night and food for animals became scarce.

Nor was it only food for the animals that was scarce. Despite what Cymberly knew to be the intense efforts of Lord Wellington to keep his army properly supplied, the men were often hungry. In the villages they would beg or buy what foodstuffs they could. When these options failed, they stole, despite threats of floggings.

The Winthrop tent was now always erected near the MacIvers' camp. Reggie stood with Cymberly before her meager fire one evening and complained about this. "You should be closer to officers and their wives, people of your own rank, not stuck away here with riffraff," he told her.

"I do not consider the MacIvers riffraff," Cymberly replied coldly.

"I did not mean them precisely." Fleming toned down his contempt. "It is just . . ." He waved a hand inclusively.

"I *prefer* to be near Molly and her husband. They have been very kind to me. And to the three sisters." This was how people had come to regard the three younger nuns.

"You could marry me and take your rightful place."

"I have told you—"

"It has been almost a month, Cymberly. A month is a long time during a war. I want you with me, my love." He slipped his arm around her waist and held her to him despite the possibility of their being seen from neighboring camps. It flashed through her mind that such a public gesture would surely establish in the minds of an audience his claim on her. Is that what Reggie intended?

She gently but quickly disentangled herself from his embrace. "Please, Reggie. It has been only three weeks. You promised not to press me."

"I am sorry, love. It is just so hard not to. You need my protection."

"I have Maggie. And Amitabha would lay down his life for me if necessary, God forbid. What is more, David MacIver is quite a capable man."

"MacIver's not even available much of the time," he said

disparagingly. "He's always off traipsing the countryside with Ryder and that lot—usually just when a battle is about to start. Neither one of *them* is much help to the rest of us, you know."

"Are you not being rather severe in your criticism?"

"I think not. Where were they three days ago when we ran into that French patrol?"

"I have no idea."

"Well, I shall tell you. They were off on some hill, probably watching as the rest of us were taking a beating."

The British had been forced to give up several positions because Wellington did not feel he had sufficient numbers to launch a full-fledged pursuit. Still, Cymberly could not reconcile Reggie's picture with what she knew of Geoffrey Ryder and David MacIver. She changed the subject.

Throughout July and August the army trudged on, fighting minor skirmishes here and there. "Hardly minor to any man seriously wounded in one," Cymberly muttered to herself. The French had gained an ally in Mother Nature, and that formidable female had several weapons of her own.

But the British had an ally in the mountains—local citizens who opposed the French and readily shared their knowledge of little-known passes through the Pyrenees. Some were so narrow and steep that wagons and carts could not go through them, though troops—sometimes single file—could. These conditions, along with scarcity of forage, obliged Wellington to split his forces, thus leaving them more vulnerable to attack.

Fiercely determined not to be a burden to anyone, Cymberly drove herself hard. It was imperative that she be useful, that she contribute her share and more to the welfare of those around her. She used the work in part to avoid facing up to her own future, but for the time being, this was simply easier.

Easier? she asked herself skeptically. Dealing with the

hardships of the trail was *easier?* She, like most others, had to walk now more than ride. The sharp stones destroyed shoes at an appalling rate. But she was lucky. At least she still had shoes. Many others did not. Cracked and bleeding feet were commonplace ailments now.

The occasional skirmish brought additional wounded. Whenever possible, they were transferred to a port to be ferried back to England. But it was not always possible. Then injured men were loaded on wagons to endure additional agony from the bumps and lumps of the trail. Those who failed to make it were buried unceremoniously at the side of the route.

Occasionally riding, but mostly walking, Cymberly did what she could to help—providing a drink of water, talking to raise a suffering man's spirits, and listening to wounded soldiers pour out their stories, their hopes, and their fears.

In camp, despite Fleming's barely suppressed impatience, she often sat to read to them from an old newspaper or her father's books. This entertainment often attracted others. Many soldiers and followers alike were illiterate, but wanted to maintain their tenuous contacts with home. Occasionally Cymberly wrote letters for them, or a note to a bereaved mother or wife, assuring her of her loved one's bravery and that he remembered his family at the end. Such assurances sometimes stretched the truth rather forcefully, but she thought a brokenhearted woman would treasure such a message.

She went to bed every night exhausted. The rigors of the trail were taking a toll on everyone, especially the women and children. When she chanced to see herself in a looking glass, Cymberly saw, and tried to ignore, a reflection of the strain she observed on others.

Mary Beth Peters had grown heavy with her pregnancy, and both Cymberly and Molly made a point of relieving the young mother of the ever-active Tommy from time to time. Cymberly worried about her. Mary Beth had fallen again and seemed always to have a bruise somewhere. She also looked especially drawn and tired. During one rest period, Cymberly joined Mary Beth and Molly. The three had spread a blanket and were sharing some bread and cheese. Tommy was allowed to play nearby.

"Tommy, you play nicely now and stay right here," Mary Beth admonished in a tired voice.

And he did—for a few minutes. The women had their eyes off him only seconds before he was attracted by some older boys and wandered in their direction.

"Tommy!" Mary Beth called, but the toddler ignored her. She started to rise, awkwardly and painfully.

"I'll get him. You stay put." Cymberly jumped up to run after the child, who saw her pursuit as a game and tried to run faster. As she swept him into her arms, he giggled. She kissed his cheek and said, "You are a naughty boy!" but her voice was not unkind. She brought the boy back to the blanket, sat him down, and offered him a piece of bread to distract him.

"Thank you." The young mother sighed. She picked up a tin cup to offer Tommy a drink. Molly silently handed Mary Beth the canteen, but as Mary Beth reached for it, she winced in pain and would have dropped it had Molly not caught it. Molly silently took the cup, filled it, and handed it to Cymberly to give to the little boy.

"Mary Beth, have you done something to your wrist?" Cymberly asked.

"I—uh—sprained it when I fell the other day."

"Oh. That is too bad." Cymberly glanced at Molly and saw the older woman's lips and jaw tighten, but Molly did not say anything, only started to gather up their things.

Major Ryder and Sergeant MacIver rejoined the regiment high in the mountains. Not best pleased to find Miss Winthrop still with the army, Geoffrey was even less pleased with himself when his heart lurched at seeing her. He was also angered by the stress he saw in her face.

They had encountered each other at the MacIver camp, where, he learned, Cymberly, Amitabha, and Maggie took most of their meals now. Sharing made short rations go farther. The MacIver group had just finished their supper when Geoffrey put in an appearance.

"Miss Winthrop." He greeted her stiffly. "I see you decided to ignore the sound advice of others to return to England." His comment sounded more accusatory than he intended, but he could not take it back.

"Yes. I am still here." He thought there was a forced gaiety in her voice, but he did not miss the slight edge when she added, "While *some* have little confidence in my abilities, others spoke up for me, you see."

"It was never a question of your *abilities,* Miss Winthrop, but of your welfare."

"I am faring quite well, thank you. I am sure you have private army business to discuss with Mac, so I shall leave you to it." Bidding everyone good night, she and her companions went to their own quarters.

"Damn!" Geoffrey muttered to himself. Then he caught Molly's twinkling gaze on him. "Sorry, Molly."

"Never mind," Molly said. "You did not handle that well, I think."

He smiled. "I think you are right. I was surprised to see her, though."

"Surprised—but not entirely disappointed, I ken?"

"I ken you know me too well." He adopted her Scots phrasing in a rueful voice. "That's what comes of serving together so many years."

"She's a lovely girl, Major. It'd be a shame to see her tied to a weak man like Fleming."

"Leave it, Molly," her husband interjected. "Folks here do not know Fleming as we who served with his pa in India know him. The gel must make her own judgment. And who knows? Mayhap he's changed."

Molly sniffed disbelievingly.

Geoffrey sat silent for a moment, unwilling to display the surge of jealousy he experienced at this pairing of Cymberly and Fleming. Then he shrugged. "You are right, Mac. It is Miss Winthrop's business, not ours."

"Well, yes it is," Molly said. "But frankly, his feelings seem stronger than hers. *He* put it out that he would make her his wife, but she has never said a word one way or the other."

"That so?" Geoffrey tried to keep his tone casual.

"Yes, that is so." Molly sounded impatient with him. "If your feelings incline that way—and I suspect they do—you would do well to make them known."

"Since I have no idea what my feelings are, I fail to see how you could know them." Geoffrey knew he sounded haughty. "In any event, I would not declare myself to any woman in the middle of a war, especially one who has every appearance of belonging to someone else. Besides, this one simply does not like me overmuch."

"Well, as to that . . ."

"Leave the man alone, Molly." MacIver's laughing tone belied the terse words. "You know how women are," he said to Geoffrey. "Once they get their own man, they have to help every other woman get one, too."

Geoffrey chuckled and said with more carelessness than he felt, "Well, if Miss Winthrop wants a husband, she should find one easily enough in this atmosphere."

"Hmmph!" Molly muttered, but she said no more on the issue as the men's conversation turned to something else.

Nine

A month after the battle of Vitoria, Wellington established his headquarters in Lesaca, scarcely a hundred miles from Vitoria, an area heavily controlled by the enemy. Despite their ignominious defeat at Vitoria, the French still commanded much of northern Spain and continued to wage aggressive campaigns against their pursuers.

Now, much to his dismay, it seemed, Wellington faced his adversary in two separate locations—in San Sebastian on the seacoast and Pamplona in the mountains. Both were heavily fortified. Moreover, the wily French General Soult held the two main passes through the mountains and insisted on engaging his opponent in any number of other places.

Still, on July 22, his lordship hosted a dinner party for his officers to commemorate the victory of the battle of Salamanca a year before.

"A dinner party? In the midst of a campaign? His lordship never ceases to amaze me," Cymberly said to Wilson, who had stopped by the quarters she shared with the MacIvers in the village.

Wilson looked very handsome in his dress uniform. Angelina had also come to visit Cymberly and was still there when Wilson arrived. Cymberly noticed Wilson could barely keep his eyes off the Spanish girl, who still wore her nun's garb. Angelina seemed awestruck by the handsome captain and responded to his greetings in shy monosyllables.

"I think," Wilson said, "this is Wellington's way of turning up his aristocratic nose at the enemy."

"A schoolboy taunt? Surely not," Cymberly said.

"Not precisely, but something of the sort. Guns and ammunition are not the only weapons of war, you know."

"Far be it from me to gainsay the commander," she replied.

"Or me. Has Mac returned yet?"

"No. Why do you ask?"

"Mere curiosity. He and Geoff were supposed to be back today, and I have not seen the traveling major."

"Did Molly know they were returning today? She did not say anything."

"Perhaps. Perhaps not. 'Tis not unusual for them to be a day late—or a day early. Geoff will hate missing the Peer's party."

"I had not realized the major was such a social being."

"He isn't. At least not like some who love the party atmosphere. You know—the music, the jokes—"

"The toasts," Cymberly interjected with a smile.

"The toasts," he agreed. "But Geoff? He loves to corner some veteran of a previous campaign to discuss strategy. Always wants to know what worked and what did not—and why."

"And people love to talk about their own experiences."

"That they do."

With that, Wilson bade the two ladies good night. Soon afterward, Angelina also took her leave. Somewhat to her surprise, Cymberly found herself worried about the missing Major Ryder. Was he all right?

She knew of the extra risks involved in his activities as a "correspondent." Going behind enemy lines to contact partisans and gather information was dangerous work, with the only real protection being the uniform he wore. A man captured in uniform would be treated honorably. One not so attired would be summarily executed.

She tried to tell herself her concern was the same for Major Ryder as for any other trooper. She tried to dismiss her memory of his kiss. That kiss had been an unfortunate aberration in behavior, and they had both immediately regretted it—had they not? Why, Ryder did not even approve of her—certainly not of her being here now. Nor should she allow herself to feel anything but distant polite interest in a Ryder. She wanted nothing to do with anyone connected to her grandfather.

Nevertheless, when the sergeant's wife came in later, clearly concerned about her husband's delayed return, Molly's worry intensified Cymberly's. But surely that was only because she felt such empathy for Molly.

Another day passed. Still no word of Molly's husband or his companion. Fleming came by to share such *on dits* and amusing tales from the commander's party as could be told to ladies. Wilson, too, put in an appearance. Cymberly could tell he was now truly worried about his friend, but Captain Wilson tried to reassure Molly.

"Ryder and Mac have come through tight situations before this. They know what they are doing. They will be all right." He was, Cymberly thought, trying to convince himself as much as his listeners.

"I hope so," Molly said, but Cymberly knew the sergeant's wife would worry until her husband was by her side again.

The next morning saw the beginning of what everyone knew would be a prolonged period of intense skirmishes. Control of the seacoast town of San Sebastian was crucial to Britain and her allies, for the port at Passages could provide easier access to supplies from England. The assault against San Sebastian was ongoing, and another skirmish erupted at a village to the south called Sorauren.

"That was a tough one." The speaker was a bandsman-stretcher-bearer. "The French are determined to keep us from Pamplona."

"Why is Pamplona so important?" she asked.

"Because it is situated at the crossroads to the Pyrenees. Even if we took sites farther north than it is, leaving the French in charge there would allow them to attack from our rear."

"Have our forces taken Pamplona?"

"Not yet. Too well fortified. But a siege is in place. Have to starve them out."

"Oh, my." Cymberly thought of mothers within the city trying to feed hungry children while men tried to hang on to territory. "Will it take long?"

"I heard General Travers tell a captain it could take a month or more."

This conversation took place in Elizondro, a village below the Maya Pass where Cymberly, Molly, and a number of other women had been deposited once that location had been secured. Once again, a church had been appropriated as a temporary hospital.

Besides those injured in the battle for Elizondro itself, wounded poured in from every point of the compass. Cymberly found it difficult to comprehend so many battles going on virtually simultaneously. She often worked in the hospital to the point of exhaustion—and far beyond.

Reggie invited her to walk out with him one evening. "Neither one of us belongs in this devil's playground," he said. "We could be so happy in London."

"But we could not just leave here now!"

"Of course we could."

"What about your position? Your career?"

"My position?" He laughed. "Perhaps you've not noticed that lieutenants are a plentiful commodity. I think they could do without me. And escorting my new wife home to England would provide a quite honorable way out of here. Once on English soil, I shall sell out and set us up in London."

"And then what?"

"What do you mean 'and then what'?"

"I mean . . ." Oh, Lord, what did she mean? The truth

was that, in contemplating marrying Reggie, she had rarely thought beyond the possibility of her saying yes. She searched her mind frantically. "I mean, what would you do? I had not thought your fortune so great . . . that is, selling your commission would not bring much . . ." She colored up in embarrassment at invading his privacy.

"Do? Why, I suppose I should do as others of our class do. My father has a bit of property that will be mine one day. Of course, it alone would not support us in a proper lifestyle, but I doubt not your father left you a suitable marriage portion."

"He did," she conceded.

"Well, then?"

"I am sorry—"

"Please, my darling. Say yes. Now. Do you not realize how very much I love you?"

"I am mindful of your affection, of course," she said slowly. "But I cannot agree to this yet. I meant it when I said I would accord my father a proper period of mourning, and I have made a commitment here. People depend on me. I cannot let them down."

"But what about us? What about me? Would you let me down?"

"Oh, Reggie. That is not fair. I am truly sorry. I just cannot give you an answer yet."

"All right, my love." He brought her hand to his lips. "Later then. By Christmas you will have completed a proper mourning even by London standards. Perhaps we can celebrate our wedding along with the Christmas season."

"I am not sure. Perhaps," she said. Why could she not give him a definitive yes or no? She did want to say yes, did she not? What made her withhold the answer that would seemingly make him so happy?

She kept herself intensely busy, and her mind was preoccupied with Reggie's proposal. Still, her thoughts often drifted to Major Ryder. Bossy and irritating though he was, she missed his quiet strength, and she worried privately over what might have happened to him.

Then one evening as she returned to the small house she, Maggie, and Amitabha shared with Molly, she found David MacIver had returned—and she breathed a sigh of relief.

Smiling, she gripped his hands. "Mac! what a welcome sight you are! We have been so worried about you—and the major. I trust you are both happy to be back with us."

MacIver squeezed her hands firmly, but gave her a bleak look. "The major didn't come back."

Cymberly drew in a sharp breath. Pain shot through her whole being. "He—he is not . . ." She could not bring herself to utter the word.

"No. He ain't dead." MacIver guided her to a chair near the dining table and took another himself. As the sergeant related his tale, Molly set cups of tea in front of them and took another chair. "He was captured by a French patrol," MacIver explained.

"Captured? How? Was he hurt?"

"No. No. He's all right. Leastwise, he was the last I saw him. They probably won't mistreat an officer in uniform, though they'll keep a close watch on him."

"The major made it possible for David to escape," Molly said. Incongruously, Cymberly noted that Molly never called her husband by the familiar "Mac."

"We were taken by surprise, you see," he said, "and Ryder, he orders me to stay low and be sure to get our report back to the Peer. Then he rode off like the hounds of hell were after 'im. Guess they were—I expect the devil's pets are French."

"Did they shoot at him? Was he wounded?" Molly asked the questions Cymberly wanted to ask.

"They fired shots, but I think they were warning shots. I saw 'em tie his hands in front of him, and one of them was leading the major's horse."

"And you think he will be treated well?" Cymberly asked, unable to keep her concern from her tone.

MacIver glanced at his wife. Apparently they had discussed the situation before Cymberly's arrival. Molly looked worried.

"Tell her the truth," she said.

MacIver cleared his throat. "Ordinarily an officer is given his parole."

"Parole? What does that mean?"

"Means if he swears he won't try to escape, his captors will treat him as one of them."

"Oh. Oh-h-h." There was a hopeful lilt in her tone.

"Tell her, David."

"Geoffrey—Major Ryder—he would never take such an oath."

"W-why? Why would he not do so?"

MacIver sighed. "Because if he took the oath, he would have to abide by it."

"Strong sense of honor in our Geoffrey. Not to mention stubbornness," Molly said.

"So he *is* in danger then?"

MacIver nodded. "Some. The frogs know who he is, so they'll keep him under close watch."

"And you think he will try to escape?"

"I *know* he will. Otherwise he could take the parole. And he won't."

"How can you be so sure?"

"He didn't before," Molly said.

"Before?"

"He was captured 'bout a year and a half ago during the siege of Badajoz. Wellington negotiated a prisoner exchange, something he does not do often."

"And if he does not take parole?"

"He'll be treated like any other prisoner—rather harshly, don't you know?"

"How terrible," Cymberly murmured.

Molly patted her hand comfortingly. "Yes, it is, my dear. But Geoff's a strong lad. Clever, too. He'll come through. You'll see."

Hope, Cymberly thought, was a thin veil through which despair shone clearly on the faces and in the voices of Major Ryder's friends. She understood their reactions to the danger Ryder encountered. After all, they had known the man for years and were very fond of him. It was the intensity of her own reaction—an echo of their despair—that surprised her.

Later that evening, Lieutenant Fleming came to visit. The next morning his regiment would leave for the seacoast. He was properly polite, if somewhat condescending, in welcoming MacIver back. MacIver seemed studiously correct in returning the lieutenant's greeting.

Fleming said nothing of Ryder's being a French prisoner, though the whole encampment knew of it. Nor did the MacIvers introduce the topic. Since Mac had broken the news to her, Cymberly had said little of it herself, though the missing major seemed never far from her thoughts. She did not ask herself why.

For over a month, the British and French forces fought intermittently in the mountains, and the sieges against San Sebastian and Pamplona remained in force. Some days the work at the hospital was almost routine. At other times it was sheer chaos. Cymberly welcomed the erratic schedule. The hard work helped ease her grief over her father's death, her uncertainty about accepting Reggie's suit, and her concern over the still missing Major Ryder.

Hospital work was not so much physically demanding as it was emotionally draining. As one of the few women caring for wounded directly, Cymberly was rarely called upon to assist in surgery, but she dealt with the surgeons' results day after day, changing bandages and offering comfort.

She tried to help men who had lost one or more limbs

cope with their losses. Yes, they could still lead useful lives. Yes, their wives and sweethearts would welcome them as whole men.

Death became an ever-present, rarely welcomed, companion. Over half the men brought to hospital died. Most perished from infection and fever which wracked their bodies after they had already suffered the excruciating pain of amputations with little more than a swig of cheap whisky to ease the trauma.

Cymberly wept over many a loss, often tears of frustration as well as grief. The medical people had so few weapons. She hated feeling so helpless. Yet there was an occasional triumph when a man seen as having no chance miraculously survived.

Sister Angelina proclaimed these as instances of God's mercy. Cymberly was more inclined to attribute them to chance—or to the wounded man's willingness to continue to fight against great odds.

She felt overwhelmed by activities outside her self-made shell of hospital work. Did individuals involved in major occurrences of history ever understand at the time? Did even leaders like Lord Wellington need historians to help them later make sense of the panorama of events? She rather thought they did. Meanwhile, her own eclectic mix of impressions came primarily from the wounded.

The lower ranks gave her their images and opinions of particular engagements. Their views were, of necessity, limited, but they were honest and often insightful. One of the most hard-fought contests had seen the British triumph at Maya Pass, one of two main passes through the mountains.

"The fightin' was fierce, Miss. Them Frenchies was all over the place."

"That damned Captain Larson—uh, beg your pardon, Miss—Larson oughtn't ta have sent us out with no backing."

"Yeh. We was just slaughtered."

"Jimmy got it right in front of me. Blew half his head

right off. An' I told his ma I'd look after him." Ending on a sob, this came from a young man whose own head was bandaged and one of his arms in a sling. Cymberly patted his good hand in a comforting gesture.

"If ol' Nosey had been at the pass with us, wouldn't a been so many die."

"Or Major Ryder. He takes care of his men."

"Some o' these others—they spend lives like they was spending their family fortunes."

"Ar Arthur knows what's what. We needed him here, 'stead of on the coast." Cymberly wondered how the aristocratic Wellington would react to this conversation.

"At Vitoria, he was all over the field. Never knew when he'd show up."

"You bloody Scots," one soldier called to another in a tone more admiring than condemning. "You fellers never know when to quit, do ya?"

"Aye, we do. When the job's done, laddie. Then's the time ta quit."

"I thought them pipes would never stop their infernal screechin'."

"Inspirin', ain't they?" the Scotsman asked. There were several very English snorts in reply.

Cymberly knew this good-natured banter, rehashing a perilous event, helped relieve tension. She also knew their criticisms were valid and their pride well-founded.

Wounded officers were brought to hospital for initial treatment, but whenever possible were immediately removed to their own quarters to be cared for by their personal servants. Still, there were always several men in the chapel set aside for officers' beds.

Cymberly found it interesting that, while officers often had a broader perspective than their men, their complaints and opinions paralleled those of lesser ranks.

"Nasty bit of business that pass, eh?" said a lieutenant who had been wounded in an earlier skirmish.

"Truly terrible. And made worse by inferior leadership. Colonels squabbling among themselves and issuing conflicting orders," a wounded captain replied.

"Too bad the Peer could not be in two places at once," put in another.

"Yes. I just wish he had been here instead of elsewhere."

"Heard he was in a tear about losses at Maya Pass."

"I believe his exact words were something to the effect that too many officers are true heroes when he is on the spot to direct them, but children when he cannot be present."

"Is that not rather harsh?"

"Perhaps. But we would have lost that battle at the pass if not for the intrepid Scots. And there is no question our losses were needlessly excessive."

"Hmmph," another speaker grunted. "Things did not go exactly as planned even when Sir Arthur *was* present."

"What do you mean?"

"When San Sebstian finally fell, the looting and atrocities equalled the worst such behavior at Badajoz and Vitoria. And Wellington could not stop it."

"That will make progress more difficult as we proceed north."

"Not to mention the terrain and weather . . ."

Ten

After the fall of San Sebastian at the end of August, supplies began to flow more freely—if erratically.

"We shall be moving on soon," Dr. Cameron said as he, Cymberly, and several others sorted through a mound of newly arrived blankets, bandages, and medicines. "With both major passes open now, Wellington intends to push on."

"I thought he wanted to take Pamplona, too," Cymberly said.

"Oh, he does. It is only a matter of time, though, before it falls into our hands, especially now that French access from the north has been severely curtailed."

"But not totally blocked."

"True. Some goods are getting through to them. Merely prolongs the process. Once the town realizes the French are deserting them, they will capitulate soon enough."

"I do hope you are right." Cymberly again thought of women and children barricaded in the town with French loyalist holdouts.

"So we shall be going in several groups with local Basques guiding us through the mountains."

"But if the main passes are open . . ."

"Too many of us. Not enough forage for animals. And it would take an inordinate amount of time to be limited to two narrow passes."

"I see."

"However, some of these routes are little better than goat trails. These supplies must be packed for mules, not wagons."

Cameron's predictions and warnings proved accurate. If anything, the doctor had understated the situation, Cymberly thought.

Summer began to give way to autumn, especially in the mountains. The hot sun of the days was offset by extreme cold at night. She began to notice hoarfrost in the mornings. Those who had them pulled extra blankets out of their baggage. Others began to sleep two or three together to share body heat.

Problems in the distribution of supplies often left troops doing without. Because the army drove its meat supply "on the hoof," that commodity was usually available, but the cattle were thin, underfed, and driven hard. The meat was stringy and tough. Flour was available intermittently. Cymberly recalled seeing one soldier's "loot" after the battle of Vitoria—a shirtful of flour. Troops passing peasant gardens could often be seen in the fields, pulling up vegetables by their roots and eating them on the spot.

Shoes and boots were in such short supply that many men marched barefoot. Their uniforms, such as they were, were in tatters. Sharp red tunics had long since faded to dull, threadbare pink, and often as not had been so patched and repatched that the original identity was all but lost. There was little uniformity at all in trousers. They, too, bore multiple patches. Cymberly knew many had been jerked from the bodies of dead and near-dead soldiers where they lay on the field, with little regard for the military affiliation of the original or current wearer.

She joined forces with the MacIvers, pooling food and other necessities. When David MacIver was away on a mission, Molly happily slept in the tent with Cymberly and Maggie. Captain Wilson, who shared with two other officers—three others when Ryder had been with them—

usually managed to have his tent pitched near the Winthrop-MacIver camp. Cymberly was grateful for his unspoken support.

She wondered fleetingly why Lieutenant Fleming's quarters always seemed so distant from hers, but she reasoned that, as a junior officer, he had less control over such matters. Fleming, whose regiment had been redeployed after San Sebastian, made a point of visiting her nearly every evening when he was not out on patrol. She knew many considered their betrothal a *fait accompli,* though she had not yet made an overt commitment.

Reggie had been sweet about not pressuring her. She chastised herself for putting him off, but she could not yet bring herself to think through this decision which would, after all, determine the course of her whole life. She had little desire to start that course just yet.

So, letting others think what they would, she drifted in a sea of emotional ambivalence. Juliana teased her about Reggie's seeking the Williams' friendship to further his interest with Cymberly. The two couples occasionally played cards in the evening, after which Reggie would walk her back to her quarters. Always he would guide her into the shadows, pull her into his arms, and kiss her.

She welcomed his embraces, but she also recognized a certain lack of enthusiasm on her part. He brought her wildflowers, an apple, or other treats. He was attentive, entertaining, and amiable. She appreciated his affection and tried to return it in kind. Surely he would be a good husband. Next time he brought up the subject, perhaps she should agree to marry him.

Riding with Captain Wilson one day, Cymberly noticed his attention wandering. He was watching Sister Angelina. The young nun was cheerfully carrying a baby for its mother. Wilson was absorbed by the scene and refocused his gaze only when Cymberly chuckled. His face reddened and he gave her a sheepish look.

"Caught me out," he said.

"She is a lovely girl. Sweet-natured, too."

"I know." He gave a sigh of profound regret.

"Have you talked with her much?"

"Only to say 'good morning' or 'good evening.' I have never had a private word with her."

"Oh. You don't know, then."

"Don't know what? That she is out of my reach?"

"But she is not, my friend."

"Surely you jest. The church views her vows as binding as marriage. Even I know that."

"Angelina has not taken final vows. Nor does she desire to do so."

"What? Are you sure?" Hope rang a clarion note in his voice.

Cymberly laughed. "Yes, I am sure. She told me so herself." She told him a little of Angelina's background, taking care to respect the girl's privacy.

Wilson reached across to put his gloved hand over Cymberly's. "Thank you," he said simply. They rode in thoughtful silence until Juliana joined them and Wilson left with a laughing remark about escaping "girl talk."

A few minutes later, Cymberly smiled to see that Wilson, dismounted and leading his horse with one hand, walked beside Sister Angelina. *He* now carried the baby and smiled down at the girl as she talked and gestured with her hands.

The mountains were spectacular in their majestic grandeur. The travelers often paused just to admire the stunning views, but the very features which created such beauty for the eye created huge impediments for the foot and other means of locomotion. In friendly terrain, the army could travel fifteen miles or more a day comfortably. Now they rarely achieved even half that.

They were, of course, moving in smaller units now, but

not so small as to make them vulnerable to attack. Patrols guarded during the day and pickets were posted every night. Each day after camp had been established, Dr. Cameron made himself available to treat those needing medical attention. Cymberly often assisted him.

One afternoon as they rebandaged a shoulder wound in front of the doctor's tent, two men approached. One of them, a big man with his head down, leaned heavily on his companion, who seemed sturdy and healthy. As they were still some distance away, her brow creased in consternation. Was it . . . no, surely not. But it was.

"Hey," the healthy one called. "I need a hand here."

Cymberly dropped the scissors she held and flew to the side of the injured man.

"Major Ryder! How on earth? Here, lean on me." She slipped her arm around his waist and dragged his free arm over her shoulder.

He looked gaunt and exhausted. His bare feet showed evidence of the unforgiving harshness of the terrain. He was filthy, his hair matted, his face, hands, and feet caked with dirt. He was dressed in a tattered shirt and trousers that must once have belonged to a peasant. And he smelled.

"Miss Winthrop." His voice was surprisingly strong, though his stumbling step showed how weak he was. "I must . . . apologize . . . your finding me in such . . . disarray."

"Never mind." She felt a rush of warm gladness as she looked into gray eyes glazed with fatigue. Having him back seemed so right.

"Found 'im lying by a stream about a mile—two, maybe—back there. Thought at first he was dead," the other man said.

Cameron joined them and took Cymberly's place. She ran ahead to prepare the extra cot Cameron kept in his tent for such emergencies. She busied herself cleaning and tidying up the doctor's instruments as he examined his new patient.

Molly and Mac arrived, both out of breath. They spoke at once.

"We heard . . ."

"Geoff—is he . . ."

A few seconds later Cameron emerged and said, "He is in remarkably good shape. No broken bones. A few bruises—mostly old ones. He is suffering from exhaustion and malnutrition."

"May we see him?" Molly asked.

"Oh, yes, but he's asleep. Just collapsed on the bed and was out immediately. I expect he will sleep for ten or twelve hours—and then he will be ravenously hungry."

Neither Molly nor Mac was satisfied until they had actually seen their friend.

"Can't we at least clean him up while he is asleep?" Molly asked.

"Don't see why not," Cameron replied.

"I'll do it," Mac said.

"I'll help," Cymberly offered, then blushed as the others looked at her in surprise. "Oh. I . . . guess not."

Just then Wilson arrived. "Is it true? It really is Geoff?"

He, too, had to see this sleeping phenomenon for himself. Cymberly went with him. As they gazed down on the besmudged but peaceful countenance, she could not restrain herself from reaching to smooth a matted lock of hair back into place. At her touch, Ryder groaned softly, but did not stir. She lifted tear-filled eyes to Wilson, who smiled in return.

Geoffrey Ryder's recovery was as rapid as Cameron had predicted. He awoke the next morning somewhat disoriented, but upon realizing where he was, he wolfed down some food and promptly fell asleep again, scarcely aware that his body was clean after weeks of going unwashed.

Fortunately, this contingent of the army was to spend two

more days encamped in a valley used by herders of sheep and goats for summer grazing. Empty now, their stone and thatch huts provided temporary shelter for a few members of the army.

When Ryder woke again, it was late afternoon. He felt refreshed, but still tired. His first order of business was to report to his commander. Higgins had brought him a change of clothing, so it was a properly attired rifleman major who presented himself to General Travers. Colonel Reese, Captain Wilson, two aides to the general, and several others joined the commander to hear his report.

"I believe Sergeant MacIver gave you the most significant data we gathered, sir."

"He did. Valuable it was, too. But we were all quite concerned about your being nabbed like that, Ryder. Worried, actually."

" 'Twas not a pleasant experience."

"You should have taken parole. You'd likely be in Paris now sipping cognac and sleeping in a featherbed."

Geoffrey shrugged. "Possibly." He then proceeded to give his commander information he had gleaned after his forced parting from MacIver. "So as I see it," he finished, "it appears Marshal Soult plans one more major assault on us. More, of course, if he should win."

"I shall convey that observation, along with this new information, to Lord Wellington. I believe he hopes to winter near Bayonne, but if you are right, we may have some difficulty getting there."

"Yes, sir."

"Now, tell me about your little escapade. How long were you a prisoner—a month?"

"Actually, not quite three weeks, sir. And I was over a week on the journey back. It should not have taken so long, of course, but I had to dodge French patrols all the time—and you never know whether the loyalties of local people lie with us or the French."

"So how did you manage to escape at all? They must have had you under close watch."

Geoffrey chuckled. "That they did. Turns out *they* never quite know where local sympathies lie, either."

"That so?"

"Despite my not taking parole, the officers of the small force that took me treated me quite decently. Captain Roche has relatives in England, even. He invited me to dine with him much of the time, but always made sure I was firmly tied up at night—and they took my boots as an added precaution. We rode in close order during the day."

"Go on," the general said eagerly.

"Well, our route was very erratic, to say the least. I could not decide whether they were taking a circuitous way for my benefit or they were engaged in some clandestine business. Bit of both, perhaps."

Travers laughed. "Or they were simply lost."

"Perhaps. In any event, we spent most nights in various villages. I was often thrown into some back room and trussed up. Usually they would come get me for the evening meal. We talked a good deal. Played cards. The captain carried a small chess set with him. Then it was back to the ropes for me."

"What finally happened?"

"You will find this hard to believe." Geoffrey looked around at his listeners and smiled. "One of the villages they stopped in was one of ours!"

Travers raised a quizzical eyebrow. "Ours?"

"Inhabited largely by a group of partisans who detest the French and do not have a great deal of love for the Spanish, either."

"Oh, I say," gasped Colonel Reese. There were several chuckles from others.

"And the best house in the village," Geoffrey continued, "is that of the partisan leader, a man named Juan Diego. I have worked with Juan before and with his daughter, Teresa.

She is as vehement in her hatred of the French as her father, and with reason. She and her mother were raped by the bastards and the mother was killed."

"Your French captain knew nothing of this?" someone asked disbelievingly. "Poor intelligence work, I say."

"Apparently he took our host's word that the whole village hates the invading English. The stories coming out of San Sebastian helped convince him and the others."

"Bad business, that," someone muttered.

"Go on, Ryder," Travers said.

"Well, sir, Juan plied his guests with drinks and they shared stories about the swinish English. Juan made a point of refusing to have me in his house. I was trussed up again and tossed into a goat shed in the back."

"No wonder you smelled so ripe when you arrived," Wilson said.

"*You* go for three or four weeks without a bath and see—"

"Get on with the story." Travers made no attempt to disguise his impatience.

"Roche and his fellows must have felt very comfortable. Someone checked on me early in the evening and they posted a guard, but then—nothing. After midnight, Teresa sneaked out to the shed. She incapacitated the guard—"

"*Incapacitated* him?" someone asked, curious.

"She conked him on the head with a block of wood. Fell like a brick."

"Ah."

"She freed me and gave me some of her father's clothing, which I changed into. We dragged the guard into the shed, then took my clothing and buried it under a boulder as she showed me the way out of the area. She left me just before dawn—said she had to be there to prepare breakfast for their guests."

"And that's it? The whole story?" Travers asked.

"Mostly. I've traveled cautiously, of course. Usually at night. Without a map—they took my compass—I've been lost a good deal of the time." Geoffrey felt somewhat chagrined at this admission.

"Rescued by a woman. And under the very noses of the French." Travers gave a hoot of laughter. "The Peer will love this story."

Later, Geoffrey thought the Peer was not the only one to love the story, for various versions of it flew like dandelion spores throughout the camp. Some of them even approximated the truth.

Eleven

Cymberly welcomed Major Ryder as he and Wilson, adding their own rations to the meal, joined her and the MacIvers for supper that evening.

"I must say you are looking much improved, Major," she observed, smiling.

"Amazing what clean clothing and a decent meal will do." His eyes twinkled as he looked directly into hers.

She felt the now familiar rush of pleasure at his attention and forcibly pulled her gaze away.

There had been letters and newspapers from England in the last shipment of supplies to reach them, so the evening was spent pleasantly in bringing Major Ryder up to date on events great and small.

He listened with apparent amusement to the month-old *on dits* of London gossip, including the Prince Regent's ongoing conflict with his capricious wife and Lady Caroline Lamb's shameless pursuit of the poet Byron. He showed considerably more interest in the news of the allies' amassing troops for a major encounter with Napoleon.

"That Russian debacle did not slow Boney much," Wilson said. "Just gathered more replacements in France."

"He does seem to have an inexhaustible source of new recruits." Mac tamped tobacco into a crooked pipe.

"True. Fortunately for us, he sends *recruits* to Soult in the west and draws veterans from armies here for his assault in the east." Geoffrey handed Mac a light from the campfire for his pipe.

"Interesting that Wellington has never gone up against Napoleon directly," Wilson said.

"Wouldn't that be something?" Mac asked. "The two greatest military leaders of our time going head to head."

"That probably will not happen." Cymberly surprised herself by speaking aloud what she thought. She and Molly had sat quietly through most of this discussion. The men turned three pairs of questioning eyes on her.

"Oh? And how do you come by this amazing conclusion?"

At the major's condescending tone, Cymberly bristled. She knew she should keep her views to herself. War was, after all, considered a masculine domain. But she was her father's daughter, was she not?

"Well, you see, sir"—her tone was ultrasweet—"I read a newspaper now and then."

"And?" he challenged.

"And it appears to me," she continued, "that Lord Wellington should be grateful that the Russians, Austrians, and Prussians finally stopped arguing like a pack of belligerent schoolboys, thus enabling them to keep Bonaparte occupied in the east."

Geoffrey stared at her in amazement. Molly cast a knowing, smiling glance from one to the other and then to her husband.

Wilson guffawed. "Yes, Geoff, there is a brain in that pretty head. If you could see your expression . . ."

"Hmmph. Well—"

Whatever else he might have said was forestalled by Angelina, who arrived in a state of anxiety.

"Oh, please—do excuse me," she said in her prettily accented English. In her excitement, she barely acknowledged the gentlemen, who had risen at her entrance. "Please, Molly,

Cymberly—you will come, no? It is Mary Beth—Mrs. Peters. The baby . . ."

"Of course. Just let me get a few things." Molly dashed into her tent for a bag she kept ready for such emergencies.

As she grabbed a shawl from her own tent, Cymberly heard Angelina shyly explaining to the men, "The baby . . . he comes too soon."

She heard Mac add, "Molly's had considerable experience as a midwife. Folks often call on her, don't you know?"

Bidding hasty and apologetic good nights to Major Ryder and Captain Wilson, Cymberly and Molly followed Angelina to the tent the Peters and their son shared with three other families. Mary Beth lay moaning on a pallet. Three women stood or knelt beside her.

Cymberly took a damp cloth from Mrs. Hoskins and wiped the suffering woman's brow. "It's all right, Mary Beth. Molly will help you," she murmured.

Molly, having examined the patient briefly, gave Cymberly a worried look, but her voice was clear and reassuring. "Now you just relax, dear."

"It's too soon . . ." Mary Beth gasped between pains. "I told him . . . I begged him . . ."

Cymberly noticed a fresh bruise on Mary Beth's jaw and others on her arms. When Molly ran her hands over Mary Beth's body, the younger woman winced and sucked in her breath as Molly touched her side beneath the left breast.

"Damn him!" Molly exclaimed.

Cymberly looked up, startled. She had never heard Molly curse before, though such language—and a good deal worse—was not at all uncommon among many of the females in camp.

"He's been beating her," Molly explained. "Six months and more with child and that scurvy fellow had to prove he was a man by knocking her about. Broke her ribs."

"Who? You don't mean . . ."

"Peters, that's who," Molly said bluntly. "I should have said something. I should have told David."

"No-o-o," Mary Beth moaned. "I fell. Really. I fell." Then another pain hit her.

Cymberly knew the young woman lied to protect her husband. Why had *she* failed to see what was happening to poor, luckless Mary Beth? "Sssh. Save your strength," she said softly.

Molly wiped her hand across her own brow and looked down at Susan. "It's going to be a long night. The baby is turned wrong. Poor, dear woman." She looked at Cymberly and Angelina and added, "You two may as well go on and get some sleep. I'll stay with her."

"No. I shall stay, too," Cymberly said.

"I will go and look after the children of these others who are helping," Angelina said.

There was a commotion at the entrance to the tent. Corporal Peters stood there looking around the phalanx of women.

"I wanta see my wife." His voice was slurred with drink. "An' where's my son?"

"Tommy is with my children," Mrs. Hoskins answered. "My oldest was looking out for them."

"Wanta see Mary Beth."

"Well, you can't do so yet."

"Whaddaya mean? Ain't time. Babe's not due yet."

Molly rose and advanced on the drunken Peters. "Well, it's coming now, thanks to you. Now you just go on out of here. You're not needed."

"Please . . ." Mary Beth called from the bed.

Molly reluctantly stood aside and Peters came to stand over his wife's pallet. "Ah, God, Mary Beth, I didn't mean to hurt you. Honest, I didn't." He knelt clumsily, nearly sprawling over her, but Molly caught his shoulders and pulled him back.

"Careful!"

"I know you didn't, Johnny." Mary Beth's voice ended on a gasp as another pain took her. "It . . . it's all right, Johnny. You go on now." The weariness in her voice seemed to encompass far more than her immediate situation.

He stood, swayed, and leaned over to pat her hand. "I—I'll come back when it's all over, then." With that, he backed out of the tent, hounded by condemning looks from all the women but his wife.

Hours later Mary Beth still labored mightily. Cymberly could see the strength ebbing from their patient with each wave of pain. She knew her hand would be sorely bruised from Mary Beth's gripping it, but it was the least she could offer. Molly rose from her latest examination, an even graver look on her face. She motioned Cymberly and the other women off to the side.

"I can't do it," she said, her voice low. "I cannot turn the baby. It is trying to come the wrong way. We're going to lose them both."

"Oh, no." Cymberly hugged Molly briefly and the others murmured sympathetically.

"Best tell the corporal so's he can say good-bye to her," one of the others said and left the tent. Half an hour later she returned. "I cannot find him. Looked everywhere. He is simply not to be found."

The gray half light just before dawn was visible through the tent flaps when Mary Beth opened her eyes, looked with startling clarity at those around her, and gripped Cymberly's hand.

"Don't blame Johnny," she whispered. "And watch over my little boy. Take care of Tommy."

With that, she expired.

The five women who had witnessed her epic battle now looked at each other helplessly.

"At least she is no longer in pain," one of them said, wiping a tear from her eye.

"We'll take care of her," Mrs. Hoskins said to Cymberly and Molly.

The two of them were quiet as they returned to their own camp. " 'Don't blame Johnny' indeed!" Molly's anger spilled over. "And who else would you blame? He killed her. *He killed her!* As God is my witness, he did it."

"We didn't know," Cymberly soothed.

"I knew. And did nothing. Said nothing." Molly's bitter tone was directed at herself.

"But what *could* you have done? Even in England, a wife is her husband's property to do with as he pleases."

"Not to kill!"

"No, not to kill. But I doubt he intended her to die."

Molly sighed. "You're right. I just wish I had said something."

Later that morning, Mary Beth was buried under one of the few trees near the camp. Johnny Peters had been found in a drunken stupor in another tent. He wept profusely, but could scarcely stand upright as his wife's body was lowered into the ground.

Late that afternoon, Cymberly saw him again. He was sober, but he walked with a limp and held one arm close to his chest. Both eyes were black and there were other visible bruises.

"Someone gave him a taste of his own medicine," Molly said with deep satisfaction.

Cymberly had every intention of seeing to the care of Mary Beth's Tommy. However, Corporal Peters angrily rejected offers of assistance from her and Molly.

"You two put them fellers on me," he accused. "I know ya did. Won't do ya no good to deny it. So you just go on about your business an' leave me and mine be. I don't need your help and Tommy don't neither."

He would not budge from this view. Dr. Cameron and

other officers may have sympathized with Miss Winthrop and Mrs. MacIver, but no one was willing to usurp a father's authority over his child.

Cymberly and Molly watched helplessly as little Tommy was shunted from one camp follower to another when his father took up with women of questionable morals.

Seeing the boy crying, dirty, and wandering aimlessly one day, Cymberly called to him. He came to her readily and trustingly put his little hand in hers.

"Horsey?" he asked. Cymberly was surprised he remembered riding with her.

"Not today, sweetheart."

She took him back to the area of camp where she thought his father would be. She found Corporal Peters sharing a *bota,* a wineskin, with some other men. Peters looked up as Cymberly and Tommy approached.

"Tommy!" Peters growled. "Thought I told you to stay with Susan."

"Susan—no!" Tommy cried.

"Susan—yes!" his father said. "Now you git on over there if you know what's good for you."

"Please, Mr. Peters. Don't be harsh with him. He is just a child," Cymberly said.

"He's got ta learn ta mind what I tell him. An' I'll thank you not ta interfere, ma'am." Peters' tone was barely civil.

"As you will, Corporal," she replied tersely.

"You have the right of it." He appeared to satisfy a need to have the last word. " 'Tis a matter of what *I* will."

As Cymberly turned on her heel and walked away, she heard Peters bark a contemptuous laugh and make some comment about "damned meddlin' females."

Later that evening, walking out with Reggie Fleming, she told him of her encounter with Peters. She was still fuming about it.

"Well, frankly, my dear," he said, "I do not see why you

persist in your interest in a child that is not yours. Let his father deal with him."

"I feel I owe Mary Beth."

"You owe her nothing. Besides, she's dead and it's out of your hands. Forget it, Cymberly."

"I suppose, given the circumstances, I must."

"Look. You did what you could. Last thing you need is someone else's brat to worry over."

"But, Reggie, he's such a sweet little boy."

"You cannot go around saving all the neglected children in the world. Leave it alone, my dear." He laughed softly, stopped, and raised her chin. "Concentrate on saving a neglected lieutenant."

"Neglected, is he?" she teased, willing to turn the subject.

"Abominably."

Beneath the bantering tone, she sensed resentment in him. She recalled his unhappiness at finding her gone when he'd come to call the evening Mary Beth died. Besides his failure to understand her interest in the inferior Peters family, he had not been pleased to learn Major Ryder had joined her and the MacIvers for supper. He ignored the fact that Wilson had also been there.

Pointing out the depth and longevity of the friendship between the MacIvers and the major had done little to assuage his resentment. Somehow he felt threatened, and she wondered why. She tried to broach the topic with him, but he shrugged it off with a comment about Ryder's being "too full of himself."

Since she often shared that view of the opinionated Major Ryder, she did not contradict Fleming. But she wondered if she and Reggie had the same things in mind with such an assessment.

Pamplona fell in late October. The news rippled through the moving British army. Cymberly heard it as she trudged beside a cart carrying two wounded men as well as a mountain of baggage.

"That is good news, is it not?" she asked the very young patient lying nearest her. She had asked the question more to divert his mind from his pain than from any real interest in a response. The younger of the two men merely grunted, but the other, an older, more seasoned veteran responded.

" 'Tis good news, Miss. Means we can stop watching our backs so close. Frogs ain't likely to come at us from the south any more."

"Seems to me our worst enemy now is not the French at all," she grumbled.

Wincing as the cart went over a particularly noticeable bump, the veteran agreed with her. "Right. The mountains and the weather seem out to get us, don't they?"

A cold drizzle had plagued them for three days. It was not a real rain so much as a saturated cloud that hovered above, its dampness permeating every protection against it. At night the temperature dipped below freezing.

Cymberly knew she was not alone in wanting to stay in her blankets each morning, though truth to tell, they, too, were damp—and cold wherever her body had not warmed them. She always tried to lie still, for to move was to expose some part of her anatomy to the chill.

The trails had grown even more precipitous. Beautiful when the perpetual cloud lifted occasionally, but even more dangerous, for the muddy, half-frozen ground was alternately extremely slippery or looked deceptively firm but lacked solidity. Just the day before, they had lost a mule carrying tents. The most surefooted of beasts had slipped and fallen into a deep ravine. To the horror of many, his thrashing about had resounded in great echoes for several minutes.

Progress was slow. Each day now was noticeably shorter than the day before. Nightfall came quickly in the mountains. Cymberly marveled at the fact that she could look to the high peaks and see them bathed in light, but lower down night already had crept in. The army woke like a lumbering giant later each day and stopped earlier, for to do otherwise was too risky by half.

Besides the rugged terrain and the inclement weather, they had to deal occasionally with French patrols. Enemy patrols encountering English stragglers were quick to take prisoners—or to kill if they met resistance. Women were cautioned to keep up, for the army could not stop for them. Females caught alone would likely be treated in the worst ways imaginable. Fortunately, such patrols were usually small, more interested in keeping track of the British than in engaging in combat.

Still mourning her father, Cymberly now mourned Mary Beth as well. In fact, it seemed she mourned the young mother's death out of proportion to their friendship. While there had been no deathbed promise regarding the care of Mary Beth's son, Cymberly regretted being unable to do anything for the little boy.

That the child was being neglected, there was little doubt. Braving his scorn, she and Molly again offered Tommy's father assistance, but, still seeing them as interfering, he spurned their offer. He complained to anyone who would listen. Sergeant MacIver suggested rather forcefully that his wife and Miss Winthrop "leave it alone" unless they saw the child being severely abused. Benign neglect hardly qualified as severe abuse.

With MacIver's admonition coming on the heels of Fleming's protest, Cymberly allowed the matter to recede in the hierarchy of important concerns for her. Still, she always noted where and with whom Tommy traveled. Occasionally she spoke with him, but only fleetingly. He was now almost three years old and was, to Cymberly's inexperienced eye, amazingly resilient. Whenever she saw him, he remembered her "horsey."

Twelve

"I told you Cosette would be bad business," Molly said conversationally one evening as she and Cymberly helped Maggie and Amitabha set up their joint camp. Once again, Sergeant MacIver and Major Ryder were off doing what they did best. They were expected to return in two days.

"What happened?" Cymberly asked.

"She instigated a fight between two men last night."

"Poor Sergeant Miller." Cymberly liked the young man. Despite his reminding her of a beaten hound, he was always polite and helpful to her.

"No. Miller was not involved. 'Twas two others. Miller found out later. But he never blames *her* for what happens around her. That girl draws trouble like a dog draws fleas."

"Are the two men all right?"

"They'll survive." Molly was clearly disgusted. "Black eyes and bruises. Nothing worse. Should be saving their fighting for the French."

"Perhaps they were."

"Were what?"

"Fighting for the French—the French *girl*, that is."

"Go on with you." Molly laughed. "Still, that girl is trouble. Mark my words."

Cymberly saw Cosette from time to time. She knew there had been another altercation some weeks ago, this one with the Spanish girl Florencia. Both young women were pretty, flirtatious, and sought after by men, and both possessed volatile tempers. Perhaps Molly was right.

Cymberly tried to recall what Reggie had said recently—something to the effect that Cosette was "just asking for it," but he did not elaborate on what "it" was. Cymberly was aware of Cosette's continued interest in Reggie, for Reggie had told her of the French girl's pursuit of him once she was convinced Wilson was out of her reach.

Reggie seemed to think it all a great joke. Cymberly thought he rather liked being the focus of the French girl's attention. Since he did not appear to return Cosette's interest, Cymberly simply dismissed the whole subject from her mind.

She saw Lieutenant Fleming nearly every day. In the last few weeks, he had been true to his word not to introduce the subject of marriage again. He seemed to make a special point of entertaining her and others around them.

"Reggie is so very amusing. Is he ever truly serious?" Juliana Williams asked one day as she and Cymberly rode together. They were having what Cymberly's mother would once have described as a "comfortable coze." Cymberly knew Juliana was intensely curious about her relationship with Reggie, but was far too polite to ask about it outright.

Cymberly was reluctant to discuss the relationship. Beyond that, she admitted privately, she hesitated to examine it too closely. She was comfortable with him and she supposed they would rub on well together once they married.

But Juliana's innocent question put a small chip in the shell she had established around her feelings, a shell that had warded off even her own probing. It was true. She and Reggie rarely discussed anything serious. Reggie did not share her love of literature. He dismissed the works of some of her favorite poets as so much rubbish, and said he never could understand all that fuss about Shakespeare.

His interest in political matters was more likely to focus on the romantic adventures of certain notables than about the policies national leaders pursued. She told herself it was just that Reggie thought such topics best left to purely male discussions, but now that she considered the matter, she could not recall ever having overheard him conversing with anyone about such matters.

On the heels of this thought, several discussions with and about Major Ryder flashed across her mind. She promptly quelled them. It was just that Reggie made a greater effort to put others at ease. Besides, there was no reason to compare the two men.

Since his return from being a French captive, she had encountered the major several times. As a friend of the MacIvers, he was much in their company, and owing in part to Lord Wellington's assigning her to the MacIvers' care, she, too, was much in their company. It certainly was not as though either of them deliberately sought the proximity of the other, was it? Out of respect for the MacIvers, they treated each other with polite regard.

If the two of them often dominated a conversation—sometimes disagreeing vehemently, sometimes reinforcing each other's positions—surely there was nothing extraordinary in such behavior. And if she sometimes was loath to leave such a discussion to walk out with Reggie, what was remarkable about that? It was a Winthrop family trait to enjoy good conversation.

"Ryder seems to impose himself on your company a great deal," Reggie said one evening, his voice overly casual.

"*Impose* is a strange choice of words," Cymberly objected. "He and Captain Wilson often call together. Major Ryder's friendship with the MacIvers goes back to their days in India."

"Yes, I know. I was there, too—remember?" His tone was testy.

"Of course you were. Did you not tell me Major Ryder served under your father?"

"He wasn't a major then. He was the *perfect* lieutenant.

Then the *perfect* captain. There was simply *no one* braver or more efficient. The quintessential military man. My father doted on him." Reggie sounded increasingly bitter.

"You must have been very young."

"Old enough. I was eighteen. I had just come out from eight years in a military boarding school in England."

"Eight years? You were just a child when you went there."

"Father thought military school would make a man of his mama's boy son. And it did. I came back to India fully prepared to become my father's right-hand man."

"He must have been very proud of you."

"Hah!" The single syllable held a reservoir of long-stored resentment. "In my absence, he'd found the son he really wanted."

"Geoffrey Ryder," she said softly.

"Geoffrey Ryder." It was a sneer. "Every time I did something wrong—and I did *nothing* right, it seemed—I had him thrown in my face as the paragon of all things army."

"But you cannot blame Major Ryder—"

"No? Well, I can and I do. My father assigned me to his favorite's command. Ryder was always demanding I do something for which I'd never trained, and he did it to belittle me."

"Are you sure of his motives? That does not seem something he would do."

"Yes, I am sure. Do you think I would lie about such a matter?"

Startled by the question and his vehemence, she murmured, "No, of course not." They walked in silence until she deliberately introduced a new subject.

Later, however, as she prepared for bed, she mulled over this conversation, along with other observations and comments about the major. As an officer, he was known to be a strict disciplinarian. This did not overly concern her, for her own father had had just such a reputation. And both her father and Major Ryder were considered to be eminently fair in administering punishments.

She knew Ryder had personally decreed and overseen the flogging of one soldier. The flogging was, of course, in line with Wellington's order regarding men known to have molested local women after the battle of Vitoria. The surprising thing in this instance was that the flogged man was an officer. At the time, Cymberly had been too distraught over her father's death to accord the incident much attention.

Reggie's animosity toward Major Ryder was deep-seated. Yet her father, whose judgment Cymberly had never questioned, had admired and respected the major. Her father's last words had been about Ryder. But General Winthrop admitted he had known the major only slightly in India. Reggie had served under Ryder's command.

From her confused musings came a surprising discovery: She truly wanted to think well of Geoffrey Ryder. Why should that be so? Her father's kind words notwithstanding, what would her mother have thought?

Mama had always said one should think and speak well of everyone. "But there are exceptions, Mama, that even you would have been forced to acknowledge," she muttered just under her breath as she crawled into her cold blankets and turned out the lantern.

Major Ryder looked over at his companion and felt a distinct twinge of guilt. Mac hated riding.

"Shank's mare will get you anywhere you want to go—'til you get to the seashore," Mac grumbled good naturedly on their second day out. It was a familiar sentiment from the sergeant, who now added, "If God had really meant us to spend our lives on horseback, he would have made us one of those mythological things, you know, a—a Pegasus."

Geoffrey laughed. "You mean a centaur."

"All right. A centaur. Whatever it is, my backside protests."

"We should be back in camp tonight or tomorrow."

"None too soon, if I may say so, sir."

Geoffrey knew Mac missed Molly and worried about her whenever they were apart. He wondered if he would ever feel that way about a wife.

Oh, yes. There would be a wife one day. Being Chadwyck's heir had been thrust upon his unwilling shoulders, but he accepted his duty to see the line did not die with him.

Now why did a vision of Cymberly Winthrop float before his mind's eye? His body tightened as he remembered her response to his kiss. How could she respond to him so warmly and spend so many of her waking hours with Reggie Fleming? Word was they were just waiting for the proper period of mourning to end before announcing their engagement.

And what was it to him, anyway? *He* certainly was not interested in forming an attachment out here in God's forgotten corner of the universe and in the middle of a war, no matter how lovely and desirable the woman. Miss Winthrop was welcome to her Lieutenant Fleming.

Still—they were not married yet.

In mid-November, the weather took a turn for the worse. Cold rain mixed with snow intensified the difficulties of the trail. There were few villages this high in the mountains, and those that did exist were far too small to accommodate any but a very few of the highest ranking officers. Cymberly found herself actually envying Mrs. Reese and Mrs. Gordon-Smythe, especially when her tent began to leak directly over her bed one night.

Tempers were on short leash. The travelers no longer shared gossipy conversations on the trail, for it took most of their energy and attention just to stay *on* the treacherous route. Carts often bogged down, requiring sturdy shoulders to get them moving again. Children fussed and adults lost patience with them. Every second person, regardless of age, seemed to have sniffles, coughs, and attendant aches and pains.

In addition to the physical inconveniences, Cymberly chafed at the lack of privacy. Faced with personal concerns in the past, she had always been able to avail herself of solitude to think them through. Here, she was constantly surrounded by others. More than anything else, she wanted some time to herself.

One afternoon she found her chance. No enemy patrols had been sighted for days. The column was traveling through a fairly large, relatively flat mountain valley and would bivouac that night at the end of it. Knowing she could easily catch up later on horseback, she grabbed her sketch book and set off to spend an hour or two sketching the magnificent scenery.

She found a comfortable and surprisingly dry spot next to a huge boulder near a small mountain stream. The rushing water and her own concentration dulled her senses. The sound of horses, creaking saddles, and voices startled her. She could not make out what was being said, merely that the voices were male. Just as she realized they were speaking French, one of the riders spotted her.

"Ah! What have we here?" the man asked in his own language. He reined in his horse, dismounted, and stood before her. "A mountain nymph."

Terrified, Cymberly clambered to her feet. She glanced around, but her mare, though only a few feet from her, was too far away. Mounting hastily was impossible with a sidesaddle. She opened her mouth to scream, but the man stepped closer and clamped one hand around her waist and the other over her mouth.

"Non!"

She struggled against him, but his grip did not loosen. She squealed incoherently against the hand over her mouth.

"Quiet!" he commanded.

"English," one of the others observed. "Delectable." He looked at her as though he mentally stripped her.

"I saw her first," the one holding her said. "You can have her when I'm through. Captains before lieutenants." He laughed.

"Ah, Lieutenant," yet another man said in false sympathy, "from the looks of this one, you will have a long wait."

There seemed to be only three of them. Nearly paralyzed with fear, she willed herself to stop struggling, to save her strength, to wait for an opportunity to escape. Instinctively, she decided to feign ignorance of their language.

"Comprendre français?" her captor asked. He was a tall man, a little on the portly side. He had black hair, and his beady black eyes shone with lust.

She looked at him blankly for a moment, pretending to try to understand. Then she shook her head.

"Bring her horse over here and some rope," he ordered.

Removing his own neckcloth, he wrapped it over her mouth, tying it securely. She smelled garlic, sweat, and some sort of perfume on the cloth. He picked up her bonnet and jammed it on her head. He helped her mount, letting his hands explore her body as he did so, and giving her a mocking leer when she shuddered at his touch. He tied her hands loosely so she could grab the saddle for balance, then mounted his own horse, closely leading hers.

They traveled in this manner very slowly, climbing into more perilous terrain and being as quiet as they could. The captain was in front, leading Cymberly's horse, with the others following behind. Her fear obliterated rational thought and any concept of time.

After what seemed a very long time, they stopped for a rest near a small waterfall that pooled at its bottom before trickling off into another small mountain stream. They were at the edge of the already darkening tree line. She thought there might be an hour of daylight left, if that. Panic threatened at the thought of what nightfall might bring.

The captain dismounted and helped her dismount, again letting his hands stray. She stood stiffly and coldly. He chuckled and indicated she should sit on a log nearby as he retrieved a canteen from his own gear and sent the other two to the pool to water the horses.

Cymberly looked at him apprehensively as he came toward her and reached out to touch her. She jerked her head away.

"Easy." His voice was probably meant to be soothing. He reached for the neckcloth binding her mouth, knocking her hat off in the process. "I was merely going to remove the gag to give you a drink, *ma chérie*. There are no English around now, I think."

"Think again, you bastard." A voice she barely recognized came from the trees, and Geoffrey Ryder materialized with his rifle trained on the captain's heart.

Thirteen

Geoffrey and Mac had rejoined their own troops in the early afternoon. Major Ryder made a brief report to General Travers, then took his customary position in the column as commander of a rifle brigade.

A short time later Mac came riding hurriedly up to him. The fact that Mac was riding after nearly three days in the saddle was remarkable in itself. He also wore a worried expression.

"What is it, Mac?" Geoffrey reined in his horse as the sergeant approached.

"Cymberly. Miss Winthrop. She's gone. Molly says she went off alone three or four hours ago. Told Molly she wanted an hour or so to herself. She's not returned."

"Oh, my God!"

"Took her sketchbook and went off toward that hill." Mac pointed to a peak some distance behind the column now.

"Oh, God. What can she have been thinking?" A sick fear gnawed at Geoffrey. His decision was immediate. "I am going after her. Have Wilson inform General Travers."

"Yes, sir. Are you going alone?" MacIver's disapproval was plain.

"Yes. I shall make better time alone. There have been no 'sightings' lately."

"Still . . ."

"It will be all right, Mac."

He reined his mount toward the rear of the column and headed for the hill Mac had pointed out. Alternating between fury at the woman's stubborn independence and fear for her safety, he pushed his horse hard.

After several stops to examine likely spots where she might have found the scene attractive, he spied her sketchbook lying next to a boulder. It had obviously been dropped in a hurry. But what truly alarmed him was a proliferation of hoof prints from several horses near the stream. Examining them carefully, he determined the direction in which they had gone.

They had to be French. English soldiers would have either left her alone or returned her to the column. Most of the locals were English sympathizers. Could be renegades—deserters from the British. Oh, God. She would be no safer with those devils than with the French.

Pushing harder now, but proceeding with extreme care, he reasoned that a lone horseman could overtake what he now determined to be four riders. He just hoped he caught up to them before nightfall.

He was almost on top of them when he heard a muffled curse and the sound of rocks and pebbles falling. A horse had stumbled. He stopped and dismounted to hold his own horse's head as he listened intently. French. They were apparently trying to go quietly, but the sounds of their own horses on the trail had covered any noise he made.

Noting their direction, Geoffrey left the trail, circling around and above them. He knew this terrain from his last scouting venture. They were likely to water their horses just ahead.

And so they did.

Geoffrey smiled a tight, bitter smile on finding the three Frenchmen had behaved exactly as he thought they would. His heart lurched at seeing Cymberly tied and gagged. When the French officer helped her dismount, she seemed unharmed, though uncertainty and fear flitted across her face as the man removed the gag.

"Major Ryder." Relief and welcome showed in her voice. "There are two others," she added quickly.

"I know. Get over here behind me, Cymberly." He did not take his eyes or his aim from the French captain.

With her hands still tied, she rose from the log somewhat awkwardly. He was pleased to see she was careful not to put herself between him and her erstwhile captor.

"Stand right there and be quiet," he said to the Frenchman. Geoffrey had determined earlier that this man was the leader. He knew dealing with three of them at once was a calculated risk, but felt he had little choice. "Cymberly, in my right boot there is a knife. Can you get it?"

He sensed her bend down behind him and felt her hand fumble against his calf.

"I have it," she said.

"Can you cut that rope yourself?"

"I think so." A moment later she said, "I am freed."

"Good. Now, you, sir," he said to the French captain in the man's own language, "tell your companions to lay down their weapons and step away from the horses."

The other two men, having by now returned leading the four horses, seemed confused at the scene before them.

"Do as he says," the French captain ordered.

"But, Captain—" one started.

"Do it!" The captain's shout was laced with panic.

Reluctantly, the other two did as they had been told.

"Can you get those weapons and horses, my dear?" Geoffrey asked Cymberly, still not taking his eyes from the captain.

"I shall try." She stepped carefully around the tableau of four men.

She caught up the dropped reins of three of the horses. The other one shied away, but after two tries, she caught the fourth set of reins. Then she stooped to pick up the weapons.

They were heavy and awkward in her arms as she tried to manage the horses as well. When she had moved out of the way, Geoffrey instructed her to lay the weapons on the ground and tie the horses to a nearby bush. Then he addressed the three prisoners.

"Sit down on the ground, next to that log." Geoffrey motioned them toward the log on which Cymberly had sat earlier. When they had done as he ordered, he said, "Now, take off your jackets and shirts and toss them behind the log. Sorry, Miss Winthrop," he added, still without looking in her direction.

The three Frenchmen looked at him in consternation, but quickly unfastened their jackets and shrugged out of their upper garments, grunting and jabbing each other with their elbows as they did so. *Well, none has another weapon on him,* Geoffrey thought.

"Now, the shoes," he said. "Carefully. Toss them out here in front of you."

He heard Cymberly's sharp intake of breath. "Surely you are not . . ."

"No, Miss Winthrop, I shall not offend your sensibilities by having them strip. The shoes, gentlemen."

When the three had complied, he walked closer to them and kicked the footgear toward Cymberly, still keeping his own weapon trained on them.

"Can you shoot, Miss Winthrop?"

"Yes."

"Good." He handed her his rifle. "Keep this aimed at them. And be careful."

He could see she was nervous about this order, but she gamely did as he instructed. He whistled loudly and his own horse came trotting out of the trees. Taking a piece of rope from a saddlebag, he forced the three to sit with their backs to each other as Cymberly continued to hold the rifle on them. He wound the rope through their elbows and secured it tightly.

"There. That ought to hold them for a while."

Finally able to turn his attention away from the enemy soldiers, Geoffrey considered the woman before him. Disheveled and frightened, she was still breathtakingly attractive. And she had remained calm throughout. What other woman would have done so?

She thrust the rifle toward him. Their hands touched as he took it and returned it to its customary place on his saddle. Turning back to her, he saw she was, in the aftermath, trembling. She seemed to be fighting for control, breathing hard. He stepped closer and took her in his arms.

"Let it go, Cymberly. Let it go, love." He pressed her head against his shoulder and held her while great shuddering sobs wracked her body. He laid his cheek against her hair, breathing in the spicy scent of it. "It is all right. You are safe now." He liked the feel of her in his arms. He kept speaking to her and caressing her back until he felt her begin to relax.

She drew back to look at him, her hazel eyes glistening with tears. "I am so sorry," she said. "I did not mean to fall to pieces like this."

"Never mind," he soothed, amazed at her apology for her emotions. He surmised any other woman would be in hysterics by now—or have fainted long since.

"I . . . I am ever so grateful for your rescuing me."

"Well, as to that," he said, feeling his own emotional reaction setting in, "it should not have been necessary, as you well know."

He could see his anger surprised her. "What *were* you thinking? Going off by yourself like that was an incredibly stupid thing to do."

Her surprise faded, replaced by sudden anger blazing from her eyes. Her voice was cold. "Thank you, sir, for that helpful observation."

She turned away, wiping her eyes. He was immediately sorry for snapping at her, but he was damned if he would apologize for the truth.

Geoffrey gathered up the discarded shoes and weapons and placed them on the Frenchmen's horses. Then he turned to assist her in remounting. She accepted his aid stiffly. He mounted his horse and took up the other three sets of reins.

"Are we just going to leave them like that?" she demanded.

"It is either that or kill them." Then he tempered his bluntness by adding, "It will take them some time—and cooperation—but they will eventually free themselves. Meanwhile, we shall be away."

She bit her lip and said, "It is just . . . it gets so cold . . ."

"You are feeling sorry for them? After what they probably had planned for you?"

She blushed and looked away, her chin high.

"Sorry." His voice was brusque. "Come, we have not much daylight left."

Cymberly rode in front of Major Ryder as he instructed. He still led the three extra horses. Anger and worry dominated her thoughts. Drat the man, anyway. Yes, she had made a mistake in going off to sketch. A serious mistake, even. But did he have to be quite so high-handed in pointing it out?

He was right about one thing, she conceded grudgingly. It would be dark soon. And among the trees in these cloud-covered mountains, it would be very dark indeed. Travel would be impossible. She was out here in a virtual wilderness alone with a man and no shelter in sight. She supposed she should be frightened by such a prospect, but she was not. The man could be intimidating, but he was not frightening.

However, what would others think? She pulled her cloak tighter around her as the damp cold permeated the garment. She felt the freezing drizzle hit her face. Rain? Yes, rain—and flakes of snow. Good heavens.

She returned to her musings. She had been gone for hours

now. Mrs. Gordon-Smythe and her lot would make much of that. And when she reappeared in Major Ryder's company, what then? It was a repeat of the incident with David Taraton.

No, much worse.

That had been an accident, pure and simple. This was all her fault. She had got herself into this. And worse—oh, so much worse—Major Ryder was now involved, too. The perils of mountainous trails would be nothing to the sticks and stones of social censure.

Both of them had been silent for some time when he called out to her.

"Cymberly. Miss Winthrop."

She reined in her horse as he brought his up closer. " 'Cymberly' is fine. We agreed on that once before, I believe."

"Yes."

His eyes told her he remembered exactly when they had agreed before. She hoped he could not see her blush in the dim light as she remembered yet again the kiss they had shared.

"We must get off and walk," he told her. "This is getting far too dangerous."

They had steadily climbed a steep, narrow trail beside a deep ravine. Stopping on relatively flat spot, Geoffrey dismounted.

"Here," he said, handing her his reins, "please hold these while I take care of these other animals."

She watched him go through the equipment on the French horses.

"They must have been close to their camp," he said.

"How can you know that?"

"No bedrolls."

"Oh."

"There is some bread and cheese here, though. We will not starve." He smelled the contents of a canteen. "Ah, one of these enterprising fellows carried wine!"

He secured one of the French weapons on her saddle and

tossed the others in different directions down the ravine. Then he removed the saddles and bridles from the Frenchmen's horses and, slapping them on their rears, sent them trotting off on their own.

They traveled on foot now and in silence, but Cymberly did not feel it to be an uncomfortable silence, though she was still annoyed with him for his outburst earlier. It was nearly dark now. She could see only because the loss of light had been gradual enough for her eyes to adjust.

Her feet kept slipping on the wet, steep trail. Dislodged rocks and pebbles rolled great distances. The precipitation was increasingly more snow than rain. She was tired, wet, cold, and hungry, but she was beginning to feel grateful for his companionship. *Misery loves company—any company,* she told herself ruefully.

They rounded a bend in the trail to emerge on a shelf of land about the size of a large English estate, Cymberly guessed. And there in the middle was a manor house—a shepherd's stone and thatch summer hut with a lean-to shelter on one side.

The snow was thicker now and beginning to form a light cover over the visible world. It hung in the surrounding trees, and Cymberly marveled at its beauty even as she was aware of the danger it held. Darkness had truly arrived. Only the luminescence from the snow allowed them to pick their way to the hut.

"Welcome to your temporary home, my lady," Geoffrey said. She thought the banter in his voice seemed a trifle forced. Grabbing a knapsack off his saddle, he shoved his way into the hut and motioned her after him.

She stood still, listening to some rustling in the corners of the room, as Major Ryder rummaged through the knapsack. She heard a scratching sound she recognized as the striking of a tinder box. There was a flare. Then a light glowed, showing his face clearly.

"A candle?" she asked, disbelieving what she saw. "You had a candle in there?"

"Always do," he said smugly. "Never know when it will be handy. But it won't last long."

He raised the candle higher to splash light over the small, windowless room. It was a very spare accommodation. Cymberly noted a rough table and two stools. There was a bed in one corner, but its obviously broken ropes rendered it useless. A fireplace, with some leftover firewood off to the side and a kettle lying on the hearth, dominated the room.

"Can you get a fire started while I see to the horses?" He handed her the lighted candle.

"I think so."

When he had gone, she removed her gloves to deal with the fire. She shivered with the cold and her hands trembled, but the wood was dry and there was even a bit of kindling. "Oh, thank you, thank you," she said quietly to the unknown shepherd, holding the candle to a small dry twig. The fire caught on the second try, and she carefully nursed it into full bloom.

Geoffrey returned with one of the saddles.

"Good. You have it going," he said cheerfully. Then he left for the rest of their gear, which he tossed down in the middle of the room. "One more trip. I think there is some more firewood in the lean-to."

When he returned the third time, he carried several large chunks of wood which, after kicking the door shut, he dumped near the fireplace.

"That's all there was," he said, eyeing his find dubiously.

"The horses?"

"Crowded, but protected." He removed his gloves and held his hands toward the fire. "The snow is coming down quite furiously now."

"It is so quiet." She thought they both took refuge in the commonplace.

Indeed, the only sound was the crackle of the fire and an occasional stamp of a horse's hoof beyond the wall.

"Do you think we will be here long?" she asked tentatively.

"Until daylight, at least."

"Oh." It came out a worried sigh as she looked around the room in despair.

"We were fortunate to find shelter. This is not exactly luxury suitable for a lady of the *ton* . . ."

"No. Please. I did not mean you to think me critical. Besides," she added in a small voice, "I know this is all my fault."

Geoffrey looked up from searching his knapsack and the items he had removed from the French horses.

"Well, yes. Some of it is," he agreed, sending her spirits plummeting even lower. Then he added, "But I seriously doubt you had much control over the weather. Do you think we could heat water in that kettle?"

Eager for a distracting task, she picked up the kettle and held it to the light. She banged it upside down on the stone hearth to rid it of dust, then wiped it out with her handkerchief.

"I suppose it will do," she said. He silently handed her a canteen.

As the water heated, he brushed off the table and laid out their meal of bread and cheese, which he sliced with his pocketknife. They pulled the table and stools as close to the fire as they dared.

"I should have thought to get an extra cup from those Frenchies," he said. "We will have to share mine, I fear." He poured wine into it from the Frenchman's canteen. "Here. This will warm us up."

He handed her the cup and she took a large swallow, coughed, and handed it back. It was the strongest wine she had ever tasted. Geoffrey lifted the cup to his own lips and swallowed.

"Not exactly the fine wine on which the French pride themselves," he said conversationally, handing her the cup again along with some bread and cheese.

"Perhaps they had it from the Spanish." She smiled at him and was pleased to see his eyes twinkle in response.

"The water is hot," he said, reaching into his knapsack again. "Not much left, but perhaps enough." He poured the contents of a packet into the kettle and soon a welcome aroma filled the hut.

"Tea! Major Ryder, sir, you are a magician!" She looked at him wonderingly. "How does it happen you are so prepared for this—ah—misadventure? As I consider it, how did *you* happen on the scene at all? I thought you and Sergeant MacIver . . ."

"We returned early this afternoon. I had not unloaded my gear when Mac said you were missing." Then he added gently, "Geoffrey. Remember, Cymberly?"

"Geoffrey," she repeated softly, savoring the sound.

He offered her the last sip of wine. She refused it, so he drank it, then rinsed the cup with a tiny bit of water which he tossed into a far corner. There was something profoundly intimate about their drinking from the same vessel. He poured tea into the cup.

"Milk or lemon, my dear?" he joked, handing her the cup. "It is hot."

"Just a bit of milk, if you please." She wrapped her handkerchief around the handle. "And I should like one of those lovely lemon cakes as well."

"Only one?"

They laughed over their foolishness and shared the warmth of the tea. It occurred to Cymberly that she should feel wretchedly embarrassed and awkward, but somehow she felt wonderfully at ease with him. Despite the precarious situation, she actually felt content. Such contentment had not been hers for many weeks.

They sat in companionable silence for a few minutes. Both of them jumped when the candle sputtered and went out.

"I knew it would not last long." He rose to put another chunk of wood on the fire. "We shall have enough fuel to last until morning if we use it sparingly."

Cymberly had put her gloves back on, and her feet felt like cold bricks. In fact, she felt warm only on the part of her body nearest the fire. They had set her cloak and his greatcoat in front of the fire, and both had achieved a degree of dryness.

Geoffrey pushed the table and stools back. Then he laid the saddle blankets on the floor in front of the hearth and unrolled his bedroll on top of them.

"Our couch, my dear." He bowed grandly, but she thought he seemed ill at ease.

"There?" She had not once thought of sleeping arrangements.

"Well"—he pointed to the bed in the corner with its ropes in shreds—"*that* is quite unusable, as you can see."

She looked from the useless bed to the pallet, then at him. "Together?" she squeaked.

"Together," he said firmly. "It is no bed of roses, I know."

"Then we shall not have to repent in thorns." She completed the quotation absentmindedly and smiled tremulously as he lifted a brow in appreciation.

"Let us hope not," he said. "Take your shoes off and put these on." He handed her a pair of wool socks from his knapsack.

"This is most unorthodox, Maj—Geoffrey."

"Your virtue is safe this night, my dear." He wrapped her cloak around her shoulders and indicated she should lie nearest the feeble fire. Then he lay down beside her and pulled his greatcoat over them, tucking the edges of her cloak and his coat in around them. Her back was to him, her cheek resting on her closed palms.

"Sweet dreams, Cymberly," he said softly, his breath brushing her ear before he lay back and seemed to relax.

She lay staring at the flames. The stale dust of the floor, smoke from the fire, the smell of horses, and, more faintly and far more pleasantly, a scent she associated with Geoffrey assailed her senses. She tried to focus her mind on what tomorrow would bring. She had no doubt this capable, practical man would see them safely restored to their friends.

Finally, she dozed off.

Fourteen

Cymberly watched from afar as the three French soldiers tried to free themselves. They seemed frantic to escape, yet they moved ever so slowly and in utter silence. The younger one stared at her, his already dead eyes accusing. Great brown-gray beasts appeared on the edge of the scene, stalking the hapless men. The animals howled eerily.

"No-o-o," she cried. "Go away. No-o-o."

"Cymberly. Wake up." Someone was shaking her shoulder.

"Wha—? Oh." Fighting toward reality, she woke. In very dim light, she looked into a pair of concerned gray eyes. "Geoffrey?" she whispered wonderingly.

"You were having a bad dream."

Just then a howl erupted terrifyingly close. This startled her fully awake and she uttered a muffled scream.

"S-s-sh. It is all right," he said, enfolding her in his arms so they faced each other. "That was just a wolf. You are safe."

"Oh, Geoffrey, no." She pushed against him. "We were wrong. We should not have left those men so helpless. The wolves came for them. I saw them so clearly." She sobbed.

He pulled her back to him, stroking her arm. "You must not worry. They were not so helpless as you think."

"How can you say that?" She was glad to hear her voice was calmer now.

"Once that rope became damp, their bonds would loosen sufficiently to allow them to extricate themselves. Shouldn't have taken more than half an hour in this weather. And they probably had a knife."

"A knife?" she asked dumbly.

"The youngest one was wearing his knapsack. It went over the log with his jacket."

"Why did you not tell me?"

"I thought you saw it. Besides, I did not want to upset you further."

"Instead, you let me think you . . ."

"Cymberly." He held her head to look directly into her eyes. "As a soldier, I *have* killed. But I am not a murderer."

"I . . . I did not think you were."

"Those men will be all right—which is far more than they deserve," he said, tightening his hold on her.

He kissed her brow and her eyelids. She lay very still, thrilling to his lips sprinkling soft caresses on her face. She lifted her head slightly, deliberately inviting him to seek her lips.

"Oh, my sweet," he murmured. His lips were firm, gentle, exploring. Her hands crept up to pull his head closer, and the kiss deepened as he hungrily responded to her welcome.

She heard a whimper of utter need and was surprised to recognize it as coming from her. She pressed closer to him, wanting more and more.

He pulled back to gaze at her.

Embarrassed by the intensity of her own response, she had never imagined being overwhelmed by sheer need for another person, or that the satisfaction of such need might make one feel safe, complete—whole.

"I—I—we should not have done that," she said.

His smile was tender, his words soft. "It felt supremely right to me. I want you, Cymberly, as I have never wanted anyone before. I cannot believe you are indifferent to me."

"But it is not right," she said, evading his implied question. She turned her back to him, but she did not move away. Nor did she reject the arm that lay across her body or the one cradling her head.

"As you wish, my dear." He sighed and placed a chaste little kiss on her temple. "Let us get some sleep. The snow must have stopped. We shall leave at first light."

"It stopped?"

"Yes. Otherwise wolves would not be prowling about."

"Oh."

It was some time before sleep claimed her again. She thought he lay awake, too. It would be so easy. . . . No. They were both overwhelmed by circumstances. Fear and the aftermath of worry about what the Frenchmen would do, that was why she had lost herself for a moment. Geoffrey Ryder might not be the ogre she had thought him to be, but he was still a Ryder, after all.

When morning dawned, she was surprised and embarrassed again, for she found her face pressed into his neck and her legs entwined with his—at least insofar as their layers of clothing allowed.

Light creeping in around the door frame awoke Geoffrey. He lay still a moment, savoring the feel of her so close. Then he nudged her into consciousness.

The fire was long since dead. Anxious to be gone, they broke their fast with the last of the hard cheese and harder bread, washing it down with water.

They emerged from the hut into a sparkling world of white. The sun was shining and already the trees were shaking off their white blankets. Geoffrey guessed the snow depth at three or four inches. *Thank God it is no deeper,* he thought.

" 'Tis warmer out here than in the hut," Cymberly said.

"So long as the sun remains with us." He finished saddling the horses and arranged such of their belongings as she had gathered up. When they were both mounted, each took a last look at the hut, then gazed at each other. She lowered her eyes first.

"You were right," she said brightly. "We were lucky to find shelter."

"That we were." He gave an inward sigh. She was not going to make it easy, was she?

They rode single file in silence until the sun was quite high in the sky, and heard the army encampment long before it came into view.

Geoffrey pulled his horse up and motioned her to come even with him.

"Cymberly, we need to talk."

"About what?" She sounded evasive.

"You know. Last night."

"Nothing happened."

"That is not true, and you know it." Deny it she might, but he knew she had been as aware of something between them as he was.

"I meant . . . well, nothing that need concern us now."

"Good God, woman. We spent the night together. The whole damned army is going to know."

"Well, you need not swear at me about it." She sounded defensive and rebellious at the same time.

"Sorry." He paused, trying to muster great patience. "We shall, of course, have to marry."

"We shall, of course, do nothing of the kind!" Her voice rose in indignation.

"Cymberly, please. Be reasonable. You will be ruined. I want to do the right thing by you."

"You have done the right thing. You rescued me. I will not repay that kindness by trapping you into a forced marriage."

"What if I do not feel trapped or forced?" He was amazed at the truth of this idea.

"Well, *I* will not be so forced," she said decisively. "I did not allow it in London. I am certainly not going to allow it here. Besides, you must know I intend to accept Lieutenant Fleming's proposal."

"You cannot be serious."

"I most assuredly am serious. Now do let us go on. I doubt not there will be a few uncomfortable moments, but they will pass."

Geoffrey was furious. Fleming? She would marry Fleming after responding so ardently last night? Here he was, trying to do the right thing—he who had never set much store by society's dictates—and she was throwing his efforts back in his face.

"You have to be *the* most perverse, stubborn, willful woman of my entire acquaintance."

"Why, thank you, kind sir." Her voice oozed sweetness.

Geoffrey and Cymberly rejoined the army, camped now at the end of a valley which afforded enough forage for a two-day rest. Geoffrey stayed with her until they found the MacIvers and the Winthrop servants. Both ignored the stares as they rode through the camp.

"Oh! There you are!" Molly's delight on seeing them was unreserved.

"We were worried," Maggie said.

"That we were," Molly and Mac chorused.

"Welcome back, Miss." Amitabha gave her a warm smile.

"What happened?" Mac asked.

Briefly, Geoffrey told them of the Frenchmen, the darkness, and the snowstorm.

"You must be starving," Molly said. "Maggie, is that stew we had for lunch still warm?"

"I think so." Maggie returned a few minutes later with a tray bearing two bowls of beef stew and a loaf of bread.

During the meal, they shared more details of the adventure with the others, but both of them skirted the fact of his proposal. Then Cymberly excused herself and left Geoffrey to the MacIvers.

She wondered why Reggie did not seek her out immediately. He finally arrived in the early evening, insisting she join him for a private discussion. She wrapped herself in a clean, dry cloak to walk with him to the edge of the camp. Behind a baggage wagon, they sat on some bales of goods.

"I had thought to see you earlier," she said, careful not to sound accusatory.

" 'Twas my intent to allow you time to rest, my dear. Also, I needed to think about this incident. I am *not* best pleased, as you might have surmised."

"It was unfortunate, I know, but it is not as though I had *planned* to be kidnapped, you know."

"Are you sure there was nothing you could have done? Did you *have* to spend the night with *him?*"

"Reggie, you know what these trails are like. We might have been killed trying to get back in the dark—and in a snowstorm."

"Just looks dashed queer to me, is all." He sounded like a petulant schoolboy.

"What do you mean?"

"I mean his managing to get you off alone that way. I've seen him ogling you. Why did no one tell *me* you were missing? I would have gone after you myself."

Cymberly spread her hands helplessly. How could she answer that? "I do not know," she said softly.

"And who is to say he did not deliberately delay your rescue just so you would be out there alone with him?"

"Oh, Reggie, how ridiculous. You cannot believe that."

"Why not?" he blustered. "I would not put anything beyond that conniving bas—uh—devil."

"Reggie," she said firmly, "please believe me. Major Ryder behaved honorably." Well, there was nothing dishonorable in his kiss—*he* was not the one planning to wed another.

"They say he wants to marry you."

That news got out quickly, she thought. "He offered. He felt it was expected of a gentleman."

"Hah! Ryder never in his life has done something merely because it was expected." He paused, then asked, "What did you say?"

"I told him no."

"Why?"

"Because nothing happened to warrant such a drastic action."

"Is that the only reason?"

"No. I . . . told him my affections were engaged elsewhere." So what if that had not been her exact wording?

"But he still wanted you—is that right?"

"I believe so. Yes."

"So the lordly Major Ryder finally wants something he cannot have," Reggie sneered.

"Reggie, please. Can we talk of something else?"

She was confused and disappointed. Reggie seemed to take more joy in an imagined triumph over Major Ryder than in the return of the woman he professed to love. Well, at least Reggie had offered love.

"Let us go back, my dear. I am sure you are exhausted." He rose and hugged her to him. His kiss was strangely unmoving, and she tried to tell herself his possessiveness was not the least bit distasteful.

Cymberly expected some censure from the remnants of polite society that were part of the Peninsular Army. However, she was not prepared for the degree of ostracism to which she was subjected because she would not marry Major Ryder. She herself spoke of the matter with only Reggie and Molly, and she surmised Geoffrey would be equally discreet. However, it was soon common knowledge that Major Ryder and Miss Winthrop had spent a night marooned together.

Despite his honorable efforts to save her reputation, she—
brazen hussy that she was—spurned his noble intentions.

Certain women of the camp, influenced, no doubt, by Mrs.
Gordon-Smythe's coterie, made a point of speaking within
her hearing of "persons who were no better than they should
be" and "so-called ladies with pretensions to grandeur."
Even Molly and Juliana tried to persuade her to reconsider,
but these two dear ladies refused to join others' criticism of
her.

Other friends stood by her, as well. Howard Williams was
inclined to think she was making a mistake, but he made no
move to cut the connection she had with his wife. Dr.
Cameron said nothing and remained unchanged in welcoming her help. Their patients continued to accept her with respect and gratitude.

The MacIvers, she knew, were torn in their loyalties, but,
having said her piece, Molly did not bring up the topic again.
Molly's view was predictable—any woman should consider
herself lucky indeed if Geoffrey Ryder proposed marriage.
Angelina's eyes filled with tears whenever anyone criticized
Cymberly in her hearing.

Cymberly had seen little of Captain Wilson, but one afternoon he swung his horse around to ride with her. He
cleared his throat several times, hesitated, and then introduced one innocuous topic after another. Finally, she could
stand it no longer.

"Out with it, Captain Wilson. You did not seek my company to talk about the weather or the latest news of the *ton*.
And you cannot be asking my help in your pursuit of the
lovely Angelina."

"No." He smiled at some secret thought. "She *is* lovely,
is she not?" He paused, then cleared his throat yet again.
"No. I come on behalf of my friend Ryder."

"He sent you?"

"No. Oh, no. Be angry if he knew, I am sure."

"What leads you to believe I may not be angry as well?"

"Truth to tell, you might be," he said. "But I must say it anyway."

"All right." She gave a resigned sigh. "Say whatever it is you must."

"Geoffrey Ryder is one of the finest men I have ever known," he began.

"He seems a very fine man. Somewhat opinionated, but he is a nice person." *Aside from the fact he has all the wrong connections,* she told herself privately.

"Then why—"

"Please." She cut him off. "Suffice it to say we just would not suit."

"He can be a very determined fellow. Usually finds a way to get what he wants, you know."

"Not this time. Let us talk of something else. How goes your suit with Angelina?"

"Well, I believe. I intend to marry her if she will have me, but I do not want to rush her."

"How wonderful. I do wish you the best, Captain. She is a rare human being. Very giving."

"I know."

A few days later, their portion of the army reconnected with the main elements of Wellington's force.

Fifteen

Everyone knew a major battle was in the offing. Desperate to hold onto Bayonne, a city special to the emperor, the French could not allow the British to cross the River Nive. The battle—actually a series of hard-fought skirmishes—took place in early December. For several days Wellington sought to cross the Nive, and the French resisted with as much force and determination as they could muster.

The British army had crossed into France some days before. No one knew exactly when or where, for no one, not even the commander himself, possessed an accurate map. Wellington established his main camp some distance from the battle area on a flat plain in the center of which was what the locals called a town.

Cymberly had to admit that it *was* larger than the mountain villages they had so recently been used to. The presence of a huge cathedral, incongruous in such a small hamlet, lent credence to the citizens' claim. The addition of the tents of the allied army turned the town into a city. Here the wives and camp followers, the sutlers and herders, waited to see how events would turn out.

The commander and his staff usurped the town hall for their headquarters and once again the cathedral—an impressive edifice with a charming cloistered garden—became the hospital. Once again, Cymberly felt herself driven by some irresistible force to work with the wounded beyond the point of exhaustion.

Because the battles were fought several miles away, the most immediate medical attention had already been given by the time the injured arrived in the main camp. Surgeons on the front lines did what they could, then sent the patients on lumbering carts to be tended in the rear. Many died before reaching the hospital.

The French guarded every bridge across the Nive and every spot that might serve as a ford for the British. Often there would be a few dwellings—even an occasional inn— near these crossings. The French, on their own territory now, fought with renewed vigor, inflicting casualties at a frightful rate.

On the afternoon of the second day, Cymberly was serving a lunch of soup and bread to a group of patients, including four or five officers. The men were engaging in a time-honored military tradition—criticizing the leadership of the generals.

"Don't know why the Peer even bothers to establish a headquarters," one young ensign grumbled. "He's never there. He pops up in the most amazing places."

"He likes to keep his eye on things," another offered. "Some of those so-called officers sent out by London are fools at best, and cowards at worst."

"Aw, he just wants to run everything his way," yet another said.

"Perhaps. But so far it has worked. We're in France, ain't we?" the second speaker asked.

True, Cymberly thought, *but at a terrible price.* A vision of wounded and maimed soldiers and mass graves popped into her mind.

"His lordship subscribes to the principle of leadership that says 'Come on!' not 'Go on!' " The speaker was an older man who had been quiet until now.

"An' that Major Ryder is cut from the same cloth." The young ensign spoke again.

Cymberly had been only half listening when Ryder's name captured her full attention.

"Yes. Did you *see* him on that bridge? Out there all alone! Just inviting the frogs to shoot him."

"They tried."

"The bugger leads a charmed life, that's what."

Cymberly smiled to herself, thinking Geoffrey would be amused by the speakers' awed tones.

She left the hospital some time later, pulling her cloak tighter against the wind and fog. Her mind drifted back to the conversation she had heard. Was Geoffrey needlessly putting himself in danger? These men did not seem to think the major foolhardy. Still, the thought of Geoffrey in danger nagged at her.

Then she was impatient with herself for that very fact. What did it matter to *her*? He was a soldier. Soldiering was a worrisome business. Of course she worried about him. She worried about Reggie, about Mac, about Wilson—even about Juliana's Howard.

Ah, and your worry for these others is exactly the same as for Major Ryder, is it?

Well, of course it is.

She ignored the way her heart had flipped as the men discussed Ryder. Nor did she question her lumping Reggie with the others.

She had been thoroughly annoyed with Major Ryder on their return to camp. His comment labeling her stubborn and willful hit home. However, her ire had cooled and she now greeted him with polite civility when they chanced to meet.

A few days ago he had singled her out deliberately. She had dismounted to lead her horse over some tricky terrain. Suddenly, there he was, right beside her, leading his own horse.

"Miss Winthrop." He inclined his head in a slight bow of greeting.

"Major Ryder. What brings you back to travel with the lesser beings of this army world?"

"You, of course." He grinned and added in a lower, teasing tone, "And what happened to 'Geoffrey' and 'Cymberly' of the shepherd's hut?"

She felt her cheeks grow warm. "Perhaps they recovered their senses."

"Too bad. I rather liked them."

"Stubborn and willful though she was?"

"Perhaps the circumstances prompted him to speak too quickly."

She glanced up at him to find his friendly, smiling countenance gazing back. They walked in silence for a few moments. Then he spoke again.

"I have not heard an announcement of your engagement."

"No, not yet. Perhaps after Christmas."

"I see. Cymberly, I shall not embarrass either of us by repeating an offer you found unwelcome, but if you should change your mind—"

"Very unlikely." She saw his lips tighten and a memory of how those lips felt against hers flashed before her.

"If you should change your mind," he went on doggedly, "I shall consider my offer valid until such time as I learn of your having truly married."

"That is . . . that is very kind of you, Geoffrey, but, really, such a gesture is not necessary." Her words sounded totally inadequate to her own ears.

He paused and put a hand on her arm. His touch had its usual unsettling effect on her. "Cymberly, I do not speak from kindness—nor am I making an empty gesture. Please believe that."

Seeing only sincerity in his eyes, she murmured, "I . . . I do."

Looping his reins over his arm, he took her free hand in

his. His gray eyes held her mesmerized and, seeing desire flare there, she felt an answering response in herself.

"I still want you," he said softly.

"Willfulness and all?"

"Yes."

She withdrew her hand. "I . . . uh, thank you." Her mind could formulate nothing further.

A voice called, "Major Ryder!" and a young corporal approached. "General Beresford sent me to find you, sir."

Geoffrey was gone as suddenly as he had appeared, and she was left with her emotions in turmoil.

Reggie had been most attentive lately. Once as they had been walking about of an evening, they had seen Ryder across the way. They were not near enough to speak, but she knew Geoffrey had seen them. Reggie knew it, too, for he put a possessive arm around her shoulders and deliberately turned her in another direction.

It would have been easy to encourage Reggie to renew his proposal of marriage. Yet whenever he seemed to be tiptoeing around the topic, she adroitly changed the subject or the tenor of the discussion. When she asked herself why she did so, there was no plausible answer. After all, she was very fond of Reggie, was she not?

Now, with the battle raging along the river and increasing numbers of wounded to care for, she scarcely had time to consider her own problems. Few members of the fighting force had returned to camp at all, staying at their posts some miles away. Those left behind could hear the boom of artillery.

On the fourth day, Cymberly returned to her quarters at noon. She had just finished a quick meal with Maggie and Molly when Juliana and Howard Williams approached. Cymberly rose to greet them and bit back a saucy remark when she registered the seriousness of their expressions.

"Is something wrong?" she asked, alarmed.

"Oh, Cymberly, dear friend." Juliana hugged her. "It is Lieutenant Fleming."

"What? Has he been injured? Has he been brought to hospital?"

Juliana choked back a sob and looked beseechingly at her husband.

"It is worse, Miss Winthrop," he said. "I am afraid he is dead."

"No. No. No. It cannot be."

Her wail brought Maggie and Molly forward. Cymberly heard Lieutenant Williams repeat the news to them.

"It is true, Cymberly," Juliana murmured. "I am so sorry."

Cymberly stifled her sobs and disengaged herself from Juliana's embrace. "How . . . how did it happen?"

"He and his unit were to hold a bridge some way up the river. It was overrun just after dawn this morning. Several perished in the fight. The wounded will be in hospital today, I am sure."

"Thank you for coming to tell me," she said to Howard.

"Major Ryder sent me. He wanted you to have the news from a friend, not just hear it from one of the wounded."

"How kind of him."

"You poor dear," Molly said, putting an arm around her waist and hugging her briefly. "First your father and now this."

"I'm so sorry, Miss," Maggie said. "I know what you are feeling."

"Yes, I am sure you do, Maggie." Cymberly recalled that Maggie had lost a beloved husband at Salamanca.

"I must go," Lieutenant Williams said, with a quick kiss for his wife.

"Be careful, dear," Juliana called after him.

Cymberly did not return to the hospital that day. She closed herself away with her memories: Reggie laughingly telling others it was his charm that entitled him to a dance. Reggie taking her out for carriage rides in Lisbon, his attentions easing over the London scandal. Reggie bringing her a bouquet of wildflowers on the trail. Reggie, always joking, always entertaining.

Memories. And guilt.

Why, oh why had she not agreed to the marriage when he wanted it? Perhaps she had not loved him enough. Would she regret forever not having done so?

The next day she forced herself to report for her customary duties at the hospital. Four men from Reggie's unit were there, including his friend Ensign Warren. All expressed condolences to her. The other three were bedridden, but Warren, with a bandage around his head and another around one leg where a shot had grazed his calf, was able to hobble around.

"Might I have a private word with you, Miss Winthrop?" he asked.

"Why, of course." She grabbed her shawl and led him to the garden in the cloisters. They shared a bench half-hidden by a fir tree.

"It is not my wish to bring you further pain, Miss Winthrop, but there are things you should know about the way Reggie died."

"I am not sure I understand."

"He need not have died at all!"

"What do you mean?"

"It was all Ryder's fault. He sent us over that bridge to be killed."

"Oh . . . that cannot be true, Mr. Warren. No one would—"

"It *is* true. *He* set us at that bridge and *he* ordered us to hold it. And God knows we tried. But it was hopeless. And he knew it, too."

"I know you are upset, Mr. Warren. You lost a dear friend—"

"No. Don't you see?" he interrupted. "Everyone knows Ryder wanted you. With Reggie out of the way, the oh-so-noble major has a clear field."

"You cannot mean to say—"

"I am saying Ryder was in charge. *He* put us at that bridge against overwhelming odds. It is his fault Reggie and the others are dead—and he did it for *you.*"

Cymberly was stunned. Geoffrey's soft "I still want you" echoed in her mind. And there were other echoes as well: Reggie's *The lordly Major Ryder wants something he cannot have.* And Captain Wilson's *Geoffrey usually finds a way to get what he wants.*

Had he indeed wanted her that badly? Was he capable of such a heinous act?

"He is a hard man, Miss Winthrop. Please, for Reggie's sake, do not allow him to win." Having delivered this earnest plea, Ensign Warren rose and hobbled on his crutch out of the garden.

Cymberly sat still, tears streaming down her face.

Another day passed before she saw Ryder again. In the interim, others confirmed Major Ryder had been in command at the bridge where Lieutenant Fleming died. The major came to the hospital to visit some of his men and was leaving just as she was. He caught her on the steps of the cathedral.

"Cymberly."

She paused, unable to control a small flutter of gladness at hearing her name on his lips. But then she remembered.

"Cymberly," he said again, standing near. "Allow me to express my sympathy for your loss."

He reached to take her hand, but she jerked away from his touch.

"I wonder that you have the audacity to mouth such words."

"I beg your pardon?" He looked thunderstruck.

"I *know* what happened. You are responsible for Reggie's death. You killed him just as surely as if you fired the shot that took his life."

Anger turned his gray eyes to granite. "I have no idea

what you are talking about, madam, or how you may have come by such misinformation. And if you think me capable of what you seem to be accusing me, you are not the woman I thought you were."

With that, he turned on his heel and was gone.

"The story is all over camp," Wilson said as he and Geoffrey glumly shared their last bottle of port. "You sent the noble Reginald Fleming off to his death because you wanted his woman."

"Oh, God. And she believes it."

"It is a great story, my friend. It even has biblical dimensions."

"What is that supposed to mean?"

"You know—King David sends Uriah off to die in battle so he can have the lovely Bathsheba."

"Rubbish! Pure, unadulterated rubbish! How can she—how can anyone—believe that of me?"

"Well, Geoff, as I see it, there is just enough known truth to make the lie palatable. I mean, you *were* the commander there. That unit was ordered to hold the bridge. And it is no secret that you *did* offer for her."

"And Cymberly believes I arranged for Fleming to die." Geoffrey took a deep breath and then a long swallow of wine to try to quell the despair threatening to undo him.

"Why do you refuse to tell her the truth? Or allow the rest of us to do so?"

"No! Absolutely not."

"Why? For God's sake, why?"

"She loved him. What good would it do for her to learn the man she loved was bedding the lovely Cosette at an inn a mile and more from the bridge when it was attacked?"

"And when he and his cronies finally showed up—having been rousted by thee and me from the inn—the man he wronged challenged him and killed him."

"Very few people know that."

"The battle itself covered the truth, but it should be known—for your sake, if nothing else."

"No. She lost her father, and the death of that Mrs. Peters was another blow. Now this. You would have her know the man she loved was a scoundrel of the worst order? She does not need this burden."

"And you do?"

"I can handle it. Also, I would not have General Fleming know the truth of his son's death. The general is a fine man. One of the best. He always had such hopes for Reggie."

"This is a mistake, my friend. A serious mistake."

"So be it."

Sixteen

Cymberly distantly floated through life during the next weeks. Continuing to work with the wounded, she went through the motions of interacting with those around her. She took part in conversations, but never truly communicated. Withdrawing into herself more and more, she reread books from her father's meager hoard. She wrote in her journal, but now, instead of exploring her feelings or describing the magnificent scenery or relating some amusing anecdote, her entries focused on the number of patients seen, the number of miles traveled, or the items on the menus.

Major Ryder had made but one attempt to break through her defenses. She repulsed him coldly.

He did not try again.

Others tried to break through the shell. Molly offered motherly concern; Juliana, sisterly advice; Maggie, practical routine help; and Amitabha, a comforting tie with the past. Angelina often chatted with her just as though Cymberly were her old self. Captain Wilson also treated her warmly, but there was still a great unbridgeable gulf between her and everyone else.

Meanwhile, Wellington's allied armies took Bayonne in another hard-fought battle. Intermittent respite came as one of Europe's worst winters limited travel. Surprisingly, though the British were now in France, the locals often welcomed them. Wellington's control of the rampages of the vengeful

Spanish in his command, as well as his edicts against rape and mayhem and his insistence that his soldiers pay for food-stuffs and other necessities were now reaping great dividends.

But of all this, too, Cymberly was only dimly aware. She plodded from one task to another. She slept fitfully and ate little. Her clothing began to hang on her. She avoided peering into the looking glass because the pale image with dark circles under its eyes just was not her.

When she thought about it—and she tried not to think beyond routine, get-through-the-day matters—Reggie's death seemed lost among dozens of others. Her mind drifted to Mary Beth's death and to other deaths she had witnessed with as much regret as Reggie's. She mourned her father anew. She longed for his shoulder on which to pour out her woes. It occurred to her that Geoffrey Ryder might have offered such comfort—but he had betrayed her. There was nothing more to say on that point.

Geoffrey watched helplessly as Cymberly seemed to close herself off from others. Hurt and angry over her repudiation of *him,* he nevertheless wanted to see again the woman whose caring awareness, ready wit, and quick smile endeared her to others. He wanted to see that saucy independence and, yes, stubborn willfulness restored.

About six weeks after Fleming's death, Geoffrey was involved in "mopping up" after an intense skirmish. A French company had stumbled into a trap and nearly a hundred French prisoners were being marched to Bayonne, where they would be transported to England until the war was over.

During the midday rest, Geoffrey rode along the erratic line, checking on his own men, who were guards. One of the French prisoners caught his attention. He tried to avoid the English major.

He had ridden past the man, a captain in a mud-spattered

uniform and ill-fitting footgear. But something about him triggered a memory. He turned his horse and stopped near the man, who kept his head down.

"You." Geoffrey leaned down to tap his shoulder. The man sighed and looked up, his eyes reflecting apprehension. "I thought so," Geoffrey said in French. "I see you survived your ordeal in the mountains."

"Oui, Monsieur Commandant. Though you made it very difficult for us."

"The others?"

"One is dead—last week. The other?" He shrugged. "He fights again, I think. Perhaps you will meet him one day." He grinned a mirthless grin.

"The lady will be glad to know you did not perish on the mountain."

"Ah, the lovely *mademoiselle.* I do sorely regret losing that one."

Angered by the man's leering tone, Geoffrey swung his horse and left abruptly, followed by the Frenchman's laughter.

A few minutes later the prisoners were sitting on the side of the road, munching on a small amount of bread and cheese each had been given.

"Ay! *Anglais!"* one of them called. When Geoffrey stopped, he found a bearded French sergeant gesturing to him. "I have something of yours, *Anglais."*

Geoffrey dismounted and approached cautiously. There were sufficient guards about, but these were enemy troops and there might be a trick.

"What is it you have?"

"This." The man pointed to what at first appeared to be a pile of clothes. Then Geoffrey saw a mop of blond curls poking out of it.

"What—"

"Come on, boy." The Frenchman's voice and manner were

gentle as he lifted a small sleeping form toward the English major.

A child? An English child?

"How did you come to have this child?" Geoffrey asked.

"I have had him with me for three days. He just wandered out of nowhere—right through the line of fire during the last battle. Bullets flying everywhere."

"Amazing."

"I have been feeding him and taking care of him as best I could, but . . ." The man's voice trailed off in regret.

As the sergeant spoke, he handed the child to Geoffrey, who took him awkwardly. The boy awoke, struggled to be free of this stranger, and reached for the Frenchman with a pitiable cry.

"Non. You must go with the *Anglais, mon petit."* The Frenchman had tears in his eyes.

Geoffrey took an instant liking to the man. "Come on, little fellow," he said, gently but firmly holding the small wriggling body. "We must get you back to your mama." The boy ceased struggling on hearing his own language. He turned clear blue eyes on Geoffrey.

"Mama?" He shook his head. "Mama's gone."

Geoffrey looked more closely and suddenly recognized the boy. This was the Peters child. What was his name? Jackie? Johnny? No. Tommy—that was it.

"Tommy? We shall go and find your papa."

"Papa's gone."

This made no sense to Geoffrey. He shifted Tommy to hold him with one arm and extended his other hand to the Frenchman.

"Thank you, sergeant."

The man shook Geoffrey's hand and patted Tommy on the back. *"Au revoir, mon petit ami."*

Tommy seemed content to go with Geoffrey, particularly when he was perched before the major on a horse. Despite some amused and inquiring looks, Geoffrey completed his business, then returned to the village providing quarters this day. His first stop was the cottage where the MacIvers were staying.

"Molly." He entered with Tommy perched on his arm, the boy's arm encircling Geoffrey's neck. Molly and Mac, seated before the fireplace, looked up in surprise. "Can you help me? I have no idea where this child is supposed to be."

"Tommy!" It was Cymberly Winthrop's voice. Tommy's body had hidden her from Geoffrey's view.

"Ah, Miss Winthrop. Good evening." He schooled his voice to be strictly formal.

Cymberly reached for the boy and he readily went into her arms.

"He is probably hungry," Geoffrey said.

"I shall take care of that problem." She did not return his gaze, and there was a long pause.

"Where did you find the lad?" Mac asked, easing the tension. Geoffrey quickly explained.

"We learned only today that Tommy was missing, too," Molly said as Cymberly left the room, carrying Tommy. "Everyone assumed his father took the child with him."

"What do you mean 'too'? His father is gone?"

"Peters has gone missing. Deserted, if his mates have the right of it," Mac explained.

"You mean he just abandoned his own son?"

"Looks that way."

"He usually left Tommy with whatever woman he had taken up with at the time." Molly's disgust was plain.

When Cymberly returned, one of Tommy's hands held hers; his other held a crust of bread. She sat down, and Tommy climbed into her lap just as though he belonged there. She put her arms around him and whispered something that caused him to giggle, then kissed the top of his head.

"Well, what is to be done with him now?" Geoffrey knew he sounded helpless. Mac gave him a sympathetic smile.

"Mrs. Glover has taken in several orphans. Perhaps she—"
Molly began, but Cymberly interrupted.

"I will take care of him."

"You?" Molly's curiosity and Geoffrey's surprise were simultaneous.

"Yes. I can do it," she said, sounding defensive. "I can do this much for Mary Beth. I am sure Maggie and Amitabha will help me."

Molly and Mac exchanged a knowing look and then glanced questioningly at Geoffrey, who tore his gaze from Cymberly and the boy to find the others staring at him.

He shrugged. "If Miss Winthrop wants to do this, it is certainly not my place to gainsay her."

"Thank you, sir," Cymberly said stiffly. She rose and took Tommy with her, presumably to her own quarters.

When she had gone, Molly heaved a sigh. "This is the first time in weeks she has allowed herself to show any genuine emotion. That child may be the answer to our prayers."

Cymberly had always been fond of Tommy. Now, almost overnight, he captured her heart. She spent hours of her free time with him—she fed him, bathed him, read to him, and took him for walks. When she returned from her duties at the hospital, his eyes lit up and he demanded she take him up. She never refused him.

Tommy had her laughing again.

A few days after Major Ryder turned the boy over to her, Cymberly received a visit from a camp follower named Dolores. The woman carried a small cloth bag.

"Seeing as how you've got the brat now, here's his gear—what there is of it."

"His father left Tommy with you?"

"Well, sort of."

"How did he get into French hands?"

"Lord knows." Dolores sounded defensive. "We turned

our backs five seconds and he was gone, jus' like that." She snapped her fingers.

"We?"

"His pa 'n' me. Johnny said the kid would come back. But he didn't. Then Johnny hadda leave. An' me, I got better things ta do than go all over God's back pasture lookin' for someone else's brat."

Cymberly thought, *I'll just bet you do,* but all she said was, "So his father left, assuming you would care for the child?"

"I guess. But I never told 'im I'd do any such thing. Anyways, Johnny ain't come back an' he left this here stuff. Most of it is the kid's clothes. Couple things belonged to his ma."

She held out the bag. It was pitifully light. Cymberly found it contained only a few articles of the child's clothing. She conjectured anything of value had been lifted by Dolores or her predecessors. In the bottom of the bag were some pieces of paper which turned out to be the Peters' marriage certificate and a letter from Mary Beth's mother.

"Poor Mary Beth," Cymberly said as she related the whole incident to Molly, who clucked sympathetically in response.

Then Molly said, "So Tommy has a grandmother, at least, who will welcome him."

"Yes."

Cymberly had very mixed feelings about the discovery of family for Tommy. She knew there was little likelihood of the negligent father's ever again being a factor in the little boy's life. Deserters faced a firing squad if they were caught. But here were others who had a claim she knew could not be denied.

Molly must have read her mind. "Don't fret, dearie. Tommy needs you here and now. Who knows what the future will bring?"

Seventeen

The allied army wintered near Bayonne. It was cold. Wood for fires, scarce and green, produced little heat. Foodstuffs were in short supply. Cymberly's days became a steady round of caring for wounded. She also continued her practice of reading to the troops and writing letters for them.

She occasionally saw Geoffrey Ryder at the hospital. He never failed to visit the men of his command. One afternoon as she left the hospital, he appeared to be waiting for her.

"Miss Winthrop? May I have a moment?"

"I . . . uh, yes." She could think of no other response that would not be rude. Her heart behaved erratically at his nearness. She peered at him around the brim of her bonnet. How *could* he knowingly have sent Reggie and those others to their deaths?

Such an act seemed so completely out of character for him, yet there had been no denial of his involvement. On the other hand, there had been no official accusation and certainly no condemnation. Was the army just overlooking reprehensible behavior in one of its most able officers?

"Miss Winthrop?" Startling her out of her musings, he drew her attention to the arm he offered.

"I am sorry. I was woolgathering." She laid her hand very lightly on his sleeve, trying—unsuccessfully—to ignore his strength.

"How is Tommy getting along now?" His tone was casual, conversational.

"He is doing very well indeed—adding words to his vocabulary at a most astonishing rate." She proceeded to tell him amusing anecdotes of this most marvelous of children. Then she became aware of what she was doing and with whom. "I am sorry, sir."

"No—no. I asked."

"It is just that I . . . I do babble on about Tommy."

"Never mind. I liked it." He patted her hand on his arm. When she glanced up, he was gazing at her with such a look of questioning and longing that it quite took her breath away. She quickly lowered her lashes to hide her own reaction.

She allowed him to steer her into the semiprivacy of a walkway between two buildings. He turned to her, taking her shoulders in each hand. She should not be allowing this, but she quite simply could not help herself.

"Sir?"

"Cymberly, please. Stop this cold formality between us."

"I do not think that would be a good idea." There was a pause, during which she dared not allow herself to look at him, but neither did she back away from his touch. "Did you have something specific on your mind, Major?"

He gave a resigned sigh. "As a matter of fact, I did."

"Well?"

"You have heard the news, I am sure, that the allies seem to be winning this war with Bonaparte?"

"Yes."

"There is still some capacity for fight left in Boney and his troops, but they cannot hold on at great length."

"They might disagree with you."

"They might."

"But what has this to do with me?" she asked.

"We—that is, our army—are on our way to Toulouse. Soult will surely make a stand there."

"So?"

"At the moment, we are actually closer and with some decent roads to the ports on the bay."

"You do have a point here somewhere, I hope?" She looked up at him in slight annoyance, then looked away.

"Yes, I do. I think you should take the boy and return to England while you have the chance."

This suggestion came as a surprise. Cymberly had thought this issue to be long settled.

"Major Ryder! You never cease trying to be rid of me, do you?" Annoyed, she tried to step away, but his grip on her shoulders tightened. She looked up, angry, and caught her breath at the raw emotion in his eyes.

"Get rid of you?" he asked, disbelief plain in his voice. He pulled her roughly against him. "My God, Cymberly. I would have you near always." The words seemed wrenched out of him.

He lowered his lips to hers in a kiss that expressed weeks of denial and hunger. Nor was it *his* hunger alone. She lost all sense of time, place, and other people as she responded to this man whose embrace constituted all any woman could want from life.

"Ah, Cymberly." He deepened the kiss as she clung to him.

Suddenly, reality came crashing in. This man had killed Reggie, and she was responding to him like a wanton. She pushed against his chest. "No. I cannot do this. Please." It was a desperate cry.

He released her at once.

"As you wish, madam. I apologize for forcing my attentions on you."

"You did not force me." Her basic honesty compelled this reply. "I . . . apology accepted. I must see to Tommy." She turned to go.

He grabbed her arm. "Will you at least think about going to England?"

"I will think on it."

They made their way to her quarters in silence, each seemingly lost in thought.

Good heavens! Why had she allowed that kiss?

Allowed it? She had welcomed it. She had *wanted* it, she accused herself. She felt an engulfing wave of shame. How could she welcome the caresses of such a man?

Geoffrey walked at her side cursing himself. He had not intended to kiss her. Lord! Had she not made it quite clear his attentions were unwelcome? So what if her response seemed otherwise? Possibly she had as little control as he did. Now *that* was a hopeful thought.

Hopeful? Of what? His pride would not allow an answer to that terse question.

He saw her to her quarters, where each bade the other a stiff good afternoon.

Well, he had tried. No doubt she would continue to ignore any advice to go home with the boy. He knew Molly and Mac had at least hinted she should do so.

Part of him deplored her stubbornness. Another part of him rejoiced that she would still be near—at least for a while. They would probably never see each other once they were back in England.

That thought filled him with despair.

Cymberly could not get the scene from her mind. Actually, she thought, in a flash of total honesty with herself, it was his kiss, the feeling she perceived in it, and her own feelings in response. Those were what she could not put from her mind.

However, she also resented Major Ryder's presuming to tell her she should go home to England. She brooded about the situation all the next day. In the evening, Molly asked, "Is something wrong, my dear?"

Mac had gone out and Tommy was playing quietly with a kitten belonging to the owner of the cottage in which the MacIvers were staying.

"No," Cymberly said reluctantly, then, "yes." She told Molly about Geoffrey's suggesting she take Tommy and return to England. She did not mention the kiss.

"I see," Molly said slowly. "What will you do?"

"I simply do not know. It pains me to admit it, but Geof— uh, Major Ryder—is probably right. Tommy belongs with his own family."

"But?"

"But he is in no real danger now." Her voice had a pleading note. "There are always three or four adults who know where he is at all times and who care about him."

"Surely his grandparents in England care, too."

"His grandmother does, if that letter to Mary Beth is to be believed."

"Well, then," Molly nudged gently.

"Oh, Molly—I just cannot give him up yet. I know the moment we arrive in England, I shall have to turn him over to strangers."

"You poor dear." Molly patted her hand sympathetically, but Cymberly noted she did not contradict the notion of having to give up Tommy.

"Did you not say you planned to write the grandparents?" Molly asked.

"I did write them, but it will be weeks yet before we get a response."

"Well, you will just have to take what comes, I suppose."

"What if his grandfather rejects him?" Cymberly voiced a fear that haunted her. She remembered very well Mary Beth's talking about her stern father.

"That probably will not happen. He may have been disappointed in his daughter, but Tommy is his own flesh and blood, too. Look at him. Who could not love him?"

The two women smiled indulgently at the boy. Tommy,

sensing their eyes on him, looked up and smiled like a cherub. He came over and patted Cymberly's knee.

"Story, Auntie?"

"Auntie?" Molly asked.

"Maggie and I thought 'Auntie' was preferable to his calling me 'Mama' as he did once or twice."

"Yes, I see."

"Story," Tommy insisted more forcefully.

"All right, sugarplum. A story. Then to bed with you." She stood, lifted him into her arms, and the two of them bade Molly good night.

The winter respite lasted only a few weeks. In February, a major battle at Orthez sent hundreds of casualties to the hospital tents. Nevertheless, Arthur Wellesley, Viscount Wellington, had the enemy on the run.

By the end of March, Marshal Nicolas Soult and his forces were barricaded in the walled city of Toulouse. This news had come as those doing hospital work were taking a much needed break one afternoon.

"Hah!" Dr. Cameron snorted. "I cannot imagine they will be overly welcome in Toulouse, a stronghold of royalist sympathizers. They supported the king and were mad as hops when the republicans sent him to the guillotine."

"But that took place—what?—over twenty years ago!"

"People have long memories. They see the self-styled emperor as a usurper."

"I am told the war is nearly over." Cymberly did not reveal her source for this information.

"That is what I hear, too. News from the east says Boney is on the defensive now."

"Let us hope it finishes soon."

"It probably will. But not soon enough. Never soon enough. The Peer intends to take Toulouse, and all indications are it will be no easy task."

"Oh, dear," Cymberly murmured, knowing full well what that would mean for medical personnel.

"Yes. The casualty rate is likely to be high."

"I shall check with Dr. Hawkins and Sergeant Benson regarding supplies. I do hope replenishments arrive soon."

"Thank you, Miss Winthrop. Don't know what we'd do without you."

She smiled her appreciation of his compliment. "I am glad to help. Truly I am."

The next evening was clear and not too cold. Already a proliferation of birds during the day and the beginning of carpets of green on the hills offered the news that spring was rapidly approaching. Cymberly had just put Tommy to bed with his inescapable story. He had finally succumbed to his little body's demand for sleep when Maggie came to announce visitors.

Cymberly stepped through the flaps of her tent to find Captain Wilson and a young woman it took her only an instant to recognize.

"Angelina! Your habit—your headdress! What are you about?"

Angelina laughed merrily and clung to Captain Wilson's arm.

"And hello to you, too, Miss Winthrop," the captain teased.

"Oh, Benjamin, I am sorry. I did not mean to ignore you. It is just that this change is such a surprise. Let me look at you, Angelina."

The girl loosened her hold on Wilson and twirled in front of Cymberly. Angelina's closely cropped black hair gave her a gamin look. She wore a muslin gown of soft blue printed with white flowers. Young and feminine and incredibly lovely, Angelina had a secret, happy look in her big brown eyes when she looked at Wilson.

"We wanted you to be the first to know." He slipped his

arm around Angelina's waist. "Angelina has agreed to marry me."

"Is it not wonderful? Benjamin wants to marry me!" Her eyes fairly danced.

"Yes. That *is* wonderful news." Cymberly grasped a hand of each of them. "Very wonderful news. I am so happy for both of you." Then she added with a laugh, "That explains the change of costume."

"Benjamin gave me this lovely new dress." Angelina swished the skirt gaily. Then her expression clouded. "It is all right for me to accept such a gift?"

Cymberly laughed again. "Under the circumstances, I doubt anyone would be overly nice about such a detail."

"Could not allow my intended bride to go around dressed in nun's garb, now could I?" Wilson smiled fondly at Angelina.

"That would never do at all," Cymberly said with exaggerated approval.

"We plan to marry as soon as I can get permission," Wilson said.

"And we want you to stand up with us," Angelina added.

"I shall be honored to do so."

"Along with Geoffrey, of course." Wilson watched her face carefully.

Cymberly hesitated for only a fraction of a second before repeating her agreement. She would do nothing to dampen their spirits.

"You are sure you will not mind?" Wilson asked with a note of worry.

"Why should I mind? It is *your* wedding." Cymberly forced a note of gaiety.

Angelina hugged her tightly. "Oh, I am so glad. So happy. Thank you. Thank you."

Within days, Wilson managed to override every objection to one of His Majesty's officers marrying a Spanish national. A Catholic priest serving as chaplain to an Irish regiment was glad to officiate, and the priest of a village church kindly allowed the ceremony to take place before his altar. The small church was filled to overflowing.

The women had managed to deck the bride out creditably in a refashioned ball gown that had belonged to Cymberly. They even scraped up a lovely trousseau of sorts. Angelina would go to her wedding bed in satin and gossamer-like lace.

As she stood next to the bride, Cymberly was keenly aware of Geoffrey standing on the other side of Wilson. She could not suppress the thought this could have been the two of them being married in front of a company of military well-wishers. As they turned to walk behind the newly married couple, she caught his gaze and knew he had been thinking the same thing.

Then she immediately felt guilty because she had imagined herself marrying Major Ryder instead of Lieutenant Fleming.

As the necessary documents were signed with Cymberly and Geoffrey as witnesses, her fingers brushed his. Awareness jolted through her, and she glanced at him involuntarily.

His eyes told her he had felt it, too.

Eighteen

Early April in southern France promised warm weather. Flowering fruit trees vied with other spring flowers to present an array of color and fragrance. In sharp contrast to nature's benevolence, Geoffrey noted man's ferocious assault on his own kind.

As part of an advance scouting team, Geoffrey had earlier discerned that the French had established some formidable defenses around the walls of the city of Toulouse. The naturally hilly terrain was augmented by freshly dug trenches.

When the battle commenced, riflemen saw action in many areas. Thus Geoffrey was all over the battlefield, issuing a stern order here, encouraging a flagging detachment there, frequently jumping right into the fray with little regard for his own safety.

"Lordy, he's all over the field." The soldier's tone was both complaining and admiring.

"Sure is," another responded. "Must lead a charmed life, that one."

But on this day, in this battle, the Ryder charm was working at less than full capacity.

Men were engaged in close combat, hindered by carts to transport cannon and ammunition. Geoffrey knew that on horseback he and his mount presented a likely target for some canny Frenchman, but this was not something to think about now. Brandishing his saber, he managed repeatedly to lend assistance and protection.

Then he felt the stallion take a hit. With a terrified scream, the horse twisted, lurched, and fell. The animal thrashed about, trying to stand, then lay still. Geoffrey's superb horsemanship allowed him to keep his seat until the horse actually fell.

He nearly jumped free, but everything happened too quickly and in close proximity to an overturned artillery cart. As he fell, his leg scraped against a jagged piece of metal. He felt it tear the flesh in his thigh. He landed face down, a large stone ripping a gash in his head.

Not now, he thought. *It is nearly over.*

Struggling to a sitting position, he was vaguely aware of blood streaming into his eyes. His leg simply would not function as it should.

Then everything went dark.

The battle was over. The eery silence of the field was broken only by an occasional cry or moan from the wounded who lay beside their dead comrades, French and British, brothers in death and pain.

Cymberly had joined a distraught Molly to search for Sergeant MacIver who, his wife had been informed, lay wounded on the battlefield. The two women had been searching for over an hour, stopping frequently to tend to the needs of wounded. The smell of gunpowder lingered over the field. There was also the smell of blood and ruptured earth and the stench of death. Foresight had prompted them to bring canteens of water with them.

"It's hopeless," Molly wailed. "We will never find my David this way."

"Yes, we will." Cymberly reassured her. "You are sure the man told you this area?"

"Yes."

"Let us separate, then. There is no need to duplicate our efforts."

"All right."

Wise as the decision to separate was, Cymberly felt the despair and horror of her surroundings more strongly after Molly moved off. Tears streamed down her face as she picked her way through wounded, dead, and dying, through debris and broken bodies. The canteen was quickly emptied, but many of the fallen still had their own canteens, so replacing hers was easy.

Compounding the horror were the scavengers, civilians and soldiers alike, who were more interested in robbing the dead than in seeing to the wounded. She could see them bending over their prey here and there and knew the burial teams would find many a body stripped naked.

Rising from the side of a very young soldier who had died even as she held a canteen to his lips, she said a prayer for him and for the mother who would grieve for such a handsome lad. Then she heard a moan off to her right.

The sound came from the other side of an overturned artillery cart. Stepping over the obviously dead driver of the cart, she rounded the edge of the vehicle and beheld a man and a dead horse. Her heart turned to lead as she recognized the green uniform of a rifleman. The horse told her he was an officer.

"No!" she sobbed as she reached his side. But it was, indeed, Major Ryder. He was unconscious, but apparently in some pain, for he moaned incoherently. Using her own handkerchief, she wiped at the already drying blood on his face and head.

"That horrible bump is worse than the cut," she said aloud, despite the unlikelihood of a response. "Your leg looks serious, though."

She looked around for something to stanch the blood still seeping from his thigh. Nothing. Looking up, she caught sight of the dead driver.

"Oh, my. I hate to do this, but Major Ryder needs this shirt far more than you do at the moment." With some difficulty, she removed the dead man's shirt and tore it into strips to tie a crude bandage around the wounded Geoffrey's leg, saving a bit of the cloth to use on his head wound.

"There. Please, God, please. Let the bleeding stop. Let him be all right." She rose and spoke again to the unresponsive form. "You just wait right here, my love. I must go for help."

Her search for Molly and help took on intensity as the sun sank lower in the sky. Having herself been on the go since dawn that morning, Cymberly was exhausted. Stooping to tend wounded now and then and promising to send them help, she stumbled on. She was stooping over yet another wounded young soldier when she heard her name called.

"Cymberly? Over here."

Molly and Mac materialized as black figures against the setting sun.

"I found him." Molly's joy was unrestrained. "And he is not hurt at all. That boy was wrong."

"Actually, I found *her*," Mac said.

"What welcome news, in any event. I need your help. Geoffrey has been injured," Cymberly said, unconsciously using Ryder's Christian name.

"The major? Where?" Mac was instantly alert.

"Over beyond the cart on that little rise there."

Amazingly, some of the wagons and carts were still upright, though the donkeys hitched to them were dead. A few donkeys incongruously munched grass beside the bent and twisted bodies of the day's adversaries. Finding one such wagon and one such donkey, the MacIvers and Cymberly brought them near the still unconscious major. They had some difficulty getting his large, limp form onto the wagon. He groaned once or twice, but otherwise was blessedly unaware of what was happening to him.

As they made their way back to the hastily established camp, they picked up four more wounded and directed people engaged in the same task to other wounded. The dead could wait.

The MacIvers and Cymberly delivered their other wounded to the hospital tent, but, knowing how swamped the hospital people were, they took Major Ryder with them. Maggie and Amitabha, with the dubious help of little Tommy, had begun to set up the Winthrop-MacIver camp.

"We'd best leave the major on the wagon for now," Mac said. "We can put a covering over it and Molly and I will take turns watching over him." His wife nodded her approval.

"No. I shall help you." Cymberly was adamant.

Molly exchanged a knowing look with her husband, then said, "Of course, if you wish. You get some rest and we will call you later."

The makeshift camp completed and a quick cold meal arranged, they all fell into their beds exhausted. Despite her body's cry for rest, Cymberly found it difficult to sleep. Consumed with worry about the injured Geoffrey, she kept seeing him lying helpless, covered with blood. What if he . . . no! She could not even consider the worst. She stifled a sob.

Another thought crept in, surprising her. Why was she so devastated over his injuries? Lord knew she had mourned Reggie's death, but this, hardly a possibility as yet, brought a sense of utter loss.

Why?

The answer sneaked in just as stealthily as the original question had.

She was in love with him.

How could she be? How could she *love* someone she could not respect? And she could never respect a man who had deliberately and for selfish reasons sent another to his death. The very idea revolted her. Her revulsion was intensified by guilt, for *she* was at the heart of his self-serving actions.

Finally, she dozed off, but it seemed only minutes later Molly was waking her for her turn at watching over their patient.

"He has become rather restless in the last hour or so," Molly said.

"Is he feverish?"

"A little."

Cymberly laid her hand gently on his brow and he turned toward her touch. She wet a cloth, dribbled some water across his parched lips, and placed the cloth on his forehead.

In the gray half-light just before dawn, he began to thrash around and moan. Most of his mutterings were incoherent, but once he said very clearly, "No! They must not know." It was an order. She spoke soothing, if nonsensical, words to him and he soon quieted down, but she wondered about that order. Later, she put her hand on his leg and could feel the heat of the fever in his wound.

Molly and Mac, sleeping under the wagon, had been awakened.

"Is he conscious?" Mac asked softly.

"No, but his leg is very hot. It worries me."

"Be morning soon," Molly said. "We'll see what the doctor says then."

The harried doctor held that the leg should be amputated before the fever became a full-blown case of gangrene.

"No!" Molly and Cymberly cried in unison.

"Not until there is no chance of saving his leg," Cymberly added.

"By then it may be too late," Cameron warned, his voice infinitely tired.

"Still," Mac said, speaking quietly, "we'd best wait a while. The major's a fighter. He'd not consent to having his leg cut off on 'what if' thinking."

"Well, it's on your head, then." The weary Cameron gave them the necessary bandages and medicines from his dwindling supply.

The British army, heartily welcomed by the local French, had moved into Toulouse once the fighting stopped. While Molly and Cymberly took the still unconscious Geoffrey back to their makeshift camp, Mac took Amitabha to search for suitable quarters.

A short while later Captain Wilson appeared with another man.

"We are looking for Geoffrey," Wilson said without preamble and sounding worried. "This is Higgins, his batman. Higgins says he did not return last night. We checked the hospital. He's not there, either."

"Mr. Higgins." Cymberly acknowledged the man. "Major Ryder is here." She gestured to the wagon. "He is unconscious." She then described his wounds and told them what the doctor had said.

"Glad you did not let them amputate," Wilson said. "Geoff would have disliked that."

Cymberly smiled faintly at the captain's understatement. "Yes, we thought so."

"Higgins and I have found quarters in the town. Angelina is waiting there. Perhaps there is something available nearby for the rest of you."

"Mac and Amitabha are off looking now," Molly said.

Wilson turned to the batman. "Higgins, you know Mac-Iver. See if you can find him and the Indian and help them find a place. We will meet you back at our quarters."

"As you wish, sir."

This conversation was interrupted by loud "hurrahs" that swept through the camp. Men threw their hats in the air and grabbed each other or their women to engage in impromptu and energetic dances. They shouted gleefully to each other.

"It's all over!"

"We're a-goin' home!"

"Boney's gone!"

"We beat 'im!"

"I shall find out what this is all about while you gather your things together," Wilson said to the women.

The three women—Maggie, with Tommy astraddle one hip, had joined Cymberly and Molly—placed bedding and clothing around the unaware Geoffrey to ease his journey as much as possible, loaded their other possessions on mules, and Cymberly put a lead rope on her horse.

When Wilson returned, they were ready.

"It is true," he announced with a grin. "The general received word this morning. Boney abdicated five days ago. He is being exiled to some island. The allies are already in Paris."

"What good news," Cymberly said as Molly and Maggie nodded, smiling. Then the full impact of what he had said hit her. "Five days ago? He abdicated five days ago? Then this battle . . . Geoffrey . . . all these deaths . . . none of this need ever have happened?"

Wilson put a comforting arm around her shoulder. "Probably not, but none of us knew, did we? Communications are slow and we all—French leaders, too—go on what we know at the time. It is one of the hazards of war."

"I hate this war. I hate the army. I hate the death and destruction."

"I know," he murmured soothingly. "We all do at times."

"Are we really going home, then?" Molly asked hopefully, diverting attention from Cymberly's outburst.

"That has not been sorted out yet, but I expect so," the captain answered.

At the quarters secured by the Wilsons and Higgins, they transferred the still unconscious patient to a bed. Madame Arnoux and her widowed daughter welcomed the newcomers. She could accommodate the MacIvers, also, and she thought her neighbor could provide for the young lady, her servants, and the boy. When Mac, Amitabha, and Higgins arrived, it was all sorted out in short order.

With both Angelina and Molly as well as Higgins on the scene to tend the injured Geoffrey, Cymberly felt her services there to be decidedly *de trop*. She turned her attention to caring for Tommy and resumed her duties at the hospital. However, she checked on the major's condition repeatedly and was glad to learn the first evening that his fever had broken. There was reason to hope.

The next day Molly reported he had regained consciousness, asked for some water, and promptly fell into what was now a healing sleep. Three days later, he was up and even hobbled around the room a bit, though he leaned on Higgins to do so and complained of dizziness, Molly said.

Cymberly was pleased to hear news of his progress, but now that he was out of danger, she did not seek his company, though he was much on her mind. She knew she was being cowardly, but she could not deal with her emotions now.

Meanwhile, events on the larger canvas gathered momentum. Bonaparte would be exiled. Rumor had it Wellington's army would be disbanded.

Cymberly called on the Wilsons and MacIvers one evening.

"Oh, I think Geoffrey is asleep," Angelina said sadly. "We gave him some laudanum for the pain."

"He will be out for some time then." Perhaps this would be easier if she did not see him. "I just came by to tell you we are leaving early tomorrow morning."

"Tomorrow?" Molly's surprise was plain.

"Yes. They are moving wounded very fast now. Maggie, Amitabha, Tommy, and I have passage on one of the transport ships."

"You must give us your direction," Wilson said.

"Yes. The major will be that sorry to have missed you," Molly added.

"I . . . I am not sure where I will go. Perhaps the cottage in Amberton where my mother and I lived. I shall be in London until I see Tommy settled."

She saw Wilson raise an eyebrow at her evasiveness, but she refused to make any further explanation. She rose, hugged each of them in turn, and left with tears streaming down her face.

Nineteen

Three weeks later, Major Ryder was back in England. Chadwyck had insisted he come to Hartwell, the principal estate of the earldom, for his recovery, and Geoffrey was not averse to doing so.

His head wound had healed nicely and the headaches had finally gone away. Only this week he had given up the use of a crutch, though his leg was weak and he walked with a pronounced limp. But that, too, diminished with daily exercise.

His state of mind was another matter. He was still hurt and angry over Cymberly's leaving without even the courtesy of a good-bye. Why had she not come to see him when she knew he was unable to go to her? Did she really hate him that much?

Ah, but it was she who was largely responsible for saving him. Left on that field all night, he would likely have bled to death.

Her leaving as she had did not make sense. Did she still believe he had deliberately sent Fleming to his death? Had she been so in love with that bounder? Her response to his own kisses had clearly shown she was not indifferent to him, at least not physically. So what was it?

Whatever it was, she had made her feelings very clear when she left so abruptly. Still, he owed her his life.

There was unfinished business between them.

The Earl of Chadwyck was not a well man. In his seventh decade, he spent his day confined to a chair with a lap robe across his knees. His mind was alert and he kept up the business of the earldom. However, he knew his time was limited—a fact he had learned to accept, he told Geoffrey. He was determined to put his affairs in order and turn matters over to younger, more capable hands.

The earl and his heir had formed the habit of sitting in the library over glasses of port most evenings to discuss the events of the day and plan future projects.

"I hope your meeting with Hellman went well today," the earl said.

"Yes. Your steward is a very able man, sir."

"*Our* steward, now that you are finally home, my boy."

Geoffrey did not respond to the implied criticism, and they both drank in silence for a moment. Then the earl cleared his throat and spoke hesitantly.

"I think you knew my granddaughter in the Peninsula."

"Yes, sir, I did."

Geoffrey was surprised. This was the first mention the old man had made of his granddaughter, though he had readily discussed the son he had lost many years before.

"Tell me about her, please."

There was such yearning in the other's tone that Geoffrey felt sorry for him. "What would you like to know?"

"Everything. What she looks like, what kind of person she is. Everything. I saw her only once when she was about five or six years old."

For the next hour, Geoffrey informed Chadwyck about his granddaughter and answered many questions. He told the other of her beauty, her courage, her willingness to help others, her loyalty as a friend to Mary Beth, her wit. He related anecdotes, some of which he carefully edited.

The old man gave him a penetrating look. "You seem to admire her very much."

"Yes, I do." He could admit to that much.

"More than admire?" When Geoffrey hesitated to respond to this question, Chadwyck said, "Never mind. Your lack of answer to a question I had no business asking is in itself an answer."

In the silence that followed, Geoffrey thought with infinite sadness of the woman who had refused his suit. Chadwyck interrupted his reverie.

"I made some serious mistakes with her mother. I treated her badly."

"I knew your daughter briefly in India, sir. She was a gracious lady."

"Yes, she was. But when she married without my permission, I rejected her."

"Her husband, General Winthrop, was a fine man."

"So I am told. But I was too stubborn to accept them at the time. And now they are both gone." In his voice was profound regret. "But their daughter is not. I suppose she hates me, though."

"I . . . do not know. I never heard either her father or her mention you. I am not sure Miss Winthrop is capable of *hate*."

"If she does, I could not blame her." The old man pulled out a handkerchief and blew his nose noisily. "It is too late for me to make it up to Elise, but perhaps I can do something for her daughter. Will you help me?"

"I will do what I can."

"Good. Elise was to have had a handsome dowry on her marriage. But when she eloped, I forbade the dowry. I want her daughter to have that legacy. Will you see that she gets it?"

"I *could* do so, but is this not a matter for a solicitor to handle?"

"It is. But right after Elise died, I sent my solicitor on just such a mission. Cymberly sent him away with a flea in his ear."

Geoffrey chuckled sympathetically. "Would you say your granddaughter comes by her stubbornness honestly?"

"She probably does," Chadwyck admitted ruefully. "Will you see her and ensure she gets what was due her mother?"

"I will certainly try. It happens that I owe the lady a debt of my own."

In London, Cymberly tried to pick up the pieces of her life. On arriving back in the capital, she had gone directly to her paternal grandmother. Anna Louisa Truesdale—more accurately, Anna Louisa Morrison Winthrop Truesdale—daughter of a rich tradesman, had been twice widowed of even richer merchants. Having returned a few months before from an extended expedition to Egypt, she now lived in a modest townhouse in a respectable neighborhood.

Gracious and loving, she welcomed her granddaughter with open arms. Cymberly had arrived with Maggie, Amitabha, and Tommy. Mrs. Truesdale greeted Amitabha fondly for having served her son so well. She welcomed Maggie and demanded an explanation for Tommy, who clung for dear life to Cymberly's skirts.

"Thurston, see that Mrs. Osborne and Amitabha are provided for, and have Cook send tea and cakes to the drawing room," Anna Louisa said to her butler as she ushered Cymberly and the clinging Tommy up the stairs to the first floor drawing room, richly decorated with Egyptian artifacts.

"Gordon, you say?" she asked as Cymberly finished Tommy's story. "Hmm. I think I know the family. If I remember correctly, Gordon is a wine merchant. The family business goes back to the days of Chaucer. And there was a daughter named Mary Beth."

"Will Mr. Gordon be likely to accept Tommy?" Cymberly almost hoped her grandmother would label the man a true blackguard so she could justify not contacting the Gordons.

"I am sure he will." Mrs. Truesdale thus dashed that hope.

"Gordon has always wanted a son, but he could not abide the son-in-law his daughter presented him."

"With due cause, it turned out," Cymberly said.

"How do you want to handle this, my dear?"

Cymberly sighed. "I shall send the Gordons a note and ask them to call tomorrow."

"Good girl."

The next day, at the earliest possible hour for making calls, the Gordons were shown into the Truesdale drawing room. In their late forties, both looked sad, apprehensive, and eager. Mrs. Gordon was small, plump, and nervous. Her husband was a rather rotund sort with a fringe of gray hair around a bald pate. He exhibited a blustery manner.

"So where's the boy?" Mr. Gordon asked after initial greetings. He looked around as though expecting the child to pop out from behind a piece of furniture.

"He is still above stairs," Cymberly said. "I shall bring him down in a few minutes."

"I . . . we want to thank you for caring for him," Mrs. Gordon said quietly, "and for writing us about our poor Mary Beth." There were tears in her voice.

Her husband patted her hand. "Now, now, my dear."

"We never should have let her go off like that," his wife said.

"No, we should not have done so. 'Twas my doing, though, and I shall regret it to my dying day. Perhaps we can make it up to Mary Beth by providing well for her son."

"I do hope so," Mrs. Gordon said fervently.

This conversation quelled most of Cymberly's fears for Tommy. "Mary Beth loved her son," Cymberly said, "and she was a good wife."

"To a scoundrel," Mary Beth's father growled.

Cymberly did not respond to this. No sense in tormenting Mary Beth's parents with the truth of their daughter's miserable life with Johnny Peters.

When she brought Tommy in a few minutes later, both

Gordons had tears in their eyes, and Cymberly surmised their arms fairly ached to hold the little boy.

"Auntie Cym?" he questioned, eyeing the strangers.

Cymberly knelt down to his level. "This is your grandmother and grandfather. Can you tell them hello?"

" 'Ullo." He buried his face in Cymberly's shoulder.

"This is your mama's mama and papa." Cymberly seated herself near the Gordons.

"Mama's gone. Papa's gone."

"Yes, darling, but now you have a grandmama and grandpapa." Cymberly held him on her lap so he was facing his grandparents.

"Would you let me hold you, Tommy?" Mrs. Gordon asked.

Tommy looked at Cymberly for reassurance and when she nodded, he silently reached out to his grandmother, who clasped him to her. Mr. Gordon reached over to pat the boy's shoulder as though he just had to touch the child.

When a maid brought in a tea tray, Cymberly passed a plate of biscuits to the Gordons, encouraging them to give one to Tommy.

"He likes these."

Tommy made friends easily and soon he was sitting on his grandfather's lap giggling as the man gently tickled him.

"Miss Winthrop, we are ever so grateful to you for giving us our grandson," Mrs. Gordon said, her husband nodding his concurrence. "And while we hesitate to impose on your own homecoming, we would like to invite you to be our houseguest for a few days to help Tommy make the transition."

"Yes, and you must feel free to visit him at any time," her husband added.

"Well I—" Cymberly started, glancing at her own grandmother.

"Of course, dear. You must," Mrs. Truesdale said. "You and I will have our time together."

It was agreed, and Cymberly removed to the Gordons' home for the remainder of the week and saw Tommy happily settled there with a nurse and very doting grandparents.

"I think that is the hardest thing I have ever done," she told her grandmother on her return to Truesdale House.

"It was the right thing to do, my dear. I know how much it hurt, but I am proud of you."

"Thank you, Grandmother."

Losing the companionship, diversion, and responsibility Tommy had provided put Cymberly at loose ends. Memories haunted her during the day—all those deaths. Did they really mean anything? The nights were worse, filled as they were with the sheer carnage of the surgeon's tent and evidence of what cannon shot could do to the human body.

One face—one masculine form—dominated her memories. Fear for one man dominated her nightmares. Geoffrey. He who had come to her rescue twice. He of the breathtaking kisses. She remembered shared ideas. Camaraderie. And she remembered all too well the feel of his arms around her, the touch of his lips.

One of her recurring nightmares showed the inert major's body covered in blood beside an overturned artillery cart. In another, he stood taller and stronger than those before him. He was pointing imperiously and ordering, *Go!* Death awaited them. Her own cry of fear and horror would wake her.

She began to stay up later and later, trying to make herself tired enough for dreamless sleep. Reading had always been a happy diversion. Now she would find herself having read several pages with nary a clue as to what the words had said. Once an avid newspaper reader, she rarely picked one up now.

Her grandmother noticed, of course, and seemed determined to lift her spirits. They went out every day on some small excursion. They visited or revisited the city's major landmarks—the Tower, Westminster Abbey, St. Paul's—and museums. They even visited Lord Elgin's display of antique statuary.

"There is talk of his selling all this marble to the nation, you know," Anna Louisa said.

"Oh?"

"It was in the *Morning Post* one day this week. Did you not see it?"

"I must have missed it."

Cymberly appreciated her grandmother's efforts, but try as she might, she could not shake herself out of this mood of lethargy, this feeling of being a distant spectator rather than a participant in life.

As the daughter and twice widowed spouse of men who had engaged in trade, Anna Louisa did not move in the first circles of society as her daughter-in-law and her granddaughter had once done. Cymberly knew that Anna Louisa, who had her own circle of friends and interests, did not consider this any great loss. It therefore came as a mild surprise when her grandmother began mentioning *on dits* of the *ton* gleaned from the society columns of the newspapers that Anna Louisa *did* read every day.

Cymberly's usual response was an absentminded "Hmm" or "How interesting." Finally, Anna Louisa took a more direct approach.

"Why do you not take the carriage and go to call upon your godmother?"

"Lady Renfrow?"

Anna Louisa chuckled. "Unless you have another tucked away somewhere."

"We did not part on the best of terms, you know."

"Surely that news was old hat only days after it was noised about. Besides, Lady Renfrow managed to marry that daughter of hers off quite well in spite of it."

"I am not sure . . ."

"You could send round a note, could you not?"

"I *could*." But Cymberly felt no burning inclination to do so.

Anna Louisa had never been one to give up. Her next ploy played on Cymberly's natural propensity to be of service to those around her.

"My dear, I wonder if I could prevail upon you to help me?"

"Of course, Grandmother."

"I desperately need some new gowns. Would you be so kind as to help me choose fabrics and patterns?"

Cymberly knew she was being manipulated, but how could she refuse this dearest of ladies? "I should be glad to help you."

"And perhaps while we are about it, *you* could choose a few new things, for I must say, my dearest girl, your wardrobe is sadly out of date."

"What is that to say to anything? I have no intention of going out into society."

"Something could come up and you would change your mind and then where would you be? Besides, I will not have my friends say I keep my granddaughter in outdated rags."

"All right, Grandmother. You win. We shall *both* go shopping."

They spent that evening poring over copies of fashion magazines, and the next day found the two of them being poked and prodded by Madame Fanchon, who produced some of the *ton's* most elegant costumes.

"A ball gown? I have no need for such," Cymberly protested.

"One never knows, dear," Anna Louisa said.

"An' zee co-lor is so right for zee ma'mselle." The dressmaker's atrocious accent contrasted with her lovely creations.

"Well, there is that," Cymberly conceded, holding the fabric next to her face and observing the effect in the looking glass. It was a soft, mossy green confection that complemented her hazel eyes. "All right. I shall have it, though heaven knows where I shall wear it."

Into the spirit of the excursion now, she ended by ordering several items, including day dresses, a cloak, a riding habit, and, of course, the ball gown. From the dressmaker, Anna Louisa dragged her—protesting less now—from shop to shop for gloves, shawls, slippers, and other absolutely necessary items to complete their new wardrobes. They had been trying on bonnets for some time in a millinery shop when a new customer entered.

"Cymberly? Oh, my goodness, it *is* you!" Suzanne, Lady Kirkwood, enfolded her former school friend in a tight embrace. "Why, you naughty puss. How dare you return to London and not let me know! Where are you staying? When will you come to visit? May we go for an ice now? Oh, I am so *glad* to see you. I have missed you dreadfully."

Finally, she paused.

Laughing, Cymberly returned her hug. "Slow down, Suzanne! You remember my grandmother?"

"Yes. Mrs. Winthrop, is it not? You tolerated two quite hoydenish girls for three weeks one summer."

Anna Louisa smiled and extended her hand. "I loved every minute of it, my lady. It is Mrs. Truesdale now. I remarried several years ago."

"Oh, I beg your pardon. I am glad to see both of you. You will join me now at Gunther's? We have *so* much to catch up on."

Cymberly looked at her grandmother and, catching her nod of assent, readily agreed. They spent a very pleasant hour with the Countess of Kirkwood.

That evening, Anna Louisa politely stifled a yawn as the two sat in the drawing room.

"What a wonderful day this has been," she said. "I must say, I need to get out more."

Cymberly smiled. "You are a sneak and a prevaricator, love. I know very well your aim was to get *me* out."

"Oh, and I thought I was being so very clever."

Cymberly reached to squeeze her hand. "I loved it. And I needed it. Thank you. I promise not to be so self-absorbed in future."

"Oh, my dear, I never meant . . ."

"No, of course you did not. But I *have* been feeling sorry for myself, and that must stop."

"Your father would be so proud of you."

The next morning Cymberly started reading the newspapers again. An article on a hospital for veterans captured her attention. The editor chastised his fellow citizens severely for neglecting those who had given so much for England.

That afternoon, Cymberly presented herself at the hospital to volunteer whatever help she could provide. The hospital administrator received her civilly and sat her in his office, but it was apparent he was not welcoming her overmuch.

"Miss Winthrop, you have no idea what a woman of your class would be getting into here."

"I think I do. The newspaper suggested you need help."

"Well, yes. We do." The man ran a finger around his cravat. "But . . . well . . . it should have specified the need for money and political support."

"I see. But I am sure there are other needs in a hospital and I know I—"

"Surely you know, Miss Winthrop, that there are generally two kinds of women performing tasks in a hospital—nuns and women of . . . uncertain virtue."

"That *is* a pity, is it not?"

"Now, Miss Winthrop." The man was turning red in the face. "The men we care for have been *soldiers*. A rough lot, they can be."

"Yes, I know."

Suddenly there was knock on the door behind her and someone entered without waiting for a response from the man at the desk.

"Edwards, I need—"

Cymberly whirled on recognizing the voice. "Dr. Cameron! How nice to see you."

Cameron took both her hands in his. "Miss Winthrop. *You* are just the tonic some of my patients need."

"Now, see here, Cameron—" the administrator began.

"I have been trying to convince Mr. Edwards that I might be of some service here," Cymberly said. "Perhaps you can put in a word for me."

"Edwards, don't be a fool," Cameron said bluntly. "You have heard that Wellington's presence on a battlefield is worth thousands of troops?"

"Well, yes, but what is that to say of—"

"This lady's presence in a hospital is worth dozens of physicians. She was invaluable to us in the Peninsula."

"Well, but—"

"We need her."

Edwards threw up his hands in defeat. "All right. All right."

"Thank you, Mr. Edwards." Cymberly rose and extended her hand to Edwards and Cameron in turn. "Dr. Cameron. I shall see you in the morning."

She smiled and knew it to be a smile of genuine happiness.

Twenty

Led by the Prince Regent, who now viewed himself as a bona fide war hero, the *ton* was in a fair way of making a cake of itself over its newest favorite, Wellington. Parliament had voted him the title of duke and a generous monetary award. In July, the Prince held a grand ball to fete the new duke.

With only a slight limp now—and then only when he had overexerted himself—Geoffrey had come to town to join in the celebrations. He had other missions to complete, as well. He spent a good deal of time with the Chadwyck solicitor and bankers. The earl wanted the eventual transition to go smoothly.

When he became a titled landowner, Geoffrey fully intended to take his place in the House of Lords. Already armed with ideas about reforms he thought necessary, he deliberately cultivated men who would share those views.

Also, the former rifleman major made himself available to men who had been in his Peninsular command. He saw that many of them had jobs, some at Hartwell, others elsewhere. He interceded at the War Office for pensions due former soldiers or their widows. He visited those who were still in the hospital.

As an eligible bachelor and the known heir to one of the richest titles in the realm, he was much in demand by hostesses of the *ton*. Initially, he accepted every invitation that came his way, hoping to encounter Cymberly at some soiree or another. She never appeared. He made discreet inquiries, but no one with whom he talked knew where she was, though many recalled her from former times.

"Lovely girl."

"Is she not the one turned down Taraton?"

"Went off to the Peninsula."

"Married some soldier, I heard."

"Had her come-out with Renfrow's girl."

At last, a name he could follow up on. But when he called at the Renfrow residence, he found the knocker had been removed from the door. A member of the skeletal staff told him the Renfrows were in the country because of an illness in the family.

He went to the War Office. No. Sorry. No one knew the whereabouts of General Winthrop's daughter.

Benjamin Wilson and the lovely Angelina had not seen her, but they, too, had only recently come to town. They knew nothing of Cymberly, but if Geoffrey should find her, he would remember them to her, would he not?

At the Brantleys' ball, he ran into Howard Williams.

"Heard you were in town," Williams said. "The Peer is making quite a splash, is he not? A duke yet."

"He earned it," Geoffrey said.

"That he did."

As they discussed other officers with whom they had served in the Peninsula, Geoffrey asked casually, "Does your wife see any of the other women who were with us in Spain?"

"She encounters that old harridan Mrs. *Colonel* Gordon-Smythe occasionally, I think. Heaven help you if you forget the rank her husband holds. But I imagine you had in mind a certain general's daughter, eh?"

"As a matter of fact, I did." Lord, did it show that much?

"Wait here a moment and I shall try to bring Juliana to

you so you can ask her." Williams began to weave his way through the crush of Brantley guests.

When the Williamses returned, Geoffrey was trying politely to rid himself of an ambitious mama and her simpering young daughter.

"Howard tells me you were asking about Cymberly," Juliana said as soon as the encroaching mother and child were dispatched.

"Yes. Chadwyck has some business with her, and we have not been able to locate her."

"Oh, I see. *Chadwyck* has business with her," Juliana said in a knowing tone.

"Julie, behave. Just tell the man what he needs to know." Her husband's words were stern, but his tone was laughing. "Women!" he said to Geoffrey.

Juliana became serious. "I am truly sorry. I have not seen her since our return. Her godmother is Lady Renfrow. You might consult her."

"I tried. The Renfrow house is closed. The viscount and his wife are in the country."

"Hmm." Juliana tapped her fan against her cheek. She looked around the room somewhat vacantly, and then her eyes widened in recognition. Both her husband and Geoffrey followed her gaze to observe a stunning couple just entering the ballroom. "Ah, she might know."

"Who?" Geoffrey and Howard asked in unison.

"The Countess of Kirkwood. Cymberly once mentioned her as a school friend."

"A school friend? Not likely," her husband scoffed.

"It is worth a try," Juliana said. "Let me see if I can arrange something."

Nearly an hour later Geoffrey, assuming Juliana's efforts had failed, was considering taking his leave when the Williamses reappeared.

"In Brantley's library in ten minutes," Juliana said.

When the three of them entered the library, the Kirkwoods

were already there. Juliana made the introductions and there was a bit of small talk. Then the Williamses excused themselves and left.

"Mrs. Williams suggested you had business with my wife," Kirkwood said, standing protectively near the beautiful blond woman.

"Yes. Thank you for agreeing to see me. I am trying to locate Miss Cymberly Winthrop, and Mrs. Williams suggested you might be able to help me."

"I see," Lady Kirkwood said in a neutral voice.

"Have you seen her? Is she all right? Can you give me her direction?" He hoped he did not sound overly eager, but Lady Kirkwood and her husband both seemed to be weighing his words.

"Yes, I have seen her," the lady said slowly. "And she is fine."

"Can you—will you give me her direction?"

"I am not sure I am free to do that," Cymberly's friend said, glancing at her husband. "You are Chadwyck's heir, are you not?"

"Yes, and it is partly on the earl's behalf that I must see her." Geoffrey knew instantly this was a mistake, for Lady Kirkwood's expression turned stony.

"You must be aware that Cymberly has nothing to do with her grandfather."

"I am aware, though I had not realized the degree of estrangement until recently."

"I doubt Cymberly's feelings on that head will have changed." Her tone suggested the discussion was ended.

"Please, Lady Kirkwood. I need your help." God help him, he was *begging.* "Cymberly—Miss Winthrop—saved my life. It is important that *I* see her."

Lady Kirkwood raised her brows at his familiar use of Cymberly's name, and something in his voice must have touched her, for her tone was more sympathetic as she said, "I am not sure I can help you, Major Ryder."

"She saved your life?" Lord Kirkwood asked.

"Yes, she did." Geoffrey gave them a brief summary, carefully omitting the horrors of the battlefield, but he could see both understood the nature of his omissions.

"She never told me," Lady Kirkwood said.

"I am not surprised," Geoffrey replied. "Perhaps you understand now why it is important to me that I see her?"

"Yes, I think I do understand, Major." She paused. "I cannot give your her direction without first securing her permission to do so. However, I shall see her soon and I will get word to you."

Geoffrey gave her his card, which she tucked into her reticule as the three of them returned to the ballroom.

"No! Absolutely not," Cymberly said in answer to Lady Kirkwood's question.

Suzanne had called the very next day and relayed Geoffrey's desire to see Cymberly.

"Now you have piqued my interest. In fact, both of you have. He says you saved his life and you are beyond vehement in refusing to see him. He seemed quite nice to me. And despite those scars, he is a very handsome man."

"Handsome is as handsome does." Cymberly sounded sanctimonious even to her own ears.

"Do not dare quote platitudes to me, Cymberly Winthrop. I have known you far too long for that."

"I apologize."

"So—are you going to tell me about you and Major Ryder?"

"There is nothing to tell."

"Yes, there is. You may be unwilling to share with me, but I am quite convinced there is much to tell."

"Suzanne . . ." Cymberly felt her resolve weakening. In truth, she *wanted* to talk, and she and Suzanne had shared their secrets for years.

"Come on, Cymberly. I told you when I found out where babies come from."

Cymberly laughed at this bit of silliness and caved in. "All right. But you are *not* to give him my direction. I want your promise."

"Is it that important?"

"Yes. Promise."

"As you wish. I promise."

Once she started, the whole story came pouring out. Her father's death; Reggie's courtship; Geoffrey's rescuing her not once, but twice; and, finally, Reggie's death. She also told Suzanne of Mary Beth and Tommy and her work with the wounded.

Suzanne listened intently, with tears in her eyes at times. When Cymberly had poured it all out, Suzanne hugged her.

"Cymberly, I had no idea. You have been through so much."

"No more than many others. But you do understand why I cannot see Geoffrey—Major Ryder—do you not?"

"He offered for you?"

"Only because he felt I had been compromised. Not because he cares for me."

"Well, my goodness, Cymberly, you spent the night with him. You *were* compromised. This was far worse than the incident with Lord Taraton."

"Do not *you* go all missish on me. Nothing happened! I will not have some man forced to marry me no matter . . ." Her voice trailed off.

"No matter what your own feelings may be?"

"You always did cut right to the core. You are right, of course. My feelings are definitely involved, but they cannot matter."

"That bit of convoluted reasoning escapes me entirely," Suzanne declared, her voice laced with irony.

"He does not love me." Cymberly felt herself blushing as she added, "I doubt not he wants me, but that alone is not enough for a marriage. But even if it were, I could not marry *him*."

"Why not? You do care for him, do you not?"

Cymberly sighed. "Yes, Suzanne, I do. We are not allowed to *choose* whom we will love, are we? However, we *can* choose whom we will marry. I shall never marry Geoffrey Ryder."

"Even though you love him?"

"Were you not listening? He does not love me. Besides, he is a Ryder. He is Chadwyck's heir, for heaven's sake."

"What has *that* to do with anything?" Suzanne's tone was disbelieving and challenging. "He is not Romeo, and you, my friend, are not Juliet."

"True. And irrelevant, for Major Ryder caused the death of the man I intended to marry. We—I— could not possibly be happy with such a terrible thing between us."

"You are quite, quite sure you have the full story on that?"

"Oh, yes." Her voice caught on a sob, but she quickly regained her composure. "I had a firsthand report and it was never denied."

"Cymberly, I am so very sorry."

Cymberly smiled weakly and braced her shoulders. "Never mind. I shall get over it—eventually. Now tell me about the latest achievement in the Kirkwood nursery."

Three mornings a week, Cymberly reported to the hospital, where she would deliver food trays, write letters for patients, or read to them. The men eagerly awaited her reading of the newspapers. They loved it when there was mention of Lord Wellington or some other military notable. And they unabashedly reveled in popular gothic novels, sympathizing with dauntless heroines and booing dastardly villains.

The hospital was not a pleasant place. Privately, Cymberly thought England treated these men as mere goods to be warehoused, preferably out of sight. The windows were small and located high on walls which had been whitewashed in the distant past. There were too many beds in each ward, all filled.

The most depressing thing about the place was the smell. The staff tried but could not obliterate the effect of the combined odors of sweat, urine, infection, and medications. Burning candles helped camouflage the smell, and Cymberly brought in bouquets of flowers.

Her work at the hospital filled a void left when Tommy went to his grandparents. Having others appreciate her efforts, as the patients universally did, was heartening. The regular staff were at first skeptical of another do-gooder society female, but they came to grudging admiration and grateful acceptance. Soon enough, Miss Winthrop's suggestions were treated as welcome orders, especially as Dr. Cameron invariably approved her ideas.

The most popular suggestion with patients was taking those who could be moved out to the garden. Lunch was sometimes served here, turning these small excursions into impromptu picnics. In truth, it was not much of a garden, but green grass and a few trees provided a welcome change from the closed atmosphere of hospital wards.

At first, the patients blended together in an amorphous group, but gradually they became individuals, each with his own dreams and his own story. She came to know several who had served with men she knew well—with Sergeant MacIver, Captain Wilson, Lieutenant Fleming, and Major Ryder. One or two of the older men had served with her father in India. In general, the men had the usual complaints and stories about their fellow soldiers. Cymberly often listened, only half attending as they traded tales among themselves.

One day it dawned on her that, while they had much to say about almost any military personality mentioned, they rarely spoke of Lieutenant Fleming in her presence. They talked freely of this captain's courage, that major's spit-and-polish uniform, a certain general's infamous cowardice, a sergeant's rifle expertise—but they avoided speaking of Reggie Fleming in any connection.

This fact became even more intriguing when she learned that two of them had been wounded in the skirmish that cost Reggie his life, and there were others in the ward who had served there but were wounded in later encounters. Most of these same men manifested a case of hero-worship regarding Major Ryder, the very man who had ordered them into that battle and others.

She finally shrugged and decided they avoided mentioning Reggie out of deference to what they thought her feelings for him had been.

The new dresses arrived, and Cymberly was surprised at how much they improved her spirits. Knowing that she presented a striking appearance, she more readily acceded to her grandmother's suggestions for outings, though Cymberly did not accept any of the few *ton* invitations that came her way.

One evening, Lord and Lady Kirkwood invited Cymberly and her grandmother to join them for a theater outing. Cymberly looked forward to seeing Mr. Kean perform.

The evening turned out to be a disaster.

Seated with the others in the Kirkwood box, Cymberly looked eagerly, albeit discreetly, around the theater and found herself staring into the familiar gray eyes of Geoffrey Ryder, who was directly across from her in another box. Attired in stylish evening wear, he was incredibly attractive. Flustered, she nodded her head in a distant greeting and quickly lowered her eyes. Then a thought struck her, and the look she now gave her friend was both inquiring and accusing.

"Suzanne, did you know Geoffrey Ryder would be here this evening?" She kept her voice low. "Is that why you invited us?"

Suzanne looked uncomfortable. "Well, yes. I suspected he might be here, but I had already invited you."

"And you just forgot to mention it to me, is that it?"

"I did not forget. I simply did not think you would be so pudding-hearted as to cancel our engagement because of the presence in the audience of someone you find odious. Perhaps I was wrong."

"I do not find him odious, but you might have given me the choice." Cymberly gave Suzanne a look of reprimand.

"Choice of what, dear? Is something wrong?" Mrs. Truesdale asked.

Cymberly patted her hand. "No, Grandmother. Nothing is wrong. I think the curtain is going up now."

Mrs. Truesdale gave her granddaughter a penetrating look. Then their attention was diverted to the stage.

Geoffrey knew she would be here, but seeing her took his breath away momentarily. Her hair was arranged in a fashionable style that offered a frame of curls about her face but left her neck bare. She wore a low-cut gown of deep gold; her only adornment was a simple diamond pendant and diamond earrings.

Suzanne had sent him the promised note after seeing Cymberly.

I am very sorry that I cannot provide the information you requested. Miss Winthrop was quite adamant in refusing her permission at this time.

"At this time." Did that mean she seemed inclined to relent at some other time? He wanted to discuss the matter with Lady Kirkwood, but did not feel he could impose on her further.

However, two days later, he attended a dinner party given by Lord and Lady Meacham. Among the guests were Lord Kirkwood and his lovely wife. When the gentlemen rejoined the ladies after dinner, Lady Kirkwood nudged her husband into a conversation with Major Ryder.

"Are you interested in theater, Major Ryder?" Lady Kirkwood asked.

"I admit to such a weakness occasionally," he said.

"Have you seen the new production of Shakespeare's *Othello?* I am told it is quite well done," she went on.

"No, I have not. Perhaps I shall make a point of doing so, though," he answered in a polite tone. He *did* enjoy the theater, but had not planned going any time in the immediate future.

"Kirkwood and I have invited some special friends to join us on Thursday next for a performance. Perhaps we shall see you there."

Geoffrey gazed at her, raising an eyebrow quizzically. Lady Kirkwood gave him a slight nod.

"Perhaps you shall," he said, grinning.

Securing an invitation for an evening at the theater was easy. The fact that his hosts had strong military ties—and a marriageable daughter—had facilitated his request. He had no real interest in the girl, and he knew her interests to be settled elsewhere, but it never hurt for a young lady to be seen in the company of an eminently eligible *parti.*

He missed Cymberly during the first interval. He had gone round to her box, but when he got there, she had gone. He wandered the halls, but did not see her. Even before the curtain fell for the second interval, he was standing outside the door to the Kirkwood box. The door opened and Lord Kirkwood stepped out.

"Ah, Ryder. Suzanne told me they had missed you earlier."

Geoffrey's smile was a bit grim. "By design, I would wager."

Kirkwood shrugged and held the door for him. "I am off to get some refreshments for the ladies."

Geoffrey stepped inside, aware that a good number of eyes

were drawn to this box. After all, there were two very beautiful young women on display here.

"Good evening, Lady Kirkwood, Miss Winthrop," he said, drawing their attention.

Cymberly gasped, but seemed to recover her aplomb quickly enough.

Lady Kirkwood extended her hand in greeting. "Major Ryder. How nice to see you again. Are you enjoying the play? Are you acquainted with Mrs. Truesdale?"

The introduction made and greetings exchanged, he turned to Cymberly. "Miss Winthrop, might I have a word with you, please?" He was sure her sense of decorum in such a public place would preclude her refusing this request.

She rose and said to her grandmother, "I shall be just outside." Once the two of them were in the hall, he steered her to a semideserted spot and stood with his back toward any others wandering about, thus effectively shielding her and affording them some privacy.

"Well, now that you have me all but trapped, what is it you desire?" she asked.

You. I want you, some inner voice screamed, but aloud he calmly said, "I wish to call upon you to discuss some unfinished business."

"I was not aware of any unfinished business between us." Her voice seemed carefully neutral.

"There is such, and you well know it." He was trying to hold his temper in check. "This is neither the time nor the place, but if you will allow me only a few minutes of your time . . ."

She sighed in what sounded like resignation. "All right."

"Tomorrow morning, perhaps?"

"No, I cannot be available in the morning."

"Tomorrow afternoon, then?"

"That will be fine." She gave him her direction. "Now, if you will excuse me . . ."

She returned to the box, having dismissed him as one

might an errant schoolboy. He gritted his teeth. How had he ever imagined himself in love with a woman who thought so little of him?

In love?

Where in thunderation had *that* notion come from?

Impossible.

He made his way back to his hosts for this evening. Having made apologetic excuses, he hailed a hackney outside the theater and rode home in a towering rage.

He could not have said with any degree of honesty how much of his rage was directed at her and how much at himself.

Twenty-one

Her mind in turmoil, Cymberly was quiet in the carriage on the return ride as her grandmother and the Kirkwoods kept up polite conversation. Seeing Geoffrey was more unsettling than she had anticipated. Suzanne was right. He *was* devastatingly handsome, the scars notwithstanding. They merely added character.

Character?

In a man who did not think twice about deliberately sending others into mortal danger? A man who used that danger to his own ends?

All right, then. The *appearance* of character.

Whatever it was, she could not deny her reaction to him. Merely seeing him across the theater had sent a thrill through her. She had been intensely jealous of the comely young woman he seemed to accompany. Standing near him in the hall had been exquisite torture. She would have to be on her guard tomorrow.

On their arrival at Truesdale House, Lord Kirkwood handed both Cymberly and her grandmother down. Then his wife unexpectedly exited the carriage, despite the late hour.

"Cymberly, might I have a word with you?" Suzanne asked.

"Of course."

"I shall just say good night to all of you," Mrs. Truesdale

said. "Thank you, Lady Kirkwood, Lord Kirkwood, for a wonderful treat."

"I shall wait here in the foyer for you, my dear," Kirkwood said to his wife as she and Cymberly went into the library.

"What is it?" Cymberly asked.

"I am concerned that you may be upset with me over Major Ryder's presence this evening."

"Should I be?"

"If you *are* upset, yes, I bear some blame. I did not give him your direction, but I did hint you might be at the theater tonight."

"Even though you knew I would not welcome seeing him?"

"Please do not be angry with me, Cymberly. I just felt so *sorry* for him, you see . . ."

"Sympathy won out over loyalty. Is that it?" Cymberly was not quite ready to put her irritation aside.

"That is a rather extreme way of putting it."

"I suppose it is," Cymberly conceded. "And in truth, Suzanne, I am more annoyed with myself than with you. I agreed to see him."

"And now you are having second thoughts?"

"Oh, yes." It was an understatement.

"You could send him a note not to come. Or simply not be at home."

"No. I agreed."

"I am sorry to have pushed you into this. I *do* think it for the best, but I should have stayed out of it."

"Perhaps it is for the best. I would probably have encountered him somewhere, somehow. Better sooner than later."

"You do have unresolved feelings, do you not?" Suzanne's tone was gentle.

"Yes. Best I deal with those head on, too. So—I may end by thanking you for your meddling, my dear friend."

"What are friends for?" Suzanne gave a light laugh. "I *am* glad you forgive me."

Cymberly gave her a hug and said, "Go on, now. We have kept Richard waiting quite long enough."

That night Cymberly slept fitfully. Her nightmares, which had abated recently, returned. The next morning she rose early, but her grandmother was already in the breakfast room when she entered.

"Did you not sleep well, my dear?" the older woman asked.

"Well enough, I suppose. Why do you ask? Do I have circles under my eyes?"

"You look a bit tired is all. And last night you seemed quite preoccupied. I hope you are not working too hard at that hospital." Mrs. Truesdale had voiced this concern several times.

"No, Grandmother. I am not working too hard." She spared her grandmother the truth—work with the patients was the only thing giving her life meaning and purpose right now.

"I assume Major Ryder is a member of your mother's family. I do not recall her or Charles mentioning him, though."

"He is Chadwyck's heir."

"Not Chadwyck's son, though. I remember when your mother learned of her only brother's death."

"No. Major Ryder is a very distant connection, but he *is* the heir."

Something in her voice caused her grandmother to look at Cymberly sharply. "Surely you do not hold that against him?"

"Not precisely. It is just that I want nothing to do with Chadwyck or anyone connected to him."

"Oh, dear. You must not allow your bitterness against Chadwyck to spill over to another."

"It is difficult not to, Grandmother. That old man's rejection was a source of pain to Mama until she died. I even wrote him of her illness, and he failed to make any response whatsoever."

"Still, Major Ryder is not Chadwyck."

"Yet."

Her grandmother gave her an oblique look and changed the subject.

Cymberly thought she could put the man out of her mind until the afternoon. However, when she arrived at the hospital, he was the main topic of discussion among the patients, for he had visited the previous day. Apparently he had spent quite some time reminiscing with several and giving them news of others with whom they had served. It was "Major Ryder this" and "Major Ryder that" until she thought she would go mad.

She told herself she would not be the least bit nervous about his visit. However, it took three changes of outfits and much recombing of her hair before she was satisfied with her appearance in a simple gown of blue sprigged muslin.

He called promptly at the appointed hour and was shown into the drawing room, where Cymberly sat with her grandmother and three other guests, friends of Mrs. Truesdale. Carrying a small packet, he was dressed smartly in a dark blue superfine coat and buff-colored pantaloons. A lighter blue waistcoat and crisp white cravat gave him a stylish but casual air. Cymberly felt her whole body respond to his presence.

Introductions and greetings accomplished, Cymberly quietly suggested she would show Major Ryder the garden. He picked up the packet he had laid on a small table and, with appropriate apologies to the others, followed her out. Beneath the canopy of a large maple tree, she turned to face him.

"You have particular business with me, Major?"

"Yes. First, on my own behalf, I must thank you for saving my life at Toulouse."

"You give me far too much credit, Major."

"Geoffrey. I believe it was 'Geoffrey' when last we spoke in France. And, no, I think I have given credit where it is due."

"As to that, were we keeping score, you would be far ahead of me, for I seem to remember your rescuing *me* not once, but twice. In any event, you need not have made a special effort to thank me for something almost anyone might have done." She knew she sounded dismissive and curt, but she feared if she let her guard down, she would be lost—lost in the soft gray warmth of his gaze.

His jaw tightened, and he looked over her head for a moment. When he brought his gaze back to hers, his expression was carefully neutral.

"I have also come on behalf of Lord Chadwyck," he said.

Cymberly went rigid with anger. "I thought I had made it perfectly clear to the earl I want nothing to do with him—or his."

"Oh, yes, your rejection has been very clear." Geoffrey sounded both disappointed and disgusted. "However, Chadwyck feels you should have what would have been due your mother and, as his heir, I feel this to be an obligation of the estate." He held out the packet. "The legalities have been handled."

Cymberly backed away, her hands held before her, palms out. "I do not want it. Nor will I take it. The moment my mother died, it was too late for that evil old man. He would not even come to her when she was dying and begging for him." Her voice caught on a sob which she quickly smothered. "I will have nothing from him. I said as much to his solicitor nearly two years ago."

His gray eyes turned hard with an anger of their own and his voice was laced with sarcasm as he asked, "Did it never occur to you, Miss Winthrop, there could be a *reason* 'that evil old man' ignored your summons?"

She turned away, her head high. "I cannot conceive of a single reason he could not have come to his dying daughter's bedside."

"How could you do so? You returned his letters unopened."

"I certainly did!"

"Having made up your mind before you knew any facts, I doubt you could have done otherwise."

"How dare you judge me."

"It is you who seem to make a habit of leaping to judgments about others," he said flatly. He tossed the packet on a nearby bench. "Here. This is yours. Whether you want it or not, the money is in an account in your name. Let it rot there if you wish. Good day, Miss Winthrop."

He gave her an ironic bow and turned to leave. Then he turned back. "By the by, 'that evil old man'? He was seriously ill at the same time as his daughter—your mother—was. He was given your letter three or four weeks later, but it was too late. He recovered then, but perhaps you will be happy to hear he has suffered a relapse. He has not a great deal of time left."

This time he did not turn back.

The chattering birds in the branches above seemed to mock her.

As he went down the front steps of Truesdale House, Geoffrey thought life was looking very bleak. Had he *really* thought he might break through to her on Chadwyck's behalf? Could he have handled the situation differently? Probably. But he doubted the result would have been otherwise.

He thought he understood her feelings toward Chadwyck. The man *had* rejected his daughter and granddaughter early on. That fact remained, no matter how much the old earl regretted it now. He had, however, tried to make amends.

Geoffrey found it difficult to reconcile this unforgiving female with the woman who offered untiring aid to wounded soldiers in the Peninsula, who had braved the horrors of the battlefield, and who had taken in a motherless child.

Behind this stubborn willfulness, he sensed a marked degree of vulnerability. How he had wanted to hold her, to tell her everything would be all right. But he had not dared do so. In truth, had he gotten her in his arms, he might have shaken her till her teeth rattled, trying to break through the wall she had thrown up.

He had been home only a few moments when his butler announced visitors. Geoffrey groaned. The last thing he wanted was to entertain guests, but on learning these guests were Benjamin Wilson and the lovely Angelina, he readily changed his mind.

"I must say you do not look in the peak of spirits, old man," Wilson said.

"Benjamin!" his wife admonished.

"Well, he doesn't. Just look at him. What has happened to you?"

He gave them an abbreviated account of his two interviews with Cymberly.

Wilson sighed. "Coming home has not been easy for any of us."

"I suppose not," Geoffrey said.

"I do not mind so much for myself as I do for Angelina." Wilson, seated on a settee with his wife, picked up her hand.

"Things are not going well for you?" Geoffrey asked in surprise.

"Benjamin makes too much of a few old cats." Angelina patted her husband's hand reassuringly.

"It just makes me so damned angry. Sorry, darling."

"What are you talking about?" Geoffrey asked.

"I brought my bride to town to make her a part of our wonderful English society."

"What happened?"

"You know how hard it is—or was—for an English officer to get permission to marry a Spanish woman?"

"Yes. You and I both approved in principle. Think how many vulnerable young cnsigns and lieutenants might have been victimized by unscrupulous women. Many officers were just boys—less than twenty."

"But there were always exceptions."

"Of course. And your Angelina is most assuredly one of them."

"Not according to the *ton* tabbies," Wilson said bitterly.

"How could they possibly have formed a negative view of Angelina?"

"They had it formed for them by the likes of Mrs. Major Horton and Mrs. Colonel Gordon-Smythe."

"Unbelievable," Geoffrey said. "What could they have against your wife?"

"The same thing they have against Miss Winthrop." Wilson's tone became mincingly sarcastic. "Proper ladies do not follow the drum—and should they find themselves doing so, perish the thought *they* should have anything to do with vulgar soldiers. And, of course, foreign women are no better than they should be."

"It is not so very bad," Angelina protested gently.

"Yes, it is," her husband said vehemently. "And it is even worse for Cymberly."

Geoffrey raised his head. "Why?"

"Because 'Mrs. Major' and 'Mrs. Colonel' have added the juicy tidbits about her being alone with a certain major and then refusing an offer from the ever-so-eligible heir to the Earl of Chadwyck."

Geoffrey ran his hand through his hair. "Good grief."

"Yes. The vultures have had a feeding frenzy." Again Wilson aped the tones of imaginary gossips. "The girl has a very high opinion of herself—turning down first Taraton and then the Chadwyck heir. You know, her maternal grandfather smelled of the shop." Then he added in his own voice, "It is appalling. Angelina and I are going home in a few days. Our village people are less likely to be so vicious."

"I realized there was some talk, but not that it had reached such proportions."

"I doubt many would say anything directly to *you*. The word is out about your putting Porterman in his place."

"So you are planning to run away, is that it?"

"Not exactly. We need to get back. This situation is merely making us happier to leave the *ton* behind us."

In the next few days, when Geoffrey saw the Wilsons at

social affairs, he was more aware of the attitudes of others toward the couple—that is, the attitudes of the women toward Angelina, for gentlemen were rarely ostracized to any degree. He was also keenly aware of Cymberly's absence.

"You must know, Major," Lady Kirkwood said, "that at least part of the reason we so rarely see Cymberly in company is by her own design." The two of them were chatting during the interlude at a musicale.

"I suspected as much," Geoffrey replied.

Lady Kirkwood clearly supported Geoffrey's efforts to renew his acquaintance with her friend. For his part, Geoffrey welcomed the Kirkwoods' friendship. He found Suzanne knowledgeable and charming and her husband, already a member of Parliament, shared many of Geoffrey's views.

"I have invited her repeatedly," Suzanne continued. "Occasionally, she will go driving in the park with me, but she sends regrets for affairs involving others."

"Men who have seen prolonged battle duties sometimes go into a period of withdrawal," Geoffrey said.

"You think this is what is happening with Cymberly?"

"It could be. She has been through some very trying experiences and seen more suffering than anyone should—especially a lady of her background."

"Is there nothing we can do?"

"Give her time. Time is ever the great healer. And keep on doing as you have been. Friendship is also a great healer."

Suzanne touched his arm and said softly, "I think Cymberly has a better friend in you than she realizes."

Cymberly continued to work at the hospital in the mornings. In the afternoons, she occasionally agreed to an outing with her grandmother or Suzanne. She also regularly visited Tommy, who was blossoming under the loving guidance of doting grandparents. The Renfrows having returned to town, Lady Renfrow made it a point to call upon her goddaughter.

Cymberly welcomed Lady Renfrow but suspected her godmother of looking for further grist for the gossip mill.

Cymberly knew the talk about her had intensified with Major Ryder's arrival in town. The season had been extended this year by the victory celebrations, and the *ton* delighted in tales of people involved to any degree in England's triumph over Napoleon.

"Is it true you turned down an offer from Chadwyck's heir?" Lady Renfrow had never been one to hold her tongue judiciously.

"Yes, but it was not a matter of great significance."

"My dear girl, are you quite out of your mind? Such a match that would be!"

"I had my reasons. So please, ma'am, may we discuss something else?"

"All right. What is this that I hear of your working in a hospital? That will simply never do."

"It does very well for me." Cymberly raised her chin. "I worked with wounded men in the Peninsula."

"Yes, my dear, but this is London, and your continuing to spend time with so many men from the lower orders does not reflect well on you."

"In the eyes of society, you mean."

"Of course. Who else would care?"

"Who indeed?" Cymberly struggled to keep her impatience in check.

"You will give it up, will you not?"

"I am afraid not. Besides, I do not go into society much."

"But, my dear, you cannot relish being the subject of so much talk."

"No, of course not, but I cannot control what comes from the mouths of others. The talk will die down with the *next* nine days' wonder. Meanwhile"—Cymberly allowed herself an impish grin—"I shall not take it amiss if you pretend not to know me."

"Pretend not to—heavens! I could not disavow my own goddaughter!"

Hearing genuine concern in Lady Renfrow's tone, Cymberly felt more amiable toward her than she had earlier.

"For your sake, I promise I will do nothing intentionally to cause the *ton* to remark further on my activities or character," Cymberly said, but her promise mollified Lady Renfrow only partially.

"I do wish you would allow me to host a dinner party to reintroduce you to society. Just a small gathering." Lady Renfrow here renewed an idea she had broached earlier. "I could not do so well as produce an heir to an earldom, but I can think of several eligible gentlemen who would welcome an invitation to an affair in your honor."

Cymberly laughed. "I see. Now that you have Amabel settled as a baroness, you intend to turn your matchmaking skills in my direction."

"Well, why should I not do so? I am confident your mama would have me do that much for you."

"Perhaps she would have, but I do not." Cymberly's voice was sharper than she intended, so she added more gently, "Truly, I do appreciate what you are trying to do, but I cannot allow it just yet."

"Do not delay your return to society too long, my dear. There are those who would say you are already perilously close to being on the shelf."

Since this comment came free of any hint of malice, Cymberly merely smiled and said, "I know. However, you need not worry on my behalf, my lady. I am not in the position of some women who simply *must* marry. My father left me well situated."

"Well then, there will be little problem finding a husband for you."

"Not quite yet, though." Cymberly chuckled at her godmother's single-mindedness.

The idea of a husband was out of the question. Once, of

course, she had dreamed of a husband and children for herself. Along with other young girls, she had conjured up an image of a handsome, brave man who would capture her heart and carry her off to wedded bliss. The trouble was now the image had a face—Geoffrey Ryder's. And that would never do.

One day she was late leaving the hospital. Many of the patients had few or no visitors, but on this day a young man named Osmund had a visitor Cymberly knew—Ensign Warren.

Warren was dressed in civilian attire and seemed to fancy himself a veritable "pink of the *ton.*" He wore a bright green coat over tan pantaloons. His waistcoat was a highly embroidered canary yellow and his shirt points so high he could hardly turn his head. His cravat was tied in an intricate style and sported a flashy yellow jewel. Cymberly suspected he came to the hospital in part to preen before his former friends.

Warren joined Osmund and two others in the garden, where a number of other small groups of patients and their visitors had gathered, some playing cards, some just talking. Osmund insisted Miss Winthrop join his group, which seemed bent on showing off their fine friend to her and to others. There were occasional catcalls from group to group, and the Osmund lot commanded a good deal of attention.

"I say, Warren," Osmund said, admiring the other man's garb, "did you sell out? Dressed like that, I mean."

"As soon as I could," Warren replied.

"How'd you manage it? I thought all us younger sons tended to make a church mouse seem well off."

"My godmother died while I was in the Peninsula. She left me a bit of blunt. And"—he paused dramatically—"I had a bit from the hoard at Vitoria."

"You sly dog!" Osmund said enviously.

"Good job Nosey did not know about it," another said.

Warren grinned smugly and looked around, apparently to see that others knew of his cleverness and good fortune. He smiled flirtatiously in Cymberly's direction, but his expression sobered as his gaze caught something behind her.

"What is *he* doing here?" Warren asked.

Others turned to look and Cymberly caught her breath. Geoffrey. Ryder's gaze caught hers for a moment, then swept over her companions. Giving her the briefest of nods, he sought someone in a group some distance away. She noticed he handed packets to two men and then left.

"Oh, him," one of the other men in Osmund's group said. "The major comes two, three times a week."

"I am surprised he has the nerve to show himself among real soldiers," Warren sneered, glancing at Osmund.

"Yes, after Salamanca and that business you told me about at the pass," Osmund said.

Not wanting to hear any more, Cymberly rose. "I must be going."

"Hey, there, Osmund," called someone nearby. "You'd be wise not to believe ever'thing you hear."

"Aw, Cathcart, what d'you know?" Osmund's tone held challenging scorn.

"More'n you, it seems."

As Cymberly made her way out of the garden, she hardly heard the calls of "good-bye" and "see you soon" around her. Only later, as she settled in the carriage, did certain snatches of conversation register with her. She knew one of the voices was Cathcart's.

"Someone oughta tell her."

"He wouldn't like that. You know what he said."

"It ain't fair."

"Damned unfair, but that's how he wants it."

"It ain't right."

Now what was that all about?

Twenty-two

Against her will, Cymberly's mind turned again and again to that scene in her grandmother's garden. The implications of what Geoffrey had said of Lord Chadwyck caused her to feel profoundly chagrined about her behavior toward the old man. She had never had to think of herself as a vindictive person. Yet was that not precisely what she had been in relation to her grandfather?

Adding to the pain of this admission was not only the memory of her father's telling her to be more charitable to Lord Chadwyck, but the thought of her mother, who had tried for years to mend the breach. And what had she done? Willfully ignored her parents' wishes. After all, it was not *Cymberly* who had been directly affected by Lord Chadwyck's rejection.

She had blamed him and had spurned the overtures of a man who apparently wanted to right a wrong. Since when was one Cymberly Winthrop so saintly that she could judge others' motivations so? In addition, he had been ill. Fate had denied him a chance to reconcile with his daughter as they both had wished. Such pain he must have suffered.

With some reluctance, but a sizable degree of curiosity, she examined the documents in the packet Geoffrey had thrown down. She gasped at the contents. Suddenly, Miss Cymberly Anna Elise Winthrop was not just well situated. She was a *very* rich woman.

Now guilt and shame truly threatened to engulf her. Seeing

Major Ryder at the hospital had intensified those feelings. The major seemed to hold her in disgust, and this disturbed her as much as her own disgust for herself. Why did she care so much what *he* thought?

That evening her grandmother, who, Cymberly knew, had been worried about her, finally broke the Winthrop family rule about prying.

"Are you all right, my dear? You seem so . . . well, distant lately."

"I am sorry, Grandmother. Have I been rude?"

"No. Nor did I mean to imply you were," Anna Louisa said, "but I must tell you I *am* concerned. Perhaps it would help if you talked about whatever it is that disturbs you."

"Oh, Gran, I feel so ashamed." The anguish came pouring out with her use of the childhood title. "I have been so wrong."

"About what, love?"

"About my grandfather, Lord Chadwyck." She proceeded to tell Anna Louisa all that Geoffrey had told her of the earl's ill health and of the fortune that was now hers.

"Well," Anna Louisa said, "this does put a different light on his behavior."

"And on mine. I should have been willing to hear him out."

"Yes, you probably should have." Her grandmother's tone was blunt, but gentle. "Luckily, you can mend some of the damage."

"Write him, you mean?"

"Yes."

"I shall. And if he chooses to consign me to the nether regions—well, I deserve no less."

"Now, now. Do not be too hard on yourself. Your reaction was understandable."

"Wrong, but comprehensible, is that it?" Cymberly smiled for the first time in some hours.

Anna Louisa nodded. "Something like that."

"I shall draft the letter tonight."

They sat in silence for a moment. Then Anna Louisa chuckled. "If this gets about, your godmother will redouble her efforts to find you a suitable husband."

Two days later, Cymberly received another jolt to her self-assurance. She had been at the hospital for over an hour and was helping wheel patients out to the garden when Eddie Cathcart touched her hand.

"Could me 'n' Tim talk with you when you finish bringin' the others out?"

"Certainly, Mr. Cathcart." Her smile included Tim Prentiss, who looked worried.

"I don't know, Eddie," she heard Tim say.

A few minutes later, she drew up a wicker chair near the two young men. Eddie had lost a leg at Toulouse and Tim had taken a saber in the chest—a wound which should have killed him and had resulted in breathing difficulties.

"Gentlemen?" she prompted.

They looked at each other. Tim shook his head and said, "I still don't like it. He's gonna be mad as hops."

"Maybe. Maybe not." Eddie sounded determined. He took a deep breath and turned to Cymberly. "I ain't meaning to bring you any pain, Miss, but there's some things you should know about the major."

"Major Ryder?" Cymberly experienced a tremor of apprehension at Cathcart's words and manner.

"Yes. And about Lieutenant Fleming, too."

"Go on, Mr. Cathcart." She did not want to hear this, but something compelled her to listen.

"You weren't told the exact truth about how Fleming died."

"Eddie, I don't think you should do this," Tim cautioned again.

"Got to now, Tim. Miss, you know Fleming caught a bullet at a bridge our unit was guarding?"

"Yes."

"Well, the truth is he only appeared there at the very last minute and then only because the major forced him."

"Yes, I know."

"No! You don't know." Cathcart's voice contained pain and frustration. "There were only about twelve of us on that bridge watch to start with. That would have been enough, if we'd all been there. We waited on our side for hours. Dead boring it was."

"I can imagine," she said.

"So Fleming, he says to Sergeant Miller, 'You stay and keep this watch, just in case. I am convinced there will be no French this night. I shall be at that inn we passed.' He said it real casual-like, but Miller, he didn't like bein' left at the bridge. He'd left that girl, Cosette, at the inn, you see?"

"No, I don't see. What was she doing so near the fighting?"

Cathcart blushed and looked away. "Guess she found camp life boring with the men gone."

"Oh."

"Anyways, Miller, along with me 'n' Tim here and some others, were left at the bridge, and Fleming took four or five of his favorites back to the inn with him."

"Are you saying Lieutenant Fleming left his post?" As a military man's daughter, Cymberly was fully aware of the seriousness of such a breach of conduct.

"Yes, miss. And all because that French girl was leadin' him on."

"I . . . I am not sure I understand." But she did understand. She just did not want to believe.

"I'm real sorry, Miss. He made Miller stay at the bridge so's he could go back to the inn and . . . uh . . . be with Miller's woman. Some other females were there, too."

"They was havin' a real good time back there—and the French were moving up on their side of the bridge." Tim's interjection was saturated with bitterness.

"Tim's right," Eddie said. "We'd begun to take some shots

when the major arrived. When he saw what was happening, he told us to hold on, that there were troops right behind him. Then he rode back to the inn. He roused them boys out o' there right quick and sent 'em back to the bridge. He came with 'em, o' course."

Tim took up the story. "It were some pretty tough fighting, Miss. We wouldn't have made it without the major. Though if we'd all been there when the French first showed up, 'twould have been different."

"We lost eight men there, Miss," Eddie declared quietly. "Two needlessly, for Miller, he shot Lieutenant Fleming, and then a French bullet caught Miller."

"But Ensign Warren told me—"

"Warren!" Eddie spat out the name.

"Warren was with Fleming all the while, and afterward he tried to make himself look good. 'Sides, he hates the major," Tim explained.

"Why?"

" 'Cause Major Ryder had him flogged for assaulting a Spanish woman at Vitoria. Wellington's orders, you know."

"My goodness." Cymberly sat stunned as their simple truths plowed through the lies she had believed. "But the reports . . . nobody said anything . . ."

"The major wanted it that way," Tim said.

"But *why?*"

Eddie gave her a look that was at once questioning and sympathetic. "Because of you—and the general."

"Me? And the gen—what general?"

"General Fleming. The lieutenant's father. He's in the colonies now. Major Ryder served with him in India."

"But . . . *why?*" she asked again.

"The major said people who loved Fleming need not endure the pain of the circumstances of his death. I think that's the way he put it."

Tim renewed his warning. "He ain't gonna like it that anyone knows now, either."

"Miss Winthrop ain't likely to go bandyin' it about. She ain't no chatterbox."

"No, certainly not," she agreed rather absently.

"When I heard that whey-faced scoundrel, Warren, talking t' other day, it seemed to me you might think ill of the major." Eddie's tone was slightly defensive.

"I thank you for confiding in me," she told them as she took her leave.

Cymberly was mortified. She had assumed the worst of a man whose honor and courage were not to be questioned. She recalled the accusations she had hurled at him and the thoughts she had harbored. If only she could pop them back into the box from which they had sprung. But, like Pandora's release of ills on the world, the ugliness could not be recalled.

Would she ever learn not to make snap judgments about people?

Mulling over what Eddie and Tim had said, it occurred to her that Ensign Warren had cleverly accused Major Ryder of the very act Reggie had committed. Her accepting it as fact had made her an instrument of the ensign's devious revenge. Warren's version of the drama had just enough truth to make it credible, never mind that he had not placed the actors in their right places.

Laughing, charming, irresponsible Reggie had also been dishonorable. Had she sensed his deeper faults? Was that why she kept putting him off? He had shown little reluctance to use *her* resources to secure his own ends. But then, many a marriage was arranged so. Still . . .

Reggie's resentment of Major Ryder was rooted in the lieutenant's own shortcomings. While Reggie failed to live up to his father's expectations, Geoffrey, simply following the dictates of his own character, had fulfilled General Fleming's concept of the ideal soldier.

And General Winthrop's as well, she noted in a mental aside. She recalled the respect with which his fellow officers regarded Major Ryder. It contrasted sharply with their tolerant dismissal of the lieutenant. Her beloved father had shown little genuine liking for Reggie, but his last words to her had praised Geoffrey.

So there it was.

She had blindly chosen a shallow scamp over a man of character and honor. What was worse, she had willfully clung to that choice, ignoring niggling doubts about Reggie's character and about her own feelings for him.

Why had no one told her the truth?

She already had the answer to that question. *The people who loved Fleming need not endure the pain . . . But I did not* love *him,* she cried inwardly. *I was fond of him, yes, but never truly in love with him.* She could face this certainty now.

She had treated Geoffrey abominably in rejecting an offer from the only man who could ever lay claim to her heart—*an offer born of obligation, not affection,* she reminded herself.

She deserved the disgust he directed her way. She had no intention of violating his wishes by broadcasting the truth of his honorable behavior, but she could surely extend privately the profound apology she owed him.

For the second time in a few days, Cymberly spent an evening in her room struggling over a difficult letter and admitting her own mistakes. The next morning, she read over what she had written, added a postscript, and quickly sent it off with a servant.

These days Geoffrey deliberately planned his visits to the hospital so he arrived after Cymberly left for the day. Seeing her, knowing of her disdain for him, was simply too painful. Also, he suspected his presence made her uncomfortable.

Returning from a hard ride in the park one morning, he picked up the mail to read during a late breakfast. It included several invitations, some missives regarding estate business, and two letters. One he recognized as coming from Chadwyck. The other he recognized not at all, though the handwriting struck him as feminine. Puzzled, he opened it first, glanced at the signature, and drew in a sharp breath.

Dear Major Ryder,

I know an apology at this stage will seem a paltry gesture. However, having only today learned the circumstances of Lieutenant Fleming's death, I am aware that I misjudged you terribly. I am sincerely sorry for having done so.

Please do not blame those who gave me the truth of the matter. They acted in what they thought to be your best interests. I believe they did the right thing.

Please accept my profound apology.

                                        Miss Cymberly Winthrop

P. S.

You may be interested to know that I have written my grandfather to thank him for his generosity toward me.

Dumbfounded, Geoffrey reread the letter three times. He was almost afraid to read too much into it, but he could not contain a flicker of hope. He marveled at the courage it had taken to write it. And she had written Chadwyck, too. This was the woman with whom he had fallen in love.

He picked up Chadwyck's letter. Sure enough, he had heard from his granddaughter. His tone was at once ecstatic and apprehensive. He implored Geoffrey to approach her and ask her to come to Hartwell for a visit. In fact, Chadwyck proposed to have his sister, the Dowager Baroness Sanford, host a house party "so the gel will not feel pressured or overwhelmed by an old curmudgeon like me."

The next day, not without some trepidation, Geoffrey visited the hospital earlier than usual. He found Cymberly joking with Cathcart and Prentiss and knew immediately from the guilty looks of the men and the apprehension in her just where Miss Winthrop had come by her information.

She seemed embarrassed as she greeted him briefly and quickly excused herself. He saw her later, bustling around among other patients. He sat down and eyed the two young men ruefully and addressed them with a show of sternness.

"You fellows are in fair way of becoming prattle-boxes, I gather."

"I told you so," Prentiss said to his companion.

"Not really, sir." Cathcart sounded defensive. "It . . . well . . . you see, Miss Winthrop was blaming you, an' she deserved the truth."

"Even if it brought her pain?" Geoffrey challenged.

"Well, yes, sir," Cathcart said doggedly. "The truth might be painful, but 'tis usually preferable to a lie. Miss Winthrop, she's a nice lady, a brave lady. She had a right to know."

"Perhaps you are correct," Geoffrey conceded. "She has a lot of stamina, that one."

He could see Cathcart and Prentiss visibly relax.

"She ain't no gabble-grinder," Prentiss said. "If General Fleming hears the truth, it won't be from her."

"No, I suppose not," Geoffrey agreed. He turned the topic to other matters, but checked his watch frequently. When it was time for her to leave, he made sure he was at the door as she came out.

"Miss Winthrop, may I see you home?"

"Why . . . but I have a carriage waiting."

"Send it on, if you please. Perhaps you will take a turn in the park with me?"

She lifted her eyes to his searchingly. "Yes. I will do so gladly." She gave her driver instructions and a message for her grandmother.

Geoffrey handed her into his vehicle, instructed his tiger to take a hackney home, and climbed in beside her. Both were silent as he took the ribbons and set the matched pair of grays into motion.

"Am I to understand we Ryders are back in your good graces?" He glanced at her and saw an embarrassed blush.

"Please, Major. I was wrong—about both of you."

"Geoffrey, remember?"

"Geoffrey," she repeated, and her blush deepened. She looked around, then said, "What a handsome team."

"Handsome is as handsome does," he said with exaggerated piety, then added, "and these two *do* very handsomely." He grinned. So far it was going well.

She gave a rather nervous little laugh and put her hand over her mouth, instantly sober, but she could not quell the twinkle in her hazel eyes.

"What is it?" he asked. She shook her head. "Come on, tell me."

"It is just"—she laughed again—"that is precisely the adage I once used to describe you to Suzanne—" Her eyes turned serious and she looked away.

He waited a moment before prodding, "I gather there is more?"

"I am afraid at the time I did not believe you to *do* handsomely."

"I see." He kept his voice neutral. "And now?"

"Now I know your behavior and motives to be as handsome as those of anyone of my acquaintance—ever," she said in a most sincere tone.

His attention was drawn to the horses as they entered the park. It was early for most of the *ton* to be parading there, but he could see that they had attracted the attention of the few who were. He concentrated on his driving until he had maneuvered them out of the way of horsemen and carriages.

He turned to her and smiled. "Now that you are sufficiently aware of my sterling qualities, may I call on you?"

"Yes, I should like that."

Twenty-three

Each day now Cymberly dressed with more care than was her wont, for each day she was likely to see Geoffrey. If he did not appear at the hospital, he called later in the afternoon. One evening he accompanied her and her grandmother to the opera.

"Major Ryder seems rather marked in his attentions to you, my dear." Mrs. Truesdale's tone was ultracasual as she glanced at Cymberly over the top of her own portion of the newspaper they shared one morning.

Cymberly shifted in her chair, looked at her grandmother, and then looked away. "I think we should not refine upon that too much."

"Oh?"

"No. As you know, Lord Chadwyck has invited you and me to a house party next month. Geoffrey—Major Ryder—is merely sharing the duties as host."

"*Before* we have become guests?"

"It would seem so." Cymberly sounded evasive even to herself.

Anna Louisa gave her a questioning look and went back to her share of the paper. A few minutes later, she said, "Oh, my, it seems Prinny is outdoing himself."

"What has he done now?"

"It is not what he has done, but what he plans," her grandmother replied. "He is to host a ball for military heroes."

"Another one? The *ton* was abuzz earlier with that grand affair at Carlton House. Suzanne told me she had never seen anything so elegantly ostentatious."

"That one was to honor Wellington. This is to honor, it says here, 'other heroes who so gallantly gave of themselves to free England and Europe of a major threat to peace and prosperity.' "

"How interesting. There are certainly enough men who deserve recognition." Cymberly thought of Geoffrey first, then of Mac and Captain Wilson and a host of others.

Reporting to the hospital later, she found the men consumed by the topic. Three gentlemen had visited earlier and talked with them about the Prince Regent's plan to honor lesser known heroes.

"That was thoughtful of them," she responded idly.

Three days later, Miss Winthrop was in a rare taking. She had received a richly engraved invitation bearing the Prince Regent's seal. Such an invitation amounted to a royal summons, so, yes, of course Miss Winthrop would happily accept the Prince's request that she attend a ball honoring Peninsula heroes.

Cymberly immediately went to pour out her apprehension to her bosom friend. "What am I to do, Suzanne? I have not been in company these several weeks, as you well know."

"The first thing to do is accept my dinner invitation for tomorrow evening." Suzanne's tone brooked no objection. "You have been seen in the park with me and with Major Ryder. It is time you widened the circle."

"Suzanne, you *know* there is still a good deal of talk."

"I promise no one would dare embarrass a guest in my home. Besides, I shall protect you—and so will Major Ryder, for I have invited him as well."

Suzanne was as good as her word. By London standards, it was a small dinner party, consisting of some fifteen couples besides the host and hostess. When she first entered the drawing room prior to dinner, Cymberly felt a moment of panic at the utter quiet that greeted the butler's announcement of her name. Suzanne instantly came to her side and deftly drew her into conversation with two other ladies.

Among the guests was Lord Taraton, who eagerly sought her out. David's acceptance, along with the obvious affection of the Kirkwoods, established—or reestablished—Miss Winthrop's credentials. No one mentioned her following the drum or her work with wounded soldiers.

When Major Ryder arrived, she was deep in conversation with Lord Taraton. Glancing up when his name was announced, Cymberly caught a glowering look cross Geoffrey's face. At dinner, he was seated near their hostess with Cymberly at the other end of the table between Lords Kirkwood and Taraton.

"I can see I did not plan the seating well," Suzanne said in an aside to Cymberly as the ladies withdrew from the dining room, leaving the men to their cigars and port.

"What do you mean?" Cymberly asked.

"Major Ryder—the ever-so-delightful Geoffrey—could hardly take his eyes from you," Suzanne teased quietly. "I should have sat him next to you, but as one of Prinny's heroes, I thought to place him in a position of honor."

"Prinny's heroes?"

"You did not know Geoffrey is being honored at this new fete?"

"No. He said nothing to me of it. But I can think of no one who deserves it more."

"Somehow I thought you would feel that way." Suzanne patted her hand and smiled enigmatically.

When the gentlemen rejoined the ladies, Geoffrey seemed determined to be first at seeking the company of Miss Winthrop and securing her as his partner for the card games to follow. Having apparently learned the Kirkwoods had sent their carriage for her earlier, he offered to see her home.

As they bade the Kirkwoods good night, Cymberly

squeezed Suzanne's hand and said, "Thank you. You were right. I need to get out more."

"I told you so." Suzanne grinned smugly and leaned closer to whisper, "I am also right about you and Major Ryder. See that you take advantage of this little *tête à tête* I have arranged."

"Suzanne—" It was a small, plaintive cry from a blushing Cymberly. Then Geoffrey handed her into the Chadwyck carriage and, after instructing the driver, seated himself beside her rather than across from her.

Alone with him in a closed carriage, Cymberly was nervous about such intimacy, but she was also intensely aware of his nearness. His long leg touched hers and he had placed an arm across the back of the seat as he turned slightly to face her. The dim light of the carriage lantern reflected off the planes of his face. His expression was serious. They both spoke at once.

"Cymberly—"

"Geoffrey—"

No further words came. He lifted her chin gently and settled his lips on hers, softly at first, then with increasing depth and hunger. Her whole being strained toward him, seeking the sense of completion, of wholeness his kiss promised. She responded blindly, with a need she had not realized she could feel until now.

He drew her closer, showering kisses on her neck, below her ear, and at the pulsing base of her throat, then brought his lips back to hers. Her hand came up to caress his cheek and bring him nearer. His tongue teased her lips and she instinctively opened, welcoming him.

The death and desolation of the last months diminished to nothingness in the life and fullness of Geoffrey's arms and his kiss. He lifted his head, but did not release her.

"I hope, my love, this means you will not reject my suit this time."

"I . . . I am not sure . . ."

"Not sure? What do you mean you are not sure?" It was more a challenge than a question. He kissed her again, fiercely claiming her lips. "Are you sure now?"

She pushed at his chest and averted her face. "Geoffrey, please. We must be sensible. You cannot marry someone who is only barely acceptable in society."

"I shall marry whom I want—and I want *you,* my dear Miss Winthrop."

"Want?"

"Want. Need. I love you, Cymberly."

"Oh, Geoffrey." Her voice caught on a sob. "I love you, too—with all my heart. But you cannot marry me. It would be disastrous for your political career."

"Pardon me, love, if I doubt that very much." He pulled her head to his shoulder and rested his check against her hair. She drew in the scent of his shaving soap and reveled in his touch. "And," he went on, "even if it were true, I could live without wielding political influence. I cannot live without you."

"Oh, Geoffrey," she whispered again, raising her lips to his, for words alone were inadequate.

He reluctantly relinquished her lips. "Besides, you have not given the *ton* much of a chance since your return."

"I know what they say." She was defensive.

"Never mind a few old tabbies. I am going for a special license in the morning. Please say you will allow us to use it at the earliest possible moment."

"But what about Lord Chadwyck's invitation?"

"I shall take you to Hartwell as my bride. Chadwyck will love it. He already loves you, you know," he added gently.

"No. Geoffrey, this is too fast. Others need you. I cannot let you do this."

"You would sacrifice my happiness because others need me?" His tone a parody of pained outrage, he chuckled and gathered her closer. "That makes little sense, my love."

"Not to you, perhaps." She lifted her chin rebelliously and

he promptly caught her lips again with his. She tried to push him away. "No. Stop. I cannot think clearly when you are kissing me."

"That is the whole idea, my sweet." He ignored her protest, and she was not sorry he did so. "Well? Will you marry me, or no?"

"Let us discuss it again after the Prince's ball."

He sighed. "As you wish. But I must warn you, I shall not readily accept a refusal." He kissed her again, deeply, willing her response. "I had best get you home. A carriage is no place for what I have in mind at the moment."

She laughed softly and snuggled closer. They were both silent until the carriage stopped at her grandmother's house.

As she prepared for bed, Cymberly was deliriously happy. Geoffrey loved her. How he had come to do so was a sweet mystery, but he did, indeed, love her. And she loved him. Oh, my, how she did love him!

Would love be enough, though, when he was thwarted in advancing some political reform because his wife was a liability? Duty and honor had compelled him to accept the obligations of the title. What would happen to their relationship—to Geoffrey—when he was prevented from living up to those obligations in full measure?

No, she could not let this happen to him. Meanwhile, though, she meant to savor every single moment of the next few days. After all, these memories would have to last a lifetime.

Geoffrey knew better than to become complacent in Cymberly's apparent acquiescence to a shared future. She had not clearly accepted his proposal, had she?

He spent the next few days paying calls and conducting business that would help him pursue the elusive Miss Winthrop. He began to view himself as engaged in a military campaign. His first step was to solicit Lady Kirkwood as his chief "staff officer," a position she was more than willing to fill.

He also spoke with Mrs. Truesdale to make known to her his honorable intentions toward her granddaughter. She, too, became his ally. He attended a musicale given by a certain Lady Hathorne simply because he had heard Lady Renfrow would be there. He found that the merest hint of his interest in Lady Renfrow's goddaughter brought her ladyship into his force.

He called at Truesdale House every day. Occasionally, it was nothing more than a short morning call, but several times he persuaded Cymberly to ride out with him. There were a few stolen kisses, but who was to say which of them was the victim and which the perpetrator of the theft?

For the Prince Regent's grand ball, Cymberly arrived at Carlton House in the company of Lord and Lady Kirkwood. A selection of some seven hundred of the Prince's closest friends had been invited, along with many of the honorees, to attend a dinner party prior to the ball.

Cymberly's natural beauty was enhanced by the gown she wore. An elegant creation in two shades of green, it set off the reddish highlights in her brown hair and made her hazel eyes take on more of the green hue than the brown in them. Her jewelry was very simple— diamond teardrop earrings and, on a gold chain, a diamond pendant that rested at the beginning of her cleavage. Geoffrey could hardly take his eyes from her.

It had required some effort—and a small bribe—but he had managed to have himself seated next to Cymberly at dinner, farther down and on the opposite side from the Kirkwoods. Geoffrey saw Suzanne give Cymberly a tiny "thumbs up" sign.

"However did you manage this seating arrangement?" she asked softly.

"What makes you think it was anything but the luck of the draw?"

She merely rolled her eyes and turned her attention to the gentleman on her other side—Lord Taraton. Geoffrey cursed himself for not ensuring that her other dinner companion would be some old, fat, boring dunderhead, rather than a man whose rank, appearance, and demeanor rivaled his own, and whose name had once been linked with hers.

At the head table, the Prince was flanked by high-ranking military men and their ladies, including Wellington and Beresford. In the reception line earlier, these two had made a special point of greeting Miss Winthrop and making her known to the prince.

Now the prince was on his feet proposing a toast to all England's heroes of the recent wars. With luck, their beloved island would be free of war for many years to come.

With luck and Bonaparte's continued incarceration, Geoffrey thought as he stood to join others in the toast.

Then there were individual toasts to the men chosen to be honored and to their absent friends. Among the honorees was one Major Geoffrey Ryder of the extraordinarily effective riflemen. Geoffrey glanced at Cymberly and found her eyes shining with pride—for him. Finally, he tore his eyes from hers and returned the salute he had been accorded.

The toasts over, Lord Wellington remained standing.

"Your Majesty," Wellington said, "we have honored many deserving men here for their sacrifices and contributions to our cause. As you know, our honorees were recommended to us by the harshest critics soldiers must endure—their fellow soldiers. However, we have heretofore neglected one of our number, and I am sorely concerned that I will not be able to face another battalion should we fail to rectify this mistake. With your permission, sire?"

"Of course, of course." The prince waved his hand expansively, obviously pleased to be in on a secret.

Others at the three tables extending from the head table to form a giant E craned their heads this way and that, questioning, trying to see whom "the Peer" was talking about.

Now Wellington addressed the army of guests in front of him. "When we asked our soldiers whom we should be honoring tonight, a number of names came up repeatedly. You have heard many of them, men who distinguished themselves on the battlefield and men who fought valiantly to save the lives of others, including our surgeons and other medical personnel."

He paused dramatically and looked around. His gaze rested on the table at which Geoffrey and Cymberly sat. All eyes in the room seemed to follow Lord Wellington's as he went on.

"There is one among us who, at great sacrifice and despite personal loss, stayed with the army rather than return to England and a life of ease. One who served the wounded untiringly and eased many a hero's last moments. One who continues to serve, even now, those the public seems to have forgotten. Your Majesty, ladies and gentlemen, I give you Miss Cymberly Winthrop."

A loud chorus of "Hear, hear," greeted this announcement, along with a scraping of chairs as men clambered to their feet once again to raise their glasses in a toast to Cymberly.

Geoffrey, looking down at her all the while, saw her go very pale, then blush. She turned to look at him in surprise and her eyes sparkled with tears. He put a hand under her elbow and pulled her to her feet.

Lady Kirkwood caught his eye and winked. Seeing her do so, Cymberly turned to Geoffrey.

"You and Suzanne knew of this?" she gasped.

"Yes, dear one, we did."

"And you did not tell me?"

"What? Spoil the surprise?"

There was no time for further discussion. Smiling, Cymberly graciously accepted the accolades being flung her way.

Soon, the dinner was over.

The prince chose Miss Winthrop as his partner to open

the ball which followed. Lord Wellington sought her hand as well. In fact, she was not allowed to sit out a single dance. Between sets, she was greeted warmly by men and women alike. Miss Winthrop became quite literally the belle of the ball.

Finally, late in the evening, Geoffrey managed to elbow out other contenders and claim her for a waltz. He deliberately maneuvered them around the edge of the dance floor and through a set of tall open doors leading to the garden.

It was one of those balmy, still-warm summer nights with just a hint of the autumn to come. Geoffrey steered her to a bench. She took the seat gratefully and stretched her feet out in front of her as he sat beside her. He kept his arm around her waist.

"Are you convinced now?" he asked.

"Convinced? Of what?"

"That you could never be a hindrance to me in any way?"

"With a prince and a duke to lend one countenance, society would not dare but tolerate me, would they?" She seemed to bubble with delight.

"All obstacles are swept away, right? You can do naught but marry me now."

"You seem extraordinarily certain of that, sir," she teased.

"If we stay secluded out here many more minutes, *you* will have little choice in the matter."

He drew her closer. "I have had little choice in the matter for over a year, love, not since you and I stood on a high hill watching the bivouac being established at Vitoria. Nor do I want a choice."

He kissed her then, and it was quite clear neither cared much about options where the heart had already chosen.

HISTORICAL NOTE

Napoleon's takeover of Spain and placing his brother on the Spanish throne fanned political fires with a split in Spanish loyalties. Wellington's distrust of *his* Spanish allies (it was mutual) is well known.

Wellington's edicts regarding looting and pillage are also well known, as are the troops' excesses at Vitoria and San Sebastian. King Joseph's loss of looted treasures at Vitoria is true.

Americans are prone to thinking of the British army of the late 18th/early 19th centuries only in terms of the redcoats. While that cavalry/infantry uniform was best known, the blue of artillerymen and green of riflemen were also prevalent.

It was rare but certainly not unknown for a woman of Cymberly's rank to follow the drum. One officer's wife is known to have accompanied her husband through the Peninsula campaign with several servants, including a nurse for her child, as well as her pet dog, a canary, and the husband's five hunting dogs!

Many of Cymberly's and Geoffrey's experiences are based on events that really happened. One of Lord Wellington's "correspondents" *was* captured and escaped, aided by a peasant woman. Wellington insisted the man come to dinner in his peasant garb. The incident in which a French prisoner turned over a child he had rescued on a battlefield really happened, with the happy result of the child's being returned to his mother. Cymberly's rescue of Geoffrey on the battlefield also had its roots in a real-life incident.

ABOUT THE AUTHOR

Wilma Counts lives in Nevada. She is currently working on her fourth Zebra Regency romance, THE WAGERED WIFE, which will be published in February, 2001. Wilma loves hearing from readers, and you may write to her c/o Zebra Books. Please include a self-addressed stamped envelope if you wish a response.